Praise for Snow Place Like Home

"Cami Brooks is trying her best to stay of trouble. Between helping with her friend's coffee shop and running her own store, Curio Finds, the mayor of Brooks Landing already has plenty to keep her busy. But when a dead body shows up in her driveway, she is once again thrust into the middle of solving a crime. And this one brings her back in contact with people from her Washington D.C. past that she would much rather just forget. The author's attention to the slightest details helps readers feel like they are right there in each scene with the characters. Avid mystery readers will appreciate the subtle clues the author sprinkles in like breadcrumbs throughout the story. However, an unexpected twist keeps us guessing right up until the very end. This is a great read from a great author." ~ Natalie Fowler, award winning author of the *Spirit's Way Home* and co-author of *Monsters of the Midwest, Ghosts of the Wild West,* and narrative non-fiction books that explore paranormal and ghostly legends from across the country.

"Well worth the wait! *Snow Place Like Home* pulls you right in - like visiting old friends. An ideal cozy mystery with just enough police procedural to keep you hooked." ~Timya Owens, author and editor, *Dark Side of the Loon, Minnesota Not So Nice, It Was A Dark And Stormy Night Dontcha Know.*

"The latest Snow Globe is my absolute favorite. I love the jelling of the characters and some are real characters that give Cami a run for her money." ~ Rhonda Gilliland, author and editor, the Cooked to Death Series.

"A cozy snow day read with wonderful characters and intriguing clues to a twisty mystery."~ Alicia Kozak, mystery reader and reviewer.

"Suspects abound! Co-workers from the past and new friends come together as Christine Husom weaves another intriguing mystery amidst snow globes & lattes in Brooks Landing. She does not disappoint!" ~ Judy Pendley, cozy mystery reader.

"In the latest Snow Globe mystery be prepared to know your Jays! This book will keep you guessing how and why they fit in and who dunnit. Can be read as a standalone without knowing any of the characters before this volume of the series." ~ Lisa Marie Farago, mystery reader and reviewer.

"Winter has settled over Brooks Landing like a life-sized Minnesota snow globe, and just as Mayor Camryn Brooks begins to relax under a comforter with a book in hand, a body is found in her backyard. Warned to stay out of the secrets surrounding the death, she's nevertheless drawn into another murder investigation. Camryn soon discovers, like snowflakes, no two suspects are identical—and the closer she examines motives and alibis, the more dangerous her curiosity becomes. She must dig deeper and piece together the truth before she, too, is put on ice. *Snow Place Like Home* is a captivating cozy read." ~ Mary Seifert, Katie and Maverick Cozy Mysteries.

"Grab your favorite brew and curl up with another action-packed adventure for Mayor Cameryn Brooks and friends. So many twists and turns, it leaves you thinking 'There's snow place like home!'" ~ Michelle Hess, reader and reviewer.

"Set against a frigid Minnesota winter, Snow Place Like Home shows that friendship and forgiveness can go a long way in chasing the chill of murder away. Camryn, Pinky, and the rest of Brooks Landing residents will make you feel right at home." *Thekla Madsen, co-author of Bad JuJu in Cleveland.*

Titles by Christine Husom

<u>**Snow Globe Shop Mystery Series:**</u>

Snow Way Out
The Iced Princess
Frosty the Dead Man
Cold Way To Go

<u>**Winnebago County Mystery Series:**</u>

Murder in Winnebago County
Buried in Wolf Lake
An Altar by the River
The Noding Field Mystery
A Death in Lionel's Woods
Secret in Whitetail Lake
Firesetter in Blackwood Township
Remains in Coyote Bog
Death to the Dealers
Deputy #714 Is Down

Buried in the House

Snow Place Like Home

Fifth in the Snow Globe Shop Mystery Series

Christine Husom

The wRight Press

The wRight Press
46 Aladdin Circle NW
Buffalo, Minnesota, 55313

Printed in the United States of America

ISBN: 978-1-948068-27-7
ISBN: 978-1-948068-28-4

Dedication

To my dear family, friends, and faithful readers. You are very dear to my heart. I couldn't do this without your support!

Acknowledgments

My humble thanks to my faithful beta/proofreaders and editors who gave their time, careful reading, and sound advice: Arlene Asfeld, Judy Bergquist, Barbara DeVries, Rhonda Gilliland, Ken Hausladen, Elizabeth Husom, Chris Marcotte. Also, to the readers and authors who wrote reviews. Plus, a shout out to Cathy Thisius for gifting me with the fun title, *Snow Place Like Home*, for this book.

Once again, with deep gratitude to my husband and the rest of my family for your patience and understanding when I was stowed away for hours on end, researching and writing.

1

It was a crisp Monday evening in February as the temperature hovered around thirty degrees Fahrenheit. Not unusual for Minnesota that time of year. As I locked the Curio Finds shop door, I envisioned how good it would feel to chill out in a warm house for a few hours.

I had trekked to the back parking lot minutes earlier, driven my Subaru around to the front of the shop, and parked to let the engine run for a few minutes. It was toasty when I climbed in for the short distance home.

After an unsavory incident the year before, I'd lost my position as the director of legislative affairs for a senator in Washington, D.C. and returned to Brooks Landing. It had been frigid that night too, in more ways than one.

My parents had welcomed me with open arms. They'd wanted me to move back for years, and it turned out the timing was right. I stepped in as their shop manager while my mother underwent cancer treatments.

On the drive, I admired the strings of Christmas lights that lit up houses and were woven into evergreen tree branches, even weeks past the holiday. People in northern regions didn't get enough natural light in the winter and craved extra doses for mental wellbeing. The man-made exception: big box stores with bright fluorescent lights overkill.

I pulled into my detached garage, grateful for the automatic door opener I'd installed before the deep freeze set in. The house I rented had belonged to Sandra McClarity, my birth mother's best friend. Sandra had passed on a short time before I returned, and her children, the current owners, were happy to rent it to someone they knew and trusted.

Sandra and my mother Berta remained close until my parents died in a car crash when I was five. My maternal aunt Beth and uncle Eddie adopted me as their youngest of five children. Sandra was like my second aunt, and I'd confided in her from early childhood. I told her things I couldn't tell my new mother.

She empathized with how I'd struggled to cope over my parents' death and the shock to my only child system when I moved from a quiet household to an active and noisy one, given all those kids and an expressive Italian father.

My aunt Beth was a lot like Berta. She'd buffered me from the others' antics as best she could, like when they teased each other or argued or arm wrestled. I'd loved my older cousins dearly, but it took time before I loved them even more as my siblings.

From my earliest memories, whenever I visited the McClarity home, I'd felt soothed and comfortable in the friendly atmosphere. Even after Sandra's death, the house maintained its pleasant fragrance, like her essence was still there. The family had taken prized heirlooms before I moved in, and I imagined when the rest of Sandra's things were gone over time, the same level of coziness in the house would dissipate.

I hung my coat in the front closet, went to the bedroom, shed my black slacks and burgundy sweater, and pulled on black sweatpants and a burgundy sweatshirt—way more comfortable clothes to spend the evening in. The same colors choice was not on purpose; they happened to be on top of the stack in my drawer.

I headed to the kitchen to search for meal options, opened the refrigerator, and a container of leftover lasagna called my name. When it was heated in the microwave, I sat down at the kitchen table to eat. After a busy day at work, the relative silence allowed me to relax. When I'd finished and licked the plate for the last little bit—something I wouldn't do in public—I set it in the soapy-water-filled sink.

I yawned on my way to the living room, stretched out on the couch, slid a comforter over my body, and opened a book I'd been reading. I was involved in the novel's complex plot when my cell phone buzzed. I reached over and plucked it from the coffee table. My best friend Alice "Pinky" Nelson's name appeared on the screen.

I smiled and pushed the accept button. "Hey, Pink—"

She cut me off. "*Ahhhh.* Cami, you need to come out here. *Now.*" She spoke with a hushed intensity. Was she hurt; in trouble?

My heart sank as I dropped the book, threw back the comforter, and jumped off the couch. "Come out *where*? Where *are* you, Pinky?"

"Kitchen . . . window. . . yours. . . look." It took me a second to process her words, comprehend what she meant. She was in *my back yard?* Had she tripped and fallen?

I crossed the ten feet in a flash, slipped my feet into boots by the back entry, cast all apprehension aside, and pushed the door open. The early evening sky was cloaked in darkness, and with the help of the alley's street lamp, I spotted a vehicle I didn't recognize parked by my garage. What in the world?

Pinky's car sat next to it. The motion detection light hadn't turned on, so I flipped the switch, and saw Pinky sitting in her car. When I went down the steps and moved toward her, she jumped from her driver's seat and pointed at the other vehicle. "I think he might be dead."

My heart sank even lower as I glanced at a bulky form in the other vehicle's passenger seat. I was unable to move, frozen to my spot on the snow-covered lawn. Pinky closed the gap between us, and threw her arms around me. We turned our heads in sync toward the vehicle, occupied by an unknown—dead or alive—person.

Thoughts ricocheted in my mind. What came out my mouth was, "What brought you here tonight, Pink?"

"Cami, why would you ask me a question like that when we've got a major *crisis* on our hands?"

"Because I need to know if this is a dream, or if it's for real."

"Oh. Um . . . I picked up groceries, and had your dish I wanted to return, you know, from when you sent that chicken and rice casserole home with me."

I nodded and continued, "You got here. Then what?"

"When I pulled in, I saw that car I didn't recognize, and wondered who it was. For a minute, I thought maybe it belonged to someone in your family. I looked closer and noticed somebody inside.

"Why would a random person be parked in your driveway? It startled me, scared me. There was enough light from the alley lamp so I could see it was a man. His head was tilted back, and his mouth was wide open."

I lifted my hand toward the vehicle in question. "What makes you think he might be dead, and not sleeping?" *Not to mention, why is he here in the first place?*

"Maybe he's not dead. If he's passed out, we need to wake him, or he'll freeze to death. We have to see," Pinky said.

Like that night, temperatures had hovered above and below the freezing point all week. I shivered at the thought.

Pinky squeezed me. "Cami, you should get a jacket on, and then we'll look."

"No. We need to call the police to take care of that." I'd set my phone on the kitchen counter. "I'll go in and call Clint." The Brooks Landing police chief and the man I'd started dating a few months before.

Pinky grabbed my arm. "You're not leaving me out here . . . alone . . . with him."

I dragged her along with me into the house. She pressed her face against the back door's window, and kept watch from a safe distance, while I picked up my phone.

My fingers trembled, and the seconds passed as I struggled to find Clint's number. Finally. It took three long rings before he picked up. "Camryn?"

"Clint, can you come to my house, like *right now*? We think there's a . . . a dead guy in my back yard."

He let out a loud huff. "What in tarnation are you talking about, and who's 'we?'"

"Pinky. She found him."

"Not on purpose," Pinky protested, her eyes still fixed on the mystery car.

"I'll grab my gear and head over. Call Mark, see if he's free to meet me there. Jake's on duty, and I know he's tied up on another call." Officer Mark Weston had been our friend since high school. Officer Jake Dooley was Pinky's new crush.

"Okay," I said and realized he'd already disconnected.

When I phoned Mark, he answered with, "What's up, Cami?"

"It's bad, Mark. Can you come to my house, ASAP? Clint's on his way and he wants you to come too."

"What happened? You okay?" He spoke at rapid fire speed, his voice raised a decibel.

"Um, I'm not hurt. Pinky's with me and she's okay too," I managed.

"Be there in ten."

I pushed the end button and held up my phone. "Mark's on his way."

"I can't see that guy's face too well from the house, but I'm pretty sure he hasn't moved. What a mean thing to do, leaving a dead guy in your yard like that," she said.

"*Pinky.*"

Her hazel eyes widened. "Well, it is."

"We don't know who he is, or if he's dead for sure. That's why we need trained professionals like Clint and Mark to investigate."

She pointed. "Clint just pulled up and parked in the alley."

He lived outside of town and had no doubt driven above the speed limit to get there so fast. I braved a look and sent up a "thank you" as I focused on Clint's movements. He withdrew a flashlight from his duty belt, and my tension increased by the minute as he went to work. I couldn't bear to watch his next actions, so I moved a few feet away and leaned against a cupboard.

"He's pointing his flashlight at the ground around the car. Now he's looking in the car," Pinky informed me.

"Okay. Um, I better grab warm gear."

"I'll wait for you." Pinky turned to me when I hadn't budged. "Cami, you look a little pale. Maybe you should stay in the house. Maybe I should too."

She resumed her watch and continued her narration. "Clint opened the car door. He's bent over and might be checking for a pulse."

Even though my feet felt like cement blocks, the real-time circumstances propelled me to move. I slipped on my coat, stocking cap, mittens, and boots by the front closet.

When I returned to the kitchen, Clint was at my back door with his flashlight pointed skyward. Pinky moved back as he stepped inside.

His intense brown eyes locked on mine and narrowed. "We'll need the medical examiner to report here."

"You mean he's dead, for real?" I said.

"For very real. Any idea who he is?" he said.

My heart beat faster yet as I shook my head. "I couldn't make myself get any closer to take a good look at him, and I can't think of anyone who drives a gray SUV like that. Nor do I have a clue why it would be parked at my place."

"Or who drove it here with that guy inside," Pinky added.

"The man's identity, his cause of death, and the vehicle's driver are the major questions we'll need answers for." Clint looked at his watch. "I'll have the county run the plates, see who the vehicle belongs to. Camryn and Pinky, are you able to take a look at the man, see if you recognize him by any chance?" Clint asked.

"I will if she will," Pinky said.

I searched Clint's face a moment and nodded. *It wasn't the first time I was close to a dead body. And I hoped to high heavens it would be the last.*

Clint took the lead and stopped halfway to the vehicle. He lifted his police radio and clicked a button. "Chief Lonsbury to Buffalo County."

"Go ahead, Chief," a female answered.

"Can you run Minnesota plate number Adam-Nora-Boy-Six-Four-One. I need the owner's name and if the party has any wants or warrants."

"Ten four," the dispatcher said and was back on the radio seconds later. "The registered owner is Peter Randall Zimmer. He's valid and clear."

Peter Randall Zimmer? Peter Zimmer! No way! He was my worst nightmare in life, and to top it off, to get another dig into me, he left a dead man in my back yard. Why? As retribution because I refused to give him what he wanted?

Pinky grabbed my arm and gave it a shake.

Clint cleared his throat. "Copy, County. I'll phone you with specifics. We'll need a Buffalo County detective and the medical examiner to report to the scene."

"Ten four."

Clint phoned the sheriff's dispatch center and gave them my address. I was grateful anyone who tuned in to the sheriff's band radio would not hear the location and be tempted to check the happenings at my house. The neighbors would know soon enough.

Clint disconnected and looked at me. "Camryn, you'll need to take a closer look at the victim, see if you recognize if it's Peter Zimmer. I didn't see a wallet on either front seat, and we'll need to wait for a detective or the medical examiner to go through his pockets."

After his initial look-see, Clint had closed the SUV's door. He reopened it for me, and when I took the quickest glance needed, my vision blurred. I knew who it was but didn't believe it could be *him. Peter Zimmer.* He looked far worse in death. Not only was his mouth open wide, so were his eyes and it seemed they looked toward heaven. I willed myself not to throw up or faint. A big gulp escaped as I turned away.

"Camryn?" Clint said.

"It *is* Peter Zimmer." I rubbed my temples and tried to process a dead Peter Zimmer in my driveway. "His wife Ramona is going to freak. Majorly freak out."

"I thought the *ex*-senator had given him the boot," Pinky said.

"One of my friends in D.C., who is in contact with Ramona on occasion, told me she took Peter back again, for the umpteenth time," I said.

Pinky rested a hand on my shoulder. "Mmm. Well maybe the *ex*-senator finally had enough of his goings on and came up with a way to get rid of him for good." She grunted. "I can't believe she actually thought you were having an affair with her husband, and didn't listen when you told her the truth. On top of it all, she blamed you when she lost her re-election bid last fall." Her breath puffs were visible in the cold air.

"Those are topics we've hammered to death ever since. She believed her husband and fired me. No question how devastated she was after her election loss and it seemed reasonable to her, given her state of mind, to blame me," I said.

Pinky plunked her hands on her hips. "I have a feeling the delusional Ramona thinks you were responsible for both, seducing Peter and convincing people to not vote for her."

"Probably. After I left D.C., I did not want to look back, much less campaign against her. That's the kind of mean revenge-like thing I think she would've done, had our roles been reversed," I said.

"Huh. Then to top it off, you can't forget the way Peter came into your shop a couple of months back to see you. He even tried to ask you out, of all things."

I lifted my hand in a halt sign. "Don't go there, Pinky. I've tried to banish that, and any other thoughts of Peter Zimmer, from my mind forever."

"You know, Ramona could've killed her husband and wanted to make it look like you were a part of it, so she drove him here," Pinky said.

It felt like creepy crawlers covered every inch of my skin's surfaces. I shook my head in place of a verbal answer.

Clint overheard the exchange between Pinky and me and ended it with, "Girls, we can't jump to any conclusions. I asked for a Buffalo County detective because I need to recuse myself from this investigation. What with Camryn being Brooks Landing mayor, and me being the police chief."

"Not to mention that you two are involved," Pinky inserted.

Clint gave a single nod. "That too."

I squeezed my eyes shut tight. We'd been dragged into an awful and unbelievable circumstance. All I wanted to do was scream at the top of my lungs, run away, and not come back until the medical examiner picked up Peter, and the towing company had taken his car away.

"He might've had a heart attack," I offered, my voice a weak squeak.

Pinky rested her hand on my shoulder again. "Cami, no matter how he died, if someone left him in your driveway, any way you slice it, that's just plain mean. And wrong."

I agreed. "This doesn't look good for Senator Zimmer, does it?" *She might be crazy enough to come up with a scheme like that. Spouses were prime suspects until the authorities either had enough evidence to charge them or were able to clear them and scratch their names off the suspect list. Ramona may have considered that. She could have devised a scheme, along with what she thought was an airtight alibi.*

Clint leaned his face close to mine. "Lost you for a minute. I wanted to make sure you're okay."

I shrugged. "Um, I guess I sort of tuned out. What'd I miss?"

"I just reiterated that you and Pinky and I are not the investigators in this . . . situation, and we'll need to let those who are do their jobs. Agreed?"

Clint wouldn't make me swear to that, would he?

Instead of a direct yes or no answer, I said, "I want them to get to the bottom of this. If it's a mean prank, leaving Peter's body here, the authorities need to uncover who's responsible."

"Of course. Cops strive to get answers and solve every crime as fast as possible, which isn't always possible. One thing that struck me as suspicious when I first arrived; whoever drove Zimmer here, when they exited the driver's seat, they used something to brush away their footprints. It could've been a window scraper," Clint said.

Mark showed up in his personal vehicle and parked a ways down the alley. He jogged over to us, on Zimmer's vehicle's passenger side, glanced inside, and shook his head. "What the hell."

"And it just might be where that guy is right now. It's Peter Zimmer," Pinky added.

"*No.* What the hell," Mark repeated.

"Cami, your parents are really gonna flip over this one," Pinky added, as if that realization had finally occurred to her.

Clint turned to Pinky. "Camryn could use our support right now and not have to worry about her parents' reaction."

"You're right." She gave my hand a squeeze. "Sorry, Cami. It was a dumb thing for me to say."

I shook my head. "I thought of them right away when I realized who was dead in my driveway. My poor parents. How are they going to handle this?"

Clint moved in beside me, put his arm around my waist, and squeezed.

An unmarked Buffalo County squad car arrived and parked behind Clint's truck. Detective Tim Garrison climbed out and walked over to our group, maybe twenty feet from Peter Zimmer's SUV. He was in his upper forties, but when the house light cast shadows on his deeply lined face, he looked a decade older.

Garrison nodded at us. "Chief, Mayor, Assistant Chief, Ms. Nelson. I understand you've got a situation here."

"And it's a really bad one," Pinky blurted, like she couldn't hold it in.

Clint rubbed his forehead with the back of his gloved hand. "It is at that, and a mysterious one to boot, Detective. The deceased male is in that vehicle. Ms. Nelson made the initial discovery and phoned Camryn Brooks who was inside her home." He inclined his head toward the SUV. "The registered owner is Peter Randall Zimmer, a man Camryn knew when she worked for his wife. You remember Senator Ramona Zimmer? No longer in office."

Garrison nodded. "Sure."

"That aside, Camryn took a look at the victim and verified it was indeed Peter Zimmer," Clint added.

Garrison nodded again as he withdrew a notepad and pencil from his jacket pocket. "Go on, Chief."

"When I first arrived on the scene, I opened the car door with my gloved hand, removed my glove, and checked for a pulse. No pulse. His skin was cold as ice to the touch. It's possible the near freezing temperature was a factor."

"Have you gotten the medical examiner's ETA?" Garrison asked.

"No, but they should be here soon," Clint said.

"Okay. I'll do a visual scan of the body and the vehicle's interior; take photos. We'll do a thorough search and collect evidence at the sheriff's evidence garage after his body is removed." Garrison zeroed in on Pinky and me. "What time did you notice the vehicle was there?"

Pinky frowned. "When I stopped by, a little after seven."

I nodded. "Pinky called me right after she arrived. When I picked up my phone, I noticed it was two minutes after seven. I got home from the shop at five fifteen, and it wasn't here, of course."

"You didn't observe anything, notice it drive in after you got home?" Garrison said.

I would have called if I had. "No. I heated leftovers for dinner around ten to six, or so. If the vehicle was there by then, I should've seen it, especially with the alley light on."

"I would think so," Garrison said.

"The outside garage light would've helped but the switch is on the inside, and I rarely turn it on. Anyway, I ate my meal then headed into the living room and picked up the novel I was in the middle of. I read until Pinky called."

"Okay. I'll get more details for my report after the ME has finished up," Garrison said.

$$\text{❄}$$

2

Pinky and I moved closer to the house so Garrison could take care of his official duties, with Clint and Mark as his witnesses.

Pinky's phone buzzed from inside her pocket. She wrestled it out and looked at its face as she pushed the accept button. "It's Erin." Our third musketeer. "Hello? . . . Oh. Well, I'm with her, and she's fine . . . sort of. We're in her back yard, and she must've left her phone inside. Do you want to talk to her?" Pinky handed the phone to me.

Oh great. I need to stay strong. "Hi, Erin."

"Cami, I thought you said you'd be home all evening, so when you didn't answer my call or my text message, I got a little worried. What in the world are you and Pinky doing? It's freezing outside," Erin scolded.

"It's not something I want to talk about over the phone," I told her.

Erin made a "hum" sound. "I'll be right over."

"I don't know if that's a good idea. Clint and Mark are here with a Buffalo County detective," I said.

Pinky reached for the phone. "Erin, Peter Zimmer is dead inside his car in Cami's driveway." I heard Erin's scream as Pinky pushed the phone away from her ear. She handed it back to me.

"Erin, it's me again. I think you broke Pinky's eardrum."

Erin's voice was an octave higher when she said, "Oh dear God! Peter Zimmer? I don't get it."

"Neither do I, nor does anybody else," I said.

"Why didn't you call me right away?"

"I didn't get that far. It's been—" I started.

Erin cut me off. "I'll be right over."

"You'll need to park in front of my house and come in that way. I'll go unlock the door," I said.

"Okay, bye." She disconnected and I passed Pinky's phone to her.

She rubbed her ear. "That woman has an unbelievable set of pipes."

"We both know that well. The way you spilled all that was a big shock to her system. At least we've had a little time to sort of process this."

"Sorry again, Cami. We tell each other almost everything. After you told her the names of everyone who was here—except for Peter Zimmer—but not *why*, I knew she'd come right over. I sort of made a split-second decision to cut to the chase before she thought whatever was even worse than it is. As *bad* as it is, we're not harmed. Not physically."

"*Pinky,* it's okay." I tapped her arm. "Right now I need to meet Erin at the front door."

"I'll come with you. Erin's right, it's freezing," she said.

"We'll be inside," I called to the men.

Clint lifted his hand to acknowledge he'd heard me.

We stepped into the kitchen and slipped off our boots. "I'm going to leave my jacket on till I've warmed up," Pinky said.

I took mine off, hung it on a kitchen chair and set my gloves on the table, but kept my stocking cap on. Within a minute after I'd unlocked the door, Erin opened it and came in.

She wagged her gloved finger at us, her eyes opened wide. "I asked myself all the way here if this was a joke, but you two wouldn't be in on something like that."

The three of us gathered in a group hug as we had too many times to count over our thirty-plus-year friendship. At five-eleven, Pinky had to bend over, with me at five-six, and petite Erin at five feet. Back in our childhood years, Pinky was always the tallest and kept growing after Erin and I had stopped; Erin in seventh grade, me in eighth.

We stepped apart and I thought, for the umpteenth time—maybe as a distraction—how much our looks differed. Pinky, thin with large, round hazel eyes and brown curly hair; petite Erin, of American and Vietnamese descent, with almond-shaped, dark brown eyes, and straight black hair; me with an hourglass figure, strawberry blonde hair, green eyes, and a sprinkling of freckles across my cheeks.

Erin sucked in a breath. "Tell me the whole story."

"Let's go to the kitchen so we can keep an eye on the officers, see what they're doing. You can leave your boots on, Erin. Pinky and I will share all we know. They expect the medical examiner any time now."

Erin shrugged off her outerwear then slipped her arm around mine for the short walk. We crowded together in front of the door's window with Pinky behind Erin and me. Mark turned and nodded when he noticed us. Erin, in particular. Once upon a time we'd thought they would marry, but after high school things had fizzled out between them. Mark still held on to the hope they'd rekindle the old flame at some point.

"I'll start, since I'm the one who saw him first," Pinky said. She gave Erin the details from when she got to my house to when Clint arrived. "You tell her the rest, Cami."

I did, and Pinky inserted a comment here and there.

Erin's eyebrows drew together. "This whole thing is *so* scary. Almost worse than the other bodies you've found, Cami. It seems like this time he was *delivered* to you."

Pinky gave my back a gentle poke. "That's what I thought too, and jealous Ramona Zimmer would be my prime suspect."

I nudged her back. "Why, though? She's not stupid, and she has to know the authorities would need to question her first. It's true that she turned a blind eye to her husband's activities. But to offer her a little forgiveness, it had a lot to do with her insecurity. She really struggled to believe handsome Peter would settle for her instead of a beautiful woman, one far more attractive than she is."

"That sounds a little on the stupid side, if you ask me. We all know it's not always about looks. Besides, people believed he married her for her money, not her looks, right?" Pinky said.

My shoulders lifted. "D.C. is full of all kinds of gossip and rumors. Even though Ramona has been back in Minnesota full-time for almost two months now, we haven't kept in touch. So why would she involve me in her personal life in this way, at this point?"

Erin touched my hand. "We can certainly understand why you wouldn't want to think the worst. And we're grateful she hasn't darkened your shop's door since she broke your Marilyn Monroe snow globe last November."

"Yeah," Pinky agreed.

"At least she eventually apologized and even left me money for it," I said.

"Clint's coming in," Pinky said.

We backed away to give him more room as he stepped inside.

Clint nodded at Erin but knew better than to ask why she was there. "Camryn, do you have Ramona Zimmer's phone number, by any chance?"

"Yes. I'll get it." My phone still laid on the kitchen counter. I picked it up, scrolled through my contacts, and found her personal cell number.

"Read it to me, instead of sharing the contact," Clint said.

I turned and saw he had his notepad and pencil ready to record. I recited the numbers twice.

"Thanks. We'll see if she's home. This kind of news is better delivered in person," he said.

My eyebrows lifted. "'We?' I thought you'd recused yourself."

"Detective Garrison asked if I'd accompany him, to act as a witness."

"If you call her first, I have a feeling Ramona will demand to know what it's all about," I said.

"I'll run that possibility by Garrison," Clint said then headed out the door.

Pinky puffed a breath. "See, I told you Ramona is their number one suspect. They want to look her in the eyes when they tell her about Peter, watch how she reacts, see what she does. That's why Garrison wants Clint there, to see if she pretend cries."

Pretend cries? "Whether that's true or not, investigators have to keep an open mind, uncover things, like if she has an alibi," I said.

"She only lives like twenty miles away. She could've dropped him off and been home before anyone—like me—found her husband."

"Pinky, you're forgetting one important fact. If she drove him here, then how did she get home? With no cab service in Brooks Landing to pick her up, she'd need an accomplice. We know she couldn't walk that far, even in nice weather, and it would take hours besides," I said.

"Mmm, I'll have to think about that one," Pinky said.

Erin listened to our exchange in silence.

The medical examiner's van arrived a short time later and backed up close to Peter Zimmer's vehicle. Dr. Trudy Long, the county coroner, and a younger male assistant, climbed from their vehicle, and walked over to the SUV.

"I better go talk to the doctor, see if she has any questions for me," I said.

Pinky elbow bumped my arm. "The *doctor*? Aren't you like on a first name basis by now?" I took her comment as an attempt to ease the tension, one that didn't need an answer.

Pinky had made a good point, however. It was the fifth time I'd happened to be at an unusual death scene in as many months. In all my years in Washington, D.C.—with all its people—I had never come upon a single dead body. After I returned to Brooks Landing, my small Minnesota hometown, I had about seven months of relative calm before I found myself in the wrong place at the wrong time. Over and over. It had started a streak I'd be happy to end at any moment.

I grabbed my coat and mittens. "Send up good thoughts for the troops."

"I'll stay with Pinky," Erin said. They didn't want to get any closer to Peter Zimmer's vehicle than from their spots inside the house.

I headed out the back door, and when Dr. Long and I locked eyes, neither of us smiled, given the circumstances. She blinked and I blinked back.

"Good evening, Ms.—or I guess it's Mayor Brooks now."

"Hello Doctor, and feel free to call me Camryn."

Dr. Long nodded. "This is another unfortunate . . . situation for you to cope with."

I remembered how she'd consoled me at the first scene, and I had liked her ever since. "Yes." It was a whisper.

"I understand you know this man's identity," she said.

"I do. I worked for his wife. She thought we were romantically involved and fired me from my director of legislative affairs position last year."

Long's head jerked back. "Oh?"

"Sorry, I hadn't meant to tell you all that. I do know who he is, but have *no* idea how he got here. Or why," I added.

"And that's the job of the detectives, right?" Long said.

I lifted my hands. "Right."

Long turned to her assistant. "Marty, let's get the gurney and prepare to take Mister Zimmer's body to our office."

"Will do, Doctor," he said.

"I can help," Mark offered.

Marty and Mark were back a moment later, one on either side of the gurney. They rolled it into position. Marty laid a body bag on top, unzipped it, and spread it. I backed up halfway to the house and glanced over my shoulder at Pinky and Erin who stood by the door. Erin gave me a small wave as they continued their watch. I was both apprehensive and curious as the team discussed the best way to proceed.

After they'd formed a plan, Garrison, Marty, Clint, and Mark worked together in the effort to transfer Peter's body from the SUV to the gurney. The operation looked awkward at first; they struggled a bit to lift his body from the vehicle, then set his remains on the gurney, and positioned him on his back.

Peter wore a zippered hoodie—not warm enough for

the weather—jogger pants, and track shoes. No cap or gloves. I felt drawn to study his face, no longer handsome. With his eyes and mouth open, it looked like he'd seen a ghost and had died on the spot. Maybe he had. His hands—turned up in what seemed like a last-second attempt to ask for forgiveness—were no longer able to grab an unwilling woman into an unwanted embrace. Like he had me.

I didn't spot outward signs that indicated what had caused his death. No blood on his clothing, like from a bullet or stab wound. His skin wasn't cherry red, like from carbon monoxide poisoning. His hoodie was zipped up almost to his chin, so if he had rope burns on his neck, they weren't visible.

Dr. Long patted Peter's side pockets. "No wallet or phone. Let's roll him on his side to see if these joggers have back pockets."

Long watched the process when Marty and Garrison did as she'd asked, looked at Peter's backside, then shook her head. "No pockets."

Garrison pointed at the SUV. "I'll take a look in the glove box, see if they're in there." He leaned inside the open passenger door, did his check, and a moment later said, "Just the vehicle manual, insurance info, and other papers."

"I wonder why they left his body, but kept his wallet and phone." Mark said.

"We won't have that answer until we uncover who *they* are," Garrison said.

The team bent over the gurney. As they zipped the body bag to the top, stark reality hit me. Peter Zimmer was *dead*. He could no longer manipulate his wife, take her money, and play around with other women. He'd tried to catch me in his web, and when I wouldn't cooperate the first time, he came back and tried again.

Eew. Peter Zimmer was a letch and a leach, and I could

not bring myself to feel sorry he was dead. I didn't hate him—or anyone else—I just couldn't stand the creepy creep he'd been: a man who charmed people for the sole purpose of fulfilling his selfish needs. Not an honorable way to live, even by the lowest standards.

Marty and Mark lifted the gurney into the back of the ME's van. Dr. Long waved to us as she climbed into the passenger seat. After they'd closed the tailgate, Marty got behind the wheel. They rolled away, down the alley, and out of sight.

Eunice, my elderly widowed neighbor to the north, plodded through a snow drift and headed toward me. She was bundled up from head to foot, and started talking before she reached me. "Camryn, I went into my room to read before bed. When I was about to shut my curtains, I noticed all the goings on here, and I've been watching for a while. Land sakes!"

I glanced at the window she'd mentioned and saw the room was dark inside. The probable reason I hadn't spotted her. I wondered if anyone else in our quiet neighborhood—where people minded their own business, unless curiosity got the best of them—had seen extra vehicles, especially the unmarked squad car and the marked medical examiner's van. In the dark of winter, with windows shut, furnaces running, and television sets on, people didn't hear noises like in other seasons.

Before I gave Eunice a good explanation, Detective Garrison approached us. "Hello, Ma'am. I'm Detective Garrison with the Buffalo County Sheriff's Office. You live in the house next door?" He nodded at it.

Her eyes moved from Garrison to me then back again. "Yes?" she uttered, like she was afraid to admit it.

"Good. I planned to talk to all the neighbors." He pulled a notepad and pencil from his jacket pocket. "If I can get your full name, date of birth, and a phone number." Eunice's voice was shaky when she recited the information, and I noted her age. *Seventy-six and still spry,* I thought.

Garrison waved his hand toward Peter Zimmer's SUV. "Did you happen to see that vehicle arrive at Mayor Brooks's house this evening?"

Eunice shook her head. "No. After supper, I watched a little television in my living room, until just about ten minutes ago when I headed into my bedroom to get my night clothes on. I planned to read in bed for a while. Instead, I noticed all the lights and wondered what was going on.

"I saw you people lift someone from the front seat—it looked like a man from what I could see—and then they laid him on that stretcher. I put my jacket and boots on and came out here to ask you."

"Thank you, Eunice. We don't know much at this point. We need to make a positive identification of the victim and notify his family before we release that information," Garrison said.

Eunice touched Garrison's hand. "You're saying it *was* a man. Wait, you mean he's *dead*?" From her vantage point, she must not have seen the ME's van, or the body bag on the gurney. "Did the driver tell you what happened?"

"We haven't spoken to the driver yet. In fact, we don't know who it is, but we'll get that answer as soon as possible."

"The driver just left him there? You mean someone *killed* him . . . and we have a killer on the loose around here?" She swerved a little so I put my arm around her waist to support her.

"We aren't in a position to make any kind of speculation about how the man died. However, I can say, with a high level of confidence, we do not believe there is threat to the public." Garrison handed Eunice a business card. "If you have any concerns, or think of anything else, call me day or night."

Eunice nodded then turned to me. "I'm gonna go back home and lock my doors. You call me if you need anything."

We hadn't exchanged phone numbers, nor did I note what she'd told Garrison, but I nodded anyway. I'd ask for it another time. "Eunice, are you feeling more steady now?"

"Yes, I had a little reaction, that's all," she said.

"All righty, and please try not to worry. The officers will get to the bottom of this." At least I prayed that was true.

Eunice turned without another word and trekked back to her house. I followed and watched until she made it safely inside her back door.

Garrison, Clint, and Mark had returned to the passenger side of Zimmer's vehicle. The door was open, and they all took a final look inside before Clint shut the door.

Garrison fished his phone from his pocket. He called a towing company to pick the SUV up and deliver it to the sheriff's office. He finished the call with, "Okay, thanks," pushed the end button and told us, "They'll be here in approximately ten minutes."

"Do you guys want to wait inside?" I offered.

"I'll sit in my car and start my report. Mayor, I have your name, birthdate, and address on record. Do you have anything else to add to what you told me earlier?" Garrison said.

I shook my head. "Not that I can think of."

"Okay." He looked at the back door with Pinky and Erin still at the window. "Come to think of it, I need to get Ms. Nelson's name and DOB and see if she remembered more details."

"I'll stand guard from here," Mark said.

"Good idea." Garrison headed toward the house; Clint

and I followed.

Pinky and Erin had moved to the kitchen table by the time we made it inside. Pinky's eyes were like giant orbs as she gave Garrison her personal information. "I told you everything I noticed and everything I did, like how I called Cami."

"Thanks." He pulled a few business cards from his pocket and laid them on the table. "Call if you have questions or remember anything else."

Pinky and I said, "yes" in unison.

Garrison lifted his hand and pointed his thumb behind him. "After Zimmer's vehicle gets towed, I'll check with neighbors, ask if anyone saw the SUV pull in here, or noticed anything else in the neighborhood this evening they thought was unusual." He looked at Clint. "And Chief, before it gets too late, we'll need to notify Ramona Zimmer about her husband's death and pay our respects."

Clint glanced at his watch. "Seven forty-three now, and it's a twenty-minute drive to the City of Orten where she lives."

Garrison nodded. "We don't want to roust her out of bed if we don't have to. I wish we'd found Zimmer's wallet. Mayor Brooks recognized him, but the best practice is to get a positive identification from a family member. I'll make sure someone is at the ME's office before I drive Ms. Zimmer there. If not tonight, then tomorrow."

"Sounds like the tow truck has arrived," Clint said.

He was right. Its blinking lights lit up the alley and area houses. If neighbors hadn't noticed any activity prior, the truck's presence was bound to get their attention. I went outside with Garrison and Clint. The driver stopped behind Zimmer's SUV and rolled down his window. I recognized Saul, a middle-aged, fun-loving guy with bushy eyebrows and a bushier beard. "Evening, folks. So, which one of those vehicles am I taking, Detective?"

Pinky's older sedan hadn't been moved.

"The gray SUV," Garrison said.

"All righty, then. I'm on it. It's a little tight back here, but we'll make it work." Saul eased ahead, then backed up as close as he could to the vehicle. He climbed from his truck and looked at the SUV. "Good, he's got a trailer hitch. It's a short distance to the sheriff's office so no need to load it on my platform. The tow bar will work just fine."

Saul hooked the tow bar on his truck then attached the other end to Zimmer's hitch. "Can one of you shift the gear into neutral, and straighten the steering wheel?" he said.

"Sure," Garrison responded, pulled his gloves tighter, opened the driver's side door, reached inside for the task, and shut the door. "She's in neutral, wheel's straight."

"We'll be good to go then," Saul said.

"A deputy will be there to meet you at the sheriff's garage and open the door for you," Garrison said.

"Thanks. Adios, folks." Saul waved, climbed into his truck, and off he went with Peter Zimmer's SUV close behind.

3

People had started to assemble in my back yard. "Looks like canvassing the neighborhood will take a lot less time than I'd thought," Garrison said.

"There sure has been a lot of activity at your place, and we even saw the medical examiner's van," an older woman said.

Her husband stepped closer. "We wanted to make sure our mayor was okay."

Before I thought of how to reply, Garrison said, "Hello, everyone. As you can see Mayor Brooks is fine."

I lifted my arms, looked around, and waved so everyone saw me. "Thanks for checking."

"That's what good neighbors do," one said.

"Officers, not that we wanted to butt in, but we had to know if any of us are in danger. When we saw the medical examiner pick someone up here, and then when that tow truck left with a vehicle, it made us kind of nervous," another said.

Garrison nodded. "Of course, that would do it all right. Folks, I can't get into specifics, but I can tell you we found a deceased man in a vehicle parked in the mayor's driveway."

A few gasps erupted from the crowd.

"Who was it?" an older man asked.

"We need to make a positive identification before we release his name. Meantime, did any of you see that gray SUV drive through the alley and pull into Mayor Brooks's driveway? It would've been roughly between the hours of six and seven p.m.," he said.

One neighbor pointed at Pinky's car. "I happened to notice that one drive in right around seven o'clock. But I've seen it here plenty of times, and I know who it belongs to—Alice Nelson, the one who owns Brew Ha-Ha, the coffee and treats shop next to Camryn's shop."

"You are correct," Garrison said.

A woman from a few doors down and across the alley said, "Not the gray SUV, but I saw a big dark-colored vehicle when I let my dog out to do his business a little after six-thirty, thereabouts."

Garrison unlocked his phone, gave it a few swipes, and held up a photo of Peter Zimmer's SUV for her. "So not this vehicle?"

She shook her head. "No, it was bigger, kind of like a small bus."

"A Suburban or an Expedition, maybe?" he said.

"Maybe one like that. I noticed the headlights weren't on and that got my attention, especially since most of them are automatic nowadays," she said.

"Did you happen to see any numbers on the license plate?" Garrison said.

"No, sir. Didn't think to look at the plate. Wait, after it drove by I heard a car door slam a few seconds later. I thought maybe it was a delivery man. Lots of us order things online nowadays," she said.

Garrison nodded. "That's true. Back to the vehicle. If I showed you photos of large SUVs, do you think you'd recognize it?"

"Maybe, but I only got a quick glance," she said.

"Understood. I'll get your contact information, and we'll get back to you later, okay?"

"Okay."

"Did any of you see this vehicle?" Garrison made his way among the twelve people—I counted—and showed them Peter Zimmer's SUV photo on his phone.

It looked like most shook their heads, and I heard one say, "Nope."

"How about a larger dark vehicle with its headlights turned off, like your neighbor described?" Garrison asked.

"No," was voiced by several individuals in the group.

"Any other vehicles, anyone walk down the alley, or in the area, that you didn't recognize?" Garrison added.

Again, a round of "Nos," from the group.

"All right. I implore you to keep this incident amongst yourselves for now, so we don't hamper the investigation in any way. Nor do we want undo attention drawn to the mayor's residence and have a bunch of curious folks driving through your alley to snoop."

Good point. Neighbors nodded and made comments. I heard, "That's for darn sure," and, "We got enough traffic here the way it is," along with a few yesses.

"Garrison continued, "I need each of you to provide me with your name, birthdate, address, and phone number for my report. I have business cards for you too. If you think of anything later, be sure to call me."

Clint, Mark, and I hung back as people took turns giving Garrison the particulars he'd requested. When the last one finished, Garrison said, "Thank you all for your help. You're free to go home, warm up, relax, and we'll take it from here. As a second reminder, don't hesitate to call if something comes to mind."

People chatted as they headed to their homes. Garrison stuck his notepad and pencil in his pocket as he walked over and joined us. "That takes care of most of the neighbors. I'll contact the others tomorrow. Whether that large SUV one neighbor observed plays a part in all this, I haven't a clue. However, if that woman is able to pick out a make and the model, it would help us narrow things down."

"It could at that. So Detective, are you about ready to head to Ramona Zimmer's house?" Clint asked.

"Yes." Garrison turned to me. "I think you should come with us, Mayor."

My head jerked back of its own volition. "*Me*? I mean, why me? We didn't part on the best terms. Ramona fired me because she wrongly thought I was involved with her husband. And then when she lost her last election, she blamed me for that too."

"Two good reasons you should join us. Ms. Zimmer was either involved in this . . . crime, or she wasn't. If she was, your presence might help push her to confess."

Mark nudged me. "Detective Garrison has a point, Cami. You don't have to be a fly on the wall to see how she reacts and hear what she says. You'll be on ground zero, and have law enforcement at the ready if she goes wacko."

Mark's "ground zero" words struck a chord, and my curiosity got the best of me. "All right. Think I should change my clothes? Like put on a pair of jeans or pants?" I said.

Garrison glanced at my legs. "Your sweats are fine."

"All right, I'll grab my phone and purse, and let Pinky and Erin know where I'm headed."

Mark accompanied me into the house. Pinky and Erin each slipped an arm around my back.

"That was quite the surprise party here tonight," Pinky said.

"For all of us," I said.

"Nothing like a body in your neighbor's back yard to

roust people from their warm houses to see what's going on. And the bonus for them was getting questioned by a Buffalo County detective," Mark added.

"The whole thing is just too scary to even believe," Erin said.

I nodded. "Another thing that's almost too scary to believe is Detective Garrison asked me to go with him and Clint to Ramona Zimmer's."

Pinky jumped about three feet into the air. "No way!"

Erin frowned. "Was he serious?"

"I can verify he was, is, and Cami needs to get going," Mark said.

"I'll wait here till you get back," Pinky said.

"Me too," Erin said.

"You both have early morning alarms." Erin taught fifth graders, and Pinky rose before dawn to bake muffins and scones. "If it gets too late, I will tell you all I can tomorrow," I said.

"Like you think we could sleep until you do?" Pinky said.

"Pinky's right. We'll wait here," Erin said.

"Hugs," Pinky called as I headed out the door.

Garrison was inside his vehicle and Clint stood next to it. As Mark and I approached, Garrison rolled down the window and said, "Clint's in back, Mayor, you're in front."

"Take care," Mark called on the way to his vehicle.

"Thanks." I opened the door and got in. Clint climbed in the back, and Garrison shut the door for him. With no handles on the backseat doors, he couldn't do it himself.

I turned and looked through the cage at Clint. "Ever been in the *back seat* of a police car?" I quipped.

"Ha, ha. As a matter of fact I have; in the line of duty, for trainings and such," he said.

"It doesn't look like you've got much leg room. How

about we switch places?" I said.

"I'm good." It came out like a quiet grunt.

"On the return trip, I call back seat," I told him.

Garrison released a lighthearted groan. "Phew. With that matter settled, we can take off. I called the county dispatch center, gave them my destination, and your names as my passengers."

"Got a plan when we get to Zimmer's place, Detective?" Clint asked.

"Not a specific one, no. Death notifications can go any number of directions. You never know how a person will react. I've been surprised a time or two," he said.

"That's true, all right. I'll do my best act as an objective observer," Clint said.

"So will I," I said. *At least I would try my best.*

It was a little after nine o'clock when we pulled into Ramona's driveway. The lights were visible behind the drawn blinds inside. Garrison called dispatch and gave his location, then he and I climbed out the front seats. He opened the back door to release Clint from his cage. I don't think the relieved look on Clint's face was my imagination, not with the way he stretched his legs, one at a time, as he crawled out.

"Ready?" Garrison asked.

My heart beats pushed against my sweatshirt and pulsed in my ears.

"Detective, we'll hang back a couple steps behind you. If she doesn't see us, it might help lessen her initial shock," Clint said.

I wished for a way to lessen mine. But given the awful circumstances, how? Would my expression reveal how I felt—whatever that might be—when I saw Ramona Zimmer again? I reached over and bumped the back of my hand against Clint's. He bumped mine back.

I drew in a deep breath and tried to exhale slowly, but as Garrison reached up to push the doorbell, it rushed from my lungs like a gale force instead. The doorbell had a camera eye so Garrison held his badge up for Ramona, or whoever answered the door, to get a view.

I longed to be almost anywhere in the world except her doorstep. As relief set in that maybe she wasn't home after all, the door opened a few inches, and Ramona herself peeked around it. Her eyes landed on Garrison, and it surprised me she didn't seem to notice Clint and me on the sidewalk below. Maybe my wish to be invisible had magically come true.

Garrison held up his badge again. "Ramona Zimmer?"

She nodded and peeped out a weak, "Yes?"

"I'm Detective Garrison with the Buffalo County Sheriff's Office."

Her hand went to her throat, like she hadn't registered his badge. "What is it?"

"It's getting colder, so if we could come inside to talk?"

"We?" she asked.

Garrison stepped aside and waved his hand back at us. "You know Chief Clinton Lonsbury and Mayor Camryn Brooks?"

Her eyebrows shot up, and a small gasp escaped from her mouth. "Um, I know Camryn." She backed up in slow motion and opened the door so we could enter. Ramona stood like a stiff statue as we slipped off our footwear. She didn't tell us to take off our jackets, so we kept them on.

Ramona looked like she was ready to retire for the night, dressed in pajamas and a satin robe. I glanced at the wool Haflingers that gave her flat feet the arch support she needed and kept her feet cozy besides.

Her home was a rambler, similar to mine, but half again as big. Every room was more spacious. Piles of papers were stacked on the coffee and end tables. The dining room and living room were adjoined, divided by appropriate furniture.

Garrison lifted his hand. "Why don't we go sit at the table?" It was a sturdy light-stained oak. The six Windsor back chairs around it had padded seats and a wood finish that matched the table stain.

"You look so serious. I think I'll feel less nervous if I stand instead," Ramona said as she stopped behind a chair and locked her hands around the top rail.

Garrison nodded. "Sure. Whatever makes you more comfortable is fine."

His voice crooned the words, and I felt less nervous myself until Ramona fastened her eyes on me and frowned. Following her lead, Garrison, Clint, and I each picked a chair to stand behind. I slipped off my coat and hung it on the chair.

"Well?" Ramona said. Her impatience—I was too familiar with—had gotten the best of her.

Garrison lifted a notepad and pen from his pocket. "There's been an incident. If you can tell me the last time you saw or spoke to your husband."

"Why do you ask?" Ramona's natural voice was nasally and whiney. The kind that grated on one's nerves after a few sentences. She had a speech coach who'd made a remarkable improvement and helped Ramona sound both warm and professional. But when she was tired or irritated, her evil twin's voice came back in full force.

"First answer the question. Please."

"Maybe two-thirty. I went shopping at the mall, and when I got home around six, Peter was gone. He didn't leave a note, which is not unusual. I tried to call him but he didn't answer, so I sent him a text. He didn't respond to that either."

If that were true, the police could obtain video coverage from the stores she visited, and check phone records.

Garrison nodded. "If you'll give me your husband's cell phone number and your carrier?"

"You have to tell me if Peter's in some sort of trouble."

Garrison's expression was firm when he said, "His number and carrier, please."

Ramona frowned as she gave him the information in a near whisper.

I pondered how Garrison would break the news, what he would say. Instead, he held up his phone, pushed one button, then another, and tapped his finger on its face. He moved closer to Ramona and held it up. "Do you recognize this vehicle?"

"My husband has one like that." She gave her head a quick shake. "Is this a quiz?"

Garrison leaned a little closer to her. "It's not meant to be. Any idea why your husband's SUV would be parked in Mayor Brooks's driveway?"

Ramona's frown deepened as she shook her head. *"What are you saying?"* She pointed at me. *"Her* driveway?"

I didn't respond and tried to keep my face as blank as possible. I didn't even let myself blink. As soon as Ramona turned her attention away from me and back to Garrison, I blinked a bunch of times to make up for it.

"Yes," Garrison said.

"Are you saying *it's* there, but *he's* not?"

Garrison nodded. "That is correct, he is not."

"If Peter is missing, you should come right out and tell me so I can call him, see where he is," she said.

Garrison reached over and laid his hand on hers. "No, Ms. Zimmer, your husband is not missing. I have the sad duty to tell you that your husband Peter is deceased."

The stunned look on her face looked real to me, but if she made the decision to kill Peter, she could have practiced what she'd say and how she'd react when the authorities delivered the news to her.

Ramona was dry-eyed as she gripped the back of her chair and began to rock from one foot to the other, back and forth, forth and back, until I started to feel seasick. I glanced at Clint. His eyes were fixed on her, so I felt comfortable looking somewhere—anywhere—else for a bit. How long would Garrison let her rock before he spoke again?

Aside from the rustle of her satiny tunic, the only other sound I heard was a clock ticking in the kitchen, until Ramona hiccoughed, that is. It was so loud Garrison, Clint, and I all reacted. Garrison's and Clint's shoulders tensed like they were ready to go into battle. I grabbed the back of the chair so I didn't drop to the floor like a sack of potatoes.

Then an even worse thing happened; I felt an attack of nervous giggles about to erupt from my insides. I managed to say, "Excuse me a moment," then raced to the bathroom, closed the door, found a clean towel in the cabinet, held it over my mouth, laughed into it until my stomach muscles ached, and I didn't have enough breath left in me for more.

With it cleansed from my system, I inhaled a giant breath, held it to the count of ten, and released it. I flushed the toilet so if the others heard it, they'd think I had a valid reason for the break. I put on my "serious discussion" face and crept back into the dining room.

It had been ages since I'd had an inappropriate nervous laughing jag like that. Ramona held a glass of water, took a sip, and nodded. "They're gone."

I hoped she meant the hiccoughs.

"Good," Garrison said, and I silently agreed.

Tears sprung from Ramona's eyes in what may have

been a delayed reaction to the news, unless it was part of her act, and she remembered it at last. "How did Peter die?" she managed, as she dabbed her face.

Garrison gave her a slight head shake. "We don't have that answer yet."

"But he's only forty-eight. I thought he was in good health. *Very* good health."

"We'll learn what caused his death after his autopsy," Garrison responded in a quiet voice.

Ramona's eyes widened and a look of horror crossed her face. "No. I don't want to put him through that."

"It's standard procedure in suspicious deaths," Garrison explained.

"*Suspicious*? How? Why do you say that?" she asked.

"Because he was found in the passenger seat of his vehicle," Garrison said.

"I don't get it." Her confusion seemed genuine. Ramona started to rock again, and if she had another hiccough I'd have to go sit in Detective Garrison's freezing-cold car. I sent up a plea that wouldn't happen.

Garrison cleared his throat. "I'd like you to come to the medical examiner's office with me, so you can identify your husband's remains."

Her face scrunched up. "His *remains*? That's such an awful way to put it."

Was her response a tactic to dodge Garrison's request? Besides, "remains" sounded better to me than "corpse."

"You can ride to Brooks Landing with us. They have staff on call at the morgue," Garrison said.

He wants her to ride back with us?

Both hands went to Ramona's neck, and she gasped. "*Morgue?*"

Here we go again.

"It's inside the medical examiner's office. I'll go in with you and can give you a ride back home afterwards. That is, unless you have a friend or family member you'd rather have pick you up."

"Ah . . . no. Not really. My brother's out of the country, and I, um, haven't done much of anything with people since I moved back to Minnesota full-time last month."

Her confession tugged at my heartstrings whether I wanted it or not. From what I'd gathered, Ramona'd had few close friends over the course of her life. She blamed me for her election loss, but in truth, she had grown more unpopular as time went on. When I worked for her I'd put up with her idiosyncrasies because I loved my job, given its challenges and constant changes that kept me abreast.

Despite my dear friends and family living in Brooks Landing, it was difficult to return home, a huge adjustment, in fact. I'd floundered for months until I was able to move into the slower lane again. In retrospect, it made me question how I had survived in D.C. all those years.

In my position, I'd been active in the legislative, not the political side of things. But a year later, I was appointed as Brooks Landing mayor after the beloved Mayor Frost died, and his seat was vacated. That meant I handled both legislative and political issues that included many, many, many citizens' concerns and complaints. It surprised me how much happened behind the scenes in our small town. I soon learned drama existed in every governmental body and their agencies, like it did in private sector ventures.

❄

4

Clint touched my arm. "Ramona went to change clothes. Are you okay?"

"Oh." I realized I'd missed the last minute or so of their conversation, and it gave me a slight fright I'd tuned it out. I lifted my coat off the dining room chair and slipped it on.

Ramona returned in slacks and a sweater, opened the front closet door, and pulled her coat off a hanger. Garrison helped her put it on. It confirmed she was riding back to Brooks Landing with us—the piece I'd missed.

Why hadn't we driven separate vehicles?

We headed out the door. Garrison waited as Ramona tapped the keypad to lock the door. Clint and I reached the car first. "You called back seat," he uttered in a quiet voice.

"Yes, and Ramona will insist on the front seat, so you can sit in back with me," I whispered back.

How wrong I was. Ramona walked to Garrison's vehicle with her awkward gait. She didn't give us car seat directions, as I'd predicted; she waited for them instead.

Garrison forgot, or ignored, our earlier seat agreement and opened the front passenger door for Ramona. I released a quiet sigh of relief.

She shook her head, and in a polite tone and mild voice said, "With those long legs of his, Chief Lonsbury should sit up front. Plus, I prefer the back seat." In the literal sense, not the figurative one. A subdued incarnation of her former self had emerged.

Ramona hadn't kept a personal vehicle in Washington, and taxied all over the district, and beyond. Plus, she'd ridden in limousines to events more times than I remembered. Maybe she missed the days when someone drove her wherever she went.

Clint opened the back door for her, and I walked around to the other side. Garrison shut the door after I was in my seat. We'd settled in and buckled up in no time. Garrison started the car, then phoned Buffalo County Dispatch and told them, "I am clear the last address, en route to Brooks Landing with three passengers."

Ramona sniffled, and I snuck a sideways glance at her as she dabbed a tissue at her cheeks and nose. We had a long twenty-minute drive ahead. I had a lot to say and questions I longed to ask but couldn't. The investigation was just a few hours old, and Ramona hadn't been crossed off the suspect list. Law enforcement would need to coax all necessary information from her, and I needed to stay out of their way, like it or not.

Ramona turned to me. "You act like you think I hurt Peter. Well I didn't."

"Ramona, I am sorry for all this. It is the worst thing for you to deal with." I'd weighed my words because I was not convinced she was innocent and didn't want to lie.

It was natural to consider she had been involved in her husband's death. Maybe not his actual death—but unless he drove himself to my house, went around to the passenger side and died—then someone else had driven him there. Was Ramona that person?

Pinky was right on. Those responsible had done an awful thing.

Garrison and Clint offered no added comments from the front seat.

Ramona went back to her sniffles and dabs. I'd been honest when I told her I was sorry, and pondered whether she could come up with such a bizarre scheme. I was not an impartial judge. She had been both a good friend and a tough boss. In my heart, I knew she loved Peter, at least she had, but she still could've been pushed past the point of no return. I'd never known her to do anything illegal, but she had a temper that could flare up in a flash.

After she'd lost the election, Ramona was not in her right mind for a long while. I'd questioned her mental faculties to the point that I had suspected her, and/or her husband, as the potential killers when my employee Molly was poisoned in Curio Finds the past November. Ramona and Peter had each been in my shop at different times that day, and either one could've mistaken Molly for me.

Molly and I each had blondish hair and similar curvy bodies. Plus, Molly was wearing my dress—the one I'd worn when Ramona walked into my Washington office and saw Peter's hands all over me the year before. That realization had not hit me until later, and I questioned why I hadn't discarded the dress after that fateful night.

Ramona had accidentally, or on purpose, broken a treasured snow globe that same day. She later apologized and had given me cash for it, but we hadn't spoken since, until that night.

Garrison and Clint remained quiet in the front seat; same with Ramona and me in the back. When I felt the seat start to jiggle, I snuck a glance and saw her knees bouncing up and down, a sign I recognized from back when. When Ramona felt pressured and tense, her knee action reaction gave her away. She stayed behind the desk for tense meetings in her office, or at a table in public places, to conceal her involuntary movements.

It wasn't much better if it hit her when she was standing; she did mini knee bends—up and down a hundred times it seemed—if she felt anxious. She'd tried to hide her habit, and people familiar with her condition stopped asking if she was all right because it made the knee action increase in number and intensity.

I did not miss Ramona's flare ups, or her idiosyncrasies. Trapped in the back seat of a county detective's squad car with her, I grew tenser by the minute. Then to my dismay, my own knees started to bounce, so I pressed my hands on them and made them stop.

My load lightened when we reached the "Welcome to Brooks Landing" city limits sign. Clint said, "Detective, you can drop the mayor and me off in front of her house."

Good thinking, Clint. Then Ramona won't see extra vehicles, besides yours, in the back.

I'd turned my phone's ringer off when we left for Ramona's and had resisted the temptation to look the few times it had pulsed in my pocket. We'd soon learn if our friends had laid in wait at my place for our return. Detective Garrison came to a stop. Erin's car was still on the street in front, so Pinky's, and maybe Mark's—if he'd returned— would be in the back.

Garrison turned to Ramona, "I'll open your door so you can move to the front seat."

"It can't be too far, so I'll stay put," she said, her voice quiet and quivering.

Clint said, "We'll be in touch, Detective." He climbed out and opened the back door for me.

I reached over and touched Ramona's arm. "Take care."

She sucked in a loud sniff as her reply.

Clint offered me his hand and helped me out. We stood

on the sidewalk a moment and watched the unmarked squad car, with a frightened woman in the backseat, roll away.

"It's a challenge to nail her down, figure out if she's really in shock, or if she's that good of an actress," Clint said.

"Tell me about it. I believe as a senator she cared about legislative issues and making the right decisions, but her personal life was another story. Needless to say, that presented its own challenges and affected her professional life. When I went to work in the morning, I didn't know if she'd be Jekyll or Hyde," I said.

He stretched his arm around my shoulder. "Off the record, do you think she is capable of murder?"

"That's what I've wondered since we learned it was Peter's body in his car. I know Ramona is smart enough to come up with a plot like killing Peter and leaving his body at my doorstep. Do I think she did it? I'm on the fence. She was blindly in love with her husband. If she *did* kill him, it meant she'd reached the end of her rope and did it to protect herself from getting hurt over and over again," I said.

"Humph. It's up to the sheriff's office to investigate that. For starters, they have Peter's time of death narrowed down at least; between two-thirty and seven."

I lifted the keys from my purse as we made our way up the steps. As I turned the key in the lock, the door flew open. Pinky and Erin stood side by side, eyes opened wide. Pinky grabbed my arm and pulled me inside, with Clint close behind. My house smelled like the inside of a bakery.

"We can't stand it anymore," Pinky said as she and Erin helped Clint and me shrug off our coats. Mark appeared from the kitchen with full cheeks and a muffin in his hand. He raised his eyebrows as though he questioned why we needed their assistance. I figured he'd returned to hang with Pinky and Erin and to hear Clint's and my adventure tale.

Erin took my hand. "Pinky picked up supplies from her house and has been baking up a storm the last couple of hours. Where do you want to sit, here in the living room or the kitchen?"

"I've got muffins in the oven," Pinky said.

"I vote for the kitchen, although the aroma is making me kinda hungry," Clint said.

"You're in luck. I made extras," Pinky said.

Mark stepped aside as we trooped to the kitchen. I noticed white boxes on the counter filled with Pinky's efforts up to that point. Clint got a text beep and glanced at his phone. "It's Jake. He's on break and checking in."

"Tell him to come over," Pinky said then looked at me. "That's okay, right Cami?"

"Of course," I said.

Clint replied to Jake's message, then we took seats around the table. All except Pinky. "I'm too keyed up to sit. And my next batch will be done in five minutes."

"Does baking help calm you?" Clint asked her.

She shrugged. "I guess, but I figured if I get it done tonight I can sleep later in the morning."

"I say we wait for Jake—and until the muffins are out of the oven—before we recount what happened at the Zimmers. As much as we can share, that is," Clint said.

Pinky waved a dish towel in the air and asked, "That's fair. Who all wants a muffin? I made a pot of decaf too."

Clint nodded. "Both would be good, thanks."

Pinky put muffins on a plate. I got up and filled a cup for Clint. "Anyone else?" I asked.

The others shook their heads. I poured a half cup for myself and set the cups on the table. Before I took my first sip, Jake knocked on the back door, and Pinky opened it for him. "Hi, Jake. Welcome."

"Thanks." He came over to me and rested his hand on

my shoulder a moment. "Sorry for what happened at your place, Cami."

I drew in a breath and nodded. "Thanks, it was a shocker all right."

When the timer dinged, Pinky removed the batch from the oven, put a dozen on a plate, and set it on the table. "Jake, would you like a cup of decaf?"

Jake slipped off his jacket, sat down, and reached for a muffin. "No thanks."

Pinky tapped my hand. "The suspense is killing us, Cami. Spill it."

Clint cleared his throat. "As a reminder, the Brooks Landing Police Department is *not* the investigating agency. Detective Garrison will conduct an official investigation, interview Ramona Zimmer, and anyone else who comes to light. Everything we share will be what we observed, off the record, just a discussion between friends. Do you all agree?" They all did, then he nodded at me to start.

I gave a brief summary of my personal observations, steering away from Garrison's official questions, and Ramona's answers. I had to share my nervous response when Ramona's hiccough sounded like a bomb had gone off, and they all cracked up. The story had eased the tension among us.

Clint narrowed his eyes at me, then smiled. "I wondered why you excused yourself like that. I have to admit, after I realized we weren't in any danger, it wasn't easy for me to keep a straight face myself. I've never heard a louder hiccough in my entire life."

After the chuckles died down, Erin asked, "Cami, how could you stand to work for the senator so many years?"

"Ramona is a complicated woman, not the easiest person to work with, but I knew other elected officials who would've been tougher. I feel like I should give her the benefit of the doubt in this big mess. And like Clint said, we need to let the sheriff's office do their job," I said.

Erin gave my leg a nudge under the table. She knew me too well, that I'd be compelled to do a little digging of my own.

We chatted a few more minutes until Jake checked his watch and stood. "I guess my break's over, so I'll catch up with you guys tomorrow." He gave Pinky a wink and a smile, and out the door he went.

As if on cue, the rest of us stood too.

Clint nodded. "It's been an eventful evening to say the least, and we all need to get some rest." He headed to the living room, returned with his jacket, and touched my cheek on his way out. "Good night."

I blinked. "Good night."

Mark and Erin gave me hugs, said their "good nights," and took off, Erin out the front, Mark out the back.

Pinky started stacking her boxes. "Leave your muffins. Either you can pick them up in the morning, or I'll bring them in," I said.

"Okay." She turned, put her hands on my shoulders, and looked me square in the face. "Do you need me to stay with you tonight, keep you company?"

I tapped her hand. "Thanks, but no. And not to worry. I promise to let you know if I need anything."

She gave my shoulders a squeeze, then we dropped our hands. "I think things will get a little crazy tomorrow when word gets around about this. Sandy Gibbons will be hot on your trail for the scoop. Seeing how Ramona was a U.S. senator, national news folks are bound to contact you. Don't you think?"

Sandy was an older reporter for the local paper. Like the Energizer Bunny, she kept on hopping. I hadn't thought that far. Ramona must not have either, or she would've had a tantrum. "Pinky, we can't fret about that. The bigger deal is that Peter Zimmer died, someone drove him to my house and left him in the driveway."

"You're right, that is a bigger deal. A really, really big deal. The reason Ramona looks like the guilty one. Who else would do such a thing?"

I shook my head and shrugged. "No clue, and we're not going to find that out tonight. One thing, Pinky, I am so sorry you're the one who discovered Peter's body."

Her brows drew together. "It was bad, but I'm glad I'm the one who did instead of you." Pinky bent over so her eyes were level with mine. "Even though you do have more experience in that department."

Leave it to Pinky. "How about we follow Clint's advice and get needed rest. Or at least try to."

"Yeah, we need that. All right, I'll leave my scones and muffins here and touch base with you in the morning. But be sure to call if you need me. Promise?"

"I promise. And you do the same."

She raised her hand. "Scout's honor."

We joined our pinkies for a single finger shake.

I helped her into her coat and watched as she got into her car and drove away. I set the empty muffin plate and cups in the sink on top of my forgotten supper dishes, locked both doors, and headed into the bathroom. A long hot shower cleansed my body and helped release a little tension. After I towel dried and got into pajamas, I went into the living room. The mystery novel on the coffee table had lost its appeal, given the real-life crime that had reared its ugly head a few hours before.

I was tired and wired at the same time, the worst combination at bedtime, and returned to the kitchen. I didn't have a single athletic bone in my body but tried running in place anyway. After a few minutes, I started to pant and needed a glass of water. I downed about twelve ounces, then opened the refrigerator to look at wine options, something to relax me. When it came to alcoholic beverages, I preferred beer, but a glass of wine now and then was nice, especially if it helped calm my racing thoughts. I selected a chardonnay and poured a generous amount in a tumbler; not too much, just enough was my hope.

As I walked into the living room, the little cuckoo clock bird popped out and hollered "cuckoo" eleven times. After a year with the little guy, when the house was otherwise quiet, it still startled me at least half the time. It belonged to Sandra's family, but no one had claimed it yet, and I could not blame them.

I set the wine within reach on the coffee table, stretched out on the couch, drew the comforter up to my middle, and found classical music on my phone app to soothe me. As I took my first sip, the image of dead Peter Zimmer appeared in my mind's eye and wouldn't go away. "*Leave me alone,*" I yelled.

As if by magic, it disappeared. To my horror however, another image of him took its place; an alive Peter with a lewd expression on his face, one he wore before he locked his arms—it seemed he had between four and eight of them—around me in my office.

I had been able to thwart his less direct advances prior, had not responded to his flirts several times before that fateful day. As I took another sip of wine, a thought dawned on me and hit me like a rock. I had not been drawn in by Peter's "charms," so had he seized an opportunity to get back at me that day in the office? He must've known his wife was due back any minute. Had he set up a scene so she'd find us in what must have looked like a passionate embrace?

To top it off, another senator—on the other side of the aisle from Zimmer—had entered the room and snapped a photo of Peter and me with his cell phone camera. I was in the *wrong* place at the wrong time; the other senator was in the *right* place at the right time with the opportunity to make both Senator Zimmer's personal *and* professional life look shady. Of course, the senator who'd taken the photo wouldn't admit that he'd given it to the media.

In any case, Senator Zimmer had refused to hear my side of the story back then, and I was dismissed. As I pondered the issue further, I looked at it from a different angle. What if Ramona and Peter had set the whole thing up so she had a reason to fire me? But why? I'd had a stellar record, and other senators had told me they would like me to work for them if I was ever in the market. Until Ramona fired me, that is.

What a mess. As my thoughts cleared, I realized how the fiasco that ended my career in D.C. had made me lose sight of the broader picture. I saw trees instead of the forest. Ramona no doubt had an inkling Peter was attracted to me, along with a list of other women besides. I'd later heard via the rumor mill Ramona had developed some animosity toward me months before she fired me, and I believed it was due to Peter's attention.

One staffer told me people thought I had a brighter future to look forward to than she did. Ramona's position in the U.S. Senate was dependent on her constituents' votes and a majority to keep her job. Congressional members looked for smart, hardworking staff, and the same person told me I fit that bill. Her opinion: Ramona was intimidated by me.

I'd been tempted at the time to file a suit against Peter Zimmer to save face and protect my honor but decided not to make a bad situation worse. Instead, I returned to the home of my birth to people I loved, and who had loved and supported me. My parents were in the market for someone to manage their Curio Finds shop, one that specialized in snow globes from around the world, so it turned out to be a win-win for all three of us.

I had a few months to adjust to the slower paced role until I started the unfortunate streak of finding bodies of people who had died under suspicious circumstances. Each one had given me an unexpected jolt and scared me half to death. After I got over the initial shocks, my sense of justice prevailed and prompted me to try to uncover the person or persons responsible for each one. Then Peter Zimmer, of all people, turned out to be the fifth victim.

Pinky, poor thing, would she be able to sleep a single wink tonight?

My phone buzzed a second later. Pinky. "Hey."

"Hey. I didn't wake you, did I?" she asked.

"No, just sipping wine, listening to soft music, and doing my best to stop thinking."

"Me too, except for the wine and music. I just want to blot out Peter Zimmer's face from my memory forever," she said.

"Would it help if you spent the night?"

"Maybe. But what if Peter Zimmer's spirit stayed behind, and it's hanging around in your back yard, like Molly's is in your shop."

"*Pinky.* We don't know for sure her spirit is in the shop," I said.

"Then why do I hear you call out 'Molly' like you think she's responsible when weird things happen?" Pinky said.

Good question. "I guess it's gotten to be a habit. Like you say, when weird things happen, and we don't have a good explanation for why, I blame our imaginary ghost."

Pinky chuckled. "Imaginary ghost. Good one, Cami. Molly was sweet, and her spirit has been helpful at times. She even saved your life. But Peter Zimmer was icky. His spirit would hang around to do mean stuff, if anything. Then you'd have to call in a paranormal pro for help."

"You're letting your thoughts run wild, and we need to relax, not get all riled up about something that's not real. At least not in the physical sense."

"Cami, you're the one who thinks your mother sends you pennies from heaven to warn you, or comfort you. A penny is a physical thing."

She had me on that one. "You want to come over? You could park in the front."

"Nah, it's okay. I feel better now that we talked. Unless you want to come to my house?" she said.

"Thanks, but I'm on the couch in my pajamas." Besides, after what she'd said, I would not want to go out in the dark, past the spot where Peter Zimmer's body had been, to my car in the garage.

"Okay, good night then," she said.

"Night, Pink."

We'd no more than disconnected when my phone buzzed again. Ramona Zimmer. What to do, what to do? I pushed the accept button before I changed my mind.

"Camryn, it *was* Peter, but I hardly recognized him. How could he just *die* like that?"

"I'm sorry, Ramona. I can't imagine." Actually, I didn't have to imagine. I knew he didn't look like himself.

"I don't have the right words for how awful it is. And unreal. Not real at all. And my brother is all the way over in Africa doing his mission work. I feel SO alone," she said.

Ramona almost had me convinced she had not seen Peter's body before her trip to the morgue. Her brother, Randy Arthur, was a person I considered—for a millisecond— as the one most likely to help her. But he was a missionary, against killing, and thousands of miles away besides. He had an air-tight alibi.

"Have you been able to reach Randy to tell him about Peter?" I asked.

She sniffed. "No, it was the middle of the night for him when Detective Garrison delivered the awful news. It's morning there now, about seven, so I'll call him next. I wish he wasn't so *far away.*"

"It'd be good to talk to him. He's a minister, right? He can pray with you. Maybe make you feel better," I said.

"Yes. He can do that."

"Are you at home now?"

"Yes, Garrison brought me back here," she said.

"I'll be up a little while yet, so if you need to talk some more, call me." *Why had I added that?*

"Thank you, Camryn. You are a friend indeed," she said, and disconnected.

Once upon a time, that had been true. We may no longer be good friends, but I could still be kind to her, offer help when needed, and hope she was not pulling the wool over my eyes.

I took a last sip of wine, turned off the end table lamp, and laid back on the couch. At times I felt safer, more comfortable, on the couch than in my bed. It was one of those times. I prayed Peter Zimmer would stay out of my dreams and fell into a deep sleep.

❄

5

My front doorbell's rings jerked me awake. I glanced at the window, over the top of the blinds, and saw it was dark outside. I was disoriented, didn't know the time, or who would be at my door. A loud knock, and as Pinky's voice called out, "Cami, it's me," it coaxed my brain into full consciousness.

"Coming," I called back. It took a few seconds to untangle my body from beneath the comforter. When I stood, a cramp tightened my left calf. I stifled a howl, limped as fast as possible, and opened the door.

Pinky's eyes opened wide. "Cami, you scared me."

"What time is it?"

"Six-thirty." A half hour before sunrise. "I tried to call to tell you I was on my way to pick up the muffins and scones, but it went straight to voicemail. So I called again, same thing."

"Oh. Um, let me check." The phone laid on the coffee table, and when I picked it up, saw its face was black. "No wonder; it's dead. I was listening to music and didn't shut it off before I fell asleep."

Pinky took it from me and carried it to the kitchen. I followed behind her, with less of a limp as the cramp eased. She plugged the phone into its charger on the counter, and turned to me, hands on her hips. "There."

"Why did you come to the front door?" I asked.

"Because of what we talked about, you know the haunted part. Besides, your back yard is creepier in the dark, and way more so after last night." She cupped her hands on my elbows with her hands. "Cami, how are you holding up, really? Did you sleep at all?"

"I'm fine, I think, for now anyway. I did not expect to get much sleep, but I conked out and slept all night. I was in the middle of a dream with a bunch of people I didn't know, in a building I didn't recognize, doing nothing in particular, when you woke me up."

She dropped her hands. "Sorry about having to wake you up like that. Honestly Cami, you and your dreams. Where does your mind come up with half the stuff it does?"

"No clue, but the best part is the Zimmers weren't in that one."

"That's a good thing all right. Well, I need to get Brew Ha-Ha's door opened, and coffee beans in the grinder, before the early morning crowd starts to arrive in about twenty minutes," she said.

Pinky picked up her boxes and walked through the living room. I opened the front door for her. "You need help getting them in your car?"

"Nah, but thanks. See you later."

"Sure thing." I closed the door. And like the night before, I watched from the window until Pinky got in her car and drove away.

When my phone had enough juice, a string of pings sounded. I left it plugged in and scrolled through them. There were three text messages from the past night and the two phone calls from Pinky that morning. A message from Clint read, *I'm here if you need me.* I sent him a heart emoji back.

One from Erin said, *Sleep tight, my friend.* I responded, *Sorry, just got your message. I slept well all night, thanks!*

The last was from Ramona, sent at 3:12 a.m. *I'm scared.* That was all she wrote. My heart pitter pattered as I pondered what she meant. Was she scared because she was involved in her husband's death, or scared because her husband was dead and she was alone? It was too early to phone, so I sent her a text message. *Hi Ramona, my phone was off and I just got your message. Call me anytime.*

My phone rang before I had a chance to set it down. I pushed the accept button, then bent over to talk because the cord was too short to reach if I stood. "Camryn, I can't believe Peter is dead. I got a hold of my brother Randy. He's really worried about me, so that made me even more worried about me."

Man alive. He was supposed to be the strong one, the one to assure her. "Ramona, what did your brother say?"

"He was worried because I'm *alone,*" she said.

Had he considered that Ramona would harm herself? "Ramona, did Randy think you're in any kind of danger?"

"Well, no. I don't think so. I've just never done very well when I'm all by myself."

True, and the reason she'd hung on to Peter the past years, no matter what he did. "All right. Did your brother say anything else?"

Ramona sniffed. "He gave me some of his favorite Bible verses to read." She had concentrated on how her brother was worried about her, not the positive message he'd given that could help her.

"Those would be good to read. Ramona, you're a strong woman and you'll get through this. You can get professional help too. You've seen a therapist in the past, right?"

"You know I have."

"See if you can get an appointment. I'll be at the shop if you need to talk later, okay?" I said.

She sniffed again. "Okay, and thank you, Camryn. Goodbye."

Goodbye sounded ominous. "Later, then," I said instead of "goodbye," and disconnected. First my leg was cramped, then my neck after the awkward position bent over with the phone to my ear for a while. I put it back on the counter to finish charging, filled a pod with Pinky's extra dark coffee, set it in the single cup coffee maker, and hit the start button. As water dripped through it, I leaned my torso from one side to the other, for the best stretches I could manage. I lifted my arms, gave them some shakes, then did the same with my legs.

When my cup was filled, I lifted it to my mouth, inhaled a deep whiff, and took a sip. Mmm. I leaned back against the cupboard, took another drink, and tried to process the surreal events from a mere twelve hours before, the first three hours especially. There was no way someone just happened to leave Peter Zimmer's body in *my* yard.

An odd thought struck me. What if he'd asked a friend to drive him to my house. After they arrived, Peter suffered a sudden, fatal heart attack, the friend got scared, and ran off. Did that make sense? No, but nothing else did either. If that were the case, the other person's fingerprints would be on the steering wheel, unless he had gloves on, a likely scenario since many people wore gloves when they drove in winter.

Chills ran down my arms. Of all the bodies I'd found, it was the first one that felt personal, directed at me. Peter's body was left in my yard, like I was supposed to find it. If Ramona wasn't involved, then who was? I'd known next to nothing with regard to Peter's personal life, because I hadn't wanted to. I'd kept as much distance between us as possible.

When they located his phone, authorities would go through it for a list of his contacts, and the calls and messages they'd exchanged. It had to be someone who knew him, because the chances were slim to none a stranger was responsible. I finished my coffee and got ready for work.

As I walked to my garage, an eerie feeling about Peter Zimmer's death ran through me. I stared at the spot his SUV had sat before it was towed away. I happened to notice a small light green piece of paper—memo note size—on the ground near where Pinky had parked. Both Clint and Detective Garrison had searched the area with their flashlights. If it was there at the time, they hadn't noticed it.

I bent over and picked it up with my gloved hand. The letters JTK and what looked like a phone number, without an area code—738 4697—were scribbled on it. I studied the handwriting but didn't recognize it.

Maybe it belonged to Pinky, a note someone had given her. Or it could have blown over from a neighbor's house, or fallen from a person's hand, or from a pocket as the owner walked down the alley. Or it could've been in Peter Zimmer's vehicle and fell out when the driver fled from the scene.

What to do? I needed to turn the note over to Detective Garrison in case it turned out to be a lead, a piece of evidence. I headed back into the house, found a plastic baggie in a drawer, slid the note inside it, and put it in my purse. On the walk back to the garage, I visually scanned every inch of ground along the way for anything suspicious.

Thoughts jumped around in my mind on the drive to work. Like always, I parked in the lot behind the shops, then pushed out a long, slow breath, and tried to convince myself I'd be able to go through my normal routine and concentrate on anything besides the Zimmers. I entered Pinky's shop, and the inviting atmosphere helped settle my nerves. Brew Ha-Ha shared an interior wall with Curio Finds. It had been a soda shop decades before and sat empty for years, before my parents bought it with the intent to expand their retail space.

They'd had an eight-foot archway opened in the thick brick wall between the two. But on second thought, my parents felt the old soda fountain was better suited for food and drinks, not to display snow globes and other collectibles. Pinky had worked at the local bakery, and they'd talked her into running the coffee shop instead.

After a good cleaning, the trio discovered the black-and-white tile floor was in good condition. It inspired Pinky to use retro furniture and integrate her favorite color in the accent pieces. She didn't overdo the pink, however. In the dining area, dark gray metal chairs sat around lighter gray Formica-topped tables with metal pedestal bases. Half the chairs had black vinyl padded seats, the other half had pink. She'd also used that combination on the six counter stools.

People enjoyed the Lucy and Ethel character pictures and other memorabilia from the fifties. I glanced up at the menu board with the day's specials above a large mirror on the back wall, then at the hands on the Betty Boop clock above it: 7:52. I greeted Pinky, and she gave me a small nod back. I interpreted the expression on her face as, "Last night was bad, but we're on the other side now." I blinked in response.

I'd hoped to ask her about the memo note first thing, but that would have to wait. Patrons sat at back tables, one was on a stool at the counter, and two others waited in line. I passed through the archway between our shops, went to the back room, and hung up my purse and coat. When I returned to Brew Ha-Ha, three women in their late thirties had arrived. They were recent regulars who stopped in for their favorite brews after an early morning swim class at the local fitness center. All wore ski jackets and knitted stocking caps on their heads.

"Mayor Camryn," the one with green eyes and auburn hair said, as I slipped behind the counter next to Pinky.

I lifted my palms. "In our shops, I'm still Camryn."

"Okay, like in the old days."

Her brown-eyed, dark brown-haired friend gave her a nudge, and laughed. "By the old days, you mean like six weeks ago?"

She shrugged. "I guess. This winter's gone on forever, so it seems like it's been a lot longer than that."

The third cast her turquoise eyes downward. "I'll give you that," she muttered and tugged at the ends of her shoulder length, highlighted light brown hair.

"Okay, ladies, what can we whip up for you?" Pinky said.

All three looked up at the menu board on the wall with the special and other drink options.

"I'll have a hot chocolate with mint," number one said.

The second one tapped her lips with a pointer finger. "Hmm, too many choices that I love. I guess I'll go with today's special, the Jamaica Blue Mountain Blend. The flavor is so rich, and with the hint of chocolate, it is amazing. With cream, please."

"I think the loco mocha with a shot of espresso will help perk me up," the third one said.

"You were even too tired to make it to class this morning; not your usual peppy self," number one said.

Her shoulders lifted. "No, I guess not."

Pinky and I prepared the drinks in no time. As we set them on the serving counter, Pinky asked, "A muffin or scone today?"

They shook their heads, and one said, "No thanks."

Number two paid for the drinks, then they carried them to a back table. I hoped whatever was wrong with the one wasn't contagious. Her complexion was paler than the others, but they'd worked out, and she hadn't.

Over the next half hour, people came and went. The two swimmers waved on their way out. One had left earlier and looked drained, not well. Coffee had not helped perk her up, after all. A moment later, the bell on Pinky's door made a jingle and it seemed louder than usual.

Sandy Gibbons, the local town newspaper reporter, blew in with a gust of wind. "Camryn Brooks, you're here so early! I stopped by your house first, but you were already gone." It felt like every head in the back turned at the same moment.

Great, just great. I knew that excited tone in her voice all too well. Given the circumstances, I put on my best smile possible. "Hi Sandy. Yes, here I am."

"I need to talk to you about the dead man who was discovered in your driveway last night." Her volume made my eardrums pulsate and hurt.

"Now, Sandy, wherever did you hear that?" Pinky said.

She eyed Pinky a moment and said, "I have my sources."

Pinky turned her palms upward and looked at me. "You know it wasn't me, Cami. Not this time, at least."

Pinky had made the dreaded discovery and would not want to discuss it, especially with Sandy. As much as Pinky loved to gossip, the reality of it all had subdued her, no doubt about that.

I heard chairs scrape on the floor in the dining area as people shifted in their seats and turned toward Sandy. "Why don't we go chat in my office," I suggested.

Sandy pulled a pen from a spot in her sprayed hairdo and a notepad from her pocket. She jutted out her chin.

"Yes, let's do that, Mayor." She'd switched to a more serious, professional tone.

It was apparent every eye was on us as I led Sandy through the archway. Enough light shone in the front window and spilled out from Brew Ha-Ha, so I kept the shop lights off. Pinky's customers often thought Curio Finds was open, even with the lights off, and despite the plaque on the wall that listed the hours.

I stepped into the office, and a claustrophobic sensation came over me. Two people in the shop's compact office was max capacity. I would've preferred to stand, better yet, to be anywhere in the world but there. Instead, I settled on the chair behind the desk and aimed for a composed demeanor.

Sandy closed the door behind her then sank down in the guest chair across from me. She laid her writing tools on the desk and leaned forward. "So, off the record, are you starting to get a major complex?"

I figured out the direction she was headed but played dumb. "Complex?"

"Yes, with all the dead people you've found over the last months."

"Off the record, I can't exactly say I'm getting a complex, but it unnerves me. A whole lot, to be honest."

"I'd be a nervous wreck if I were you. I can't even imagine." She drew in a breath and poised her pen over her notepad. "All right, on the record, tell me who it was and how it happened this time."

"Sandy, you'll have to wait for the authorities to release his name. I can confirm it was a man. His body was in a vehicle in my driveway, and the sheriff's office is doing the investigation."

"Buffalo County, huh? Neighbors said they saw Chief Lonsbury and Officer Weston there, but I suppose with you being the mayor and all, our police chief must've thought it would be a conflict of interest."

"They'd be the ones to ask," I said.

"You didn't know the man, the dead one in the vehicle?"

"No comment."

Sandy leaned closer. "So you *did*. Well, that makes things more interesting."

She had no idea how true that was. "Sandy, I really can't say anything more at this point."

"Not even about what caused his death?" she said.

"I can tell you I have no idea. It's up to the medical examiner to figure that out."

"So you didn't see anything obvious, like blood?" Sandy asked.

"Sandy—"

"Okay. I've been thinking about your parents. I imagine how upset they must be."

"I agree they will be. I haven't told them yet," I said.

"Hmm. It'd be a good idea to tell them soon, so they aren't the last ones in town to hear the news."

I nodded and stood. "Thanks, Sandy. We'll talk again, but I best go help Pinky. She's pretty busy this time of day."

Gravity seemed to fight against Sandy as she struggled to stand. I put my arm around her waist and helped balance her on her feet. At seventy-plus, she was quick witted, but her muscles and joints slowed her movements, showed her age. Sandy picked up her writing tools and turned to the door.

I followed her and flipped off the office light switch. The light came back on as I crossed the threshold. *Molly.* I caught myself before I said her name out loud. After Molly died in the shop, the lights would turn off, and come on again, in random moments. Critical ones, at times, and once that saved my life, as Pinky had pointed out.

We'd had the wiring in the building checked, and the electrician found no issues with it. So we blamed, or credited, Molly the guardian ghost. I reached around and turned the light off again. It stayed off and I lifted my hand in a small wave as if Molly were there to see it.

Sandy hadn't noticed the off-on-off light action. Brew Ha-Ha's doorbell dinged as we entered the shop. I did a double take when Clint stepped inside. He was an immediate magnet pull for Sandy, and she closed the distance between them in no time.

"Chief Lonsbury! You're just the person I need to talk to about the man found in the mayor's driveway last night," she said.

To his credit, Clint didn't flinch. His brows lifted a tad, but not enough for most people to notice. I moseyed over to the serving counter. Pinky emerged from her back room carrying a glass container filled with freshly ground coffee. She looked from Clint and Sandy, then to me and rolled her eyes.

Clint tipped his head. "Sandy, there's not a lot I can say at this point. I'm thinking the Buffalo County Sheriff should have a statement by this afternoon."

"Neighbors saw you at Cami's place last night. They also observed you and Cami get into the Buffalo County detective's car and drive away. But I guess they fell asleep before you got back. Chief, what say you about that?" Sandy persisted.

Clint gave a slight nod. "Both things are true and part of the investigation."

"Well, now you've got me even more curious. Cami wouldn't say, but she acted like it was someone she knows, um, knew."

"Sandy, I know you want answers, but you'll have to be

patient and wait until the sheriff's office is ready to provide them." Clint's phone buzzed, and when he checked it, said, "I need to take this." He pushed the button. We heard him say, "Chief Lonsbury," as he walked into Curio Finds.

Sandy's face visibly twitched as she took a stool at Pinky's counter. "This is big news, and my readers want the scoop."

"And they'll get it," I said.

"I'm nearly as snoopy as you are, Sandy, and you are going to flip your lid when you get your scoop. It surely made me flip mine," Pinky said.

Pinky, open mouth, insert foot. I would have nudged her with my foot had she been closer.

Sandy dropped her pen. "You know what happened? *How*?"

Pinky's shoulders lifted. "I sort of happened to be there."

"My source must not have seen you," Sandy said.

"Sandy, before you ask her any more questions that *really is all* Pinky can say for now," I said.

She picked up her pen and pushed out her lips. "Just when I felt a ray of hope I'd get one tiny tidbit."

Given Sandy's comical pouty face, I suppressed a smile. "Clint thinks the sheriff's office will let the public know the person's name at some point today. If the sheriff holds a press conference, you'll be among the first to know," I said.

"A press conference, you mean like last month when Police Chief Newel was killed? Are you telling me it was a *prominent* member of our community, like Newel was?" Sandy asked.

I shook my head. "Can't say."

She pressed on, "Well, what then?"

Pinky snapped her dish towel. "Sandy, you'll just have to wait."

"Okay. Is it all right if I have a coffee and scone before I leave?"

"Of course. The usual blend?" Pinky said.

Sandy nodded as reached in a pocket for her wallet.

65

❄

6

We all turned at the sound of Clint's voice behind us. "Camryn, can I have a word with you?"

As I rose from the stool, Sandy grabbed my hand like it was a reflex action.

"Sure." I gently slid my hand from her grip and left the inquiring minds behind. It was a toss-up between who was worse in that department, Sandy or Pinky.

Clint and I navigated to the store room past the office. He closed the door and studied my face a moment. "That was Detective Garrison on the phone. He witnessed the autopsy and gathered evidence from the body. It appears Peter Zimmer did *not* have a natural death, so we can rule that out."

I felt a flush creep up my neck and cover my face. "He was murdered?"

Clint nodded. "That's the way it looks, all right."

I leaned against shelves for support. "Oh, wow. We knew that was a probability, but when I took a quick glance at his body, I didn't notice any blood."

"No. At autopsy, the medical examiner discovered a small bruise caused by a needle puncture into the coronary artery."

My eyebrows drew together. "He had something injected into his artery?"

"Yep. It was air."

"Air?"

Clint pulled the notepad from his pocket and looked at his notes. "To be sure I get this right." He glanced at me then at his notes. "When air bubbles get into an artery, it causes an embolism. The doctor told Garrison the bubbles can travel to a person's heart and cause a heart attack; or if they go to the brain, it can cause a stroke; or to the lungs it can cause respiratory failure. The bubbles could go to other organs and affect them as well."

A visual of those traveling air bubbles zipped through my mind. "Scary. What an awful thing."

"I'll say. The location of the needle stick gave the ME his first clue, of course. He determined Peter Zimmer did indeed suffer a heart attack from air injected into his coronary artery and ruled his manner of death a homicide."

"Homicide," I repeated.

He took another look at his notes. "They drew blood and ran a preliminary test. Alcohol was present in his system. That could've played into the series of events, made Zimmer more cooperative—or vulnerable—in whatever was going on."

"From what I've heard about Peter Zimmer, nothing much would surprise me. It could be any number of scenarios. But whatever it was, it ended in a bad, bad way. Who could have expected anything this freakish? I mean, someone stuck a syringe filled with air into his artery?" My insides trembled.

"That brings a key point to light. Zimmer would likely have been bare chested—at least the ME didn't find a minute hole in his shirt or around his wound—so the person would've had a good chance of hitting an artery."

I thought for a moment. "When a person is straining, their veins and arteries stick out. Think how weightlifters look."

"True. Zimmer must've been in a compromised state. If he felt threatened, tried to resist, and strained his muscles against whatever, that would do it," he said.

I tried to banish the picture of a bare-chested Peter Zimmer from my mind. "Clint, how long will it take the detectives to track down the names of every person Peter's been involved with? Not to mention, then go through the potentially long list of people who thought they had a good reason to want him dead?"

"You pose valid questions, Camryn. It could be a long list, all right. Besides a motive, the caveat is that the person, or persons, responsible would also need the means to pull off a murder like that. Seems like it'd involve a complex plot. Or an encounter that went downhill fast," he said.

"Peter was killed somewhere, maybe at a hotel. But how would they get him out without being spotted? And why in the world would they bring him to my house? They had to have known me. And that's one big Eew that has got me more than a little creeped out."

Clint leaned over and squeezed my shoulder. "It is a disturbing situation, to be sure. It'd take two people to pull off an operation like that. Unless it was one big, strong guy who could lift and position Zimmer in his vehicle. If the guy was alone, he'd either have to walk to wherever he came from or get a ride back from an accomplice."

"My head is starting to spin. Do you know if they've located Peter's wallet and phone?"

"According to Garrison, the sheriff's crime lab team did not find it in his vehicle. You know Garrison got Peter's number from Ramona. But when he tried to call it, it went to nowhere land. Garrison thinks it's been disabled, maybe the SIM card was removed, maybe someone ran over it. He asked Ramona if she and Peter had the same phone provider, and the answer was no, so she can't access his account. Garrison plans to get a warrant so he can get records from the phone company, but that takes time and is a rigamarole."

"Then they'd know who all he's talked to."

"Yes."

"Clint, have you heard when the sheriff's office is releasing a statement regarding the crime, along with Peter's name?"

"The plan so far is the sheriff will issue it at one o'clock, and since Zimmer was the husband of a former U.S. Senator, he plans to hold a press conference at four. The media is always looking for a story, and this could easily gain national attention."

Like Pinky had said. "Man alive. Maybe I should stay away from my house; go live with my parents for a while," I said.

"According to Garrison, the sheriff won't disclose your name or address. However, the call is recorded at the sheriff's office."

"My neighbors know. Sandy Gibbons knows. It won't be long before the whole state does too."

"I'll talk to Sandy, ask her to keep your name out of her articles," he said.

"Thanks. Well, I should get back to Brew Ha-Ha, see if Pinky needs anything before I open my shop."

Clint and I had just stepped next door when Ramona Zimmer—the last person in the world I wanted to see, given Sandy Gibbons was still at Pinky's counter—burst through the door with enough gusto to surprise even Clint.

She bee-lined toward me. "Camryn! I tried to call you, but you didn't answer, and you didn't call me back."

In her state, had she forgotten we'd talked earlier? Ramona threw her arms around me. "Detective Garrison called me and gave me the most terrible news. Somebody *killed* Peter."

Sandy was on her feet much faster than she'd managed in my office a short time before. "Senator Zimmer, does he happen to be the man they found in the mayor's back yard?"

Clint stepped forward as if to intervene, but before he could, Ramona turned to Sandy. "*Yes.* They *killed* him and left him at *Camryn's.*"

If the whole situation wasn't so serious, so dire, I could have grinned at Sandy's amusing gawk. Her mouth dropped open, her eyes widened, her eyebrows shot halfway up to her hairline, and her face froze in that expression for a drawn-out minute.

Before anyone uttered another word, Clint pointed from me to Sandy to Ramona. "I need the three of you to follow me."

He turned and headed back into Curio Finds. I caught the look on Pinky's face; it almost mirrored Sandy's. I snuck a glance at customers in the back area and noticed they all seemed tuned in to the drama as it unfolded up front. Pinky's shop was often an ideal place for local gossip, and they'd hit pay dirt that morning.

I brought up the rear when Clint led us to the store room. Sandy, Ramona, and I formed a semi-circle around him. Clint took a breath as if he needed time to weigh his words. "All right. The Buffalo County Sheriff's Office is looking into the unusual set of circumstances that turned into a homicide investigation this morning."

Ramona butted in. "The detective wouldn't tell me how Peter was killed when he called. He told me that when I meet with the medical examiner this morning, he hopes to be there too. And I want someone else with me." She turned to me. "Like you, Camryn."

I willed myself to remain calm. *How could I possibly answer her?*

Clint rescued me before I had to. "Senator, Camryn might need to open her shop before you'd be finished at their office. How about I go with you?"

Ramona studied him a moment and nodded. "Okay."

Clint returned the nod. "What I need to tell all of you is we do *not* want to compromise this investigation in any way. That means not another word about it until the sheriff issues a statement. At some point, he will ask if anyone has any information, if they heard or saw anything suspicious, or has knowledge with regard to his death. If so, he'll ask them to contact the sheriff's office. We don't want rumors or speculations of any kind circulating among our citizens."

Sandy frowned, shook her head, then glanced at Ramona who had teared up. If Sandy was about to appeal to Clint, she changed her mind and tucked in her lips.

Clint laid a hand on Ramona's shoulder. "We also want to be respectful of Senator Zimmer and her feelings. This has understandably been a major shock for her."

Sandy eyed her feet a while then homed in on Ramona. "I have been very thoughtless, Senator. I owe you my apologies and deepest sympathy."

Tears ran down Ramona's cheeks as she nodded. "Thank you, and it's okay. I've been in such a funk I didn't even notice. I probably shouldn't have even driven, now that I think about it. I got that phone call and all I could think was I needed to talk to Camryn, and when she didn't answer, I was worried something had happened to her too."

Where is my phone? I mentally ran through my morning routine and realized I'd left it on the counter at home, plugged into the charger. If I had taken Ramona's second call, we could have avoided the unscheduled store room meeting between the four of us. On the other hand, maybe it was meant to be. Clint had killed two birds with one stone, so to speak.

"So we're all on the same page?" he asked.

"Yes," I said. Ramona seconded it, and as Sandy nodded, her mouth turned downward.

"Senator, I'll drive you over to the medical examiner's office when you're ready, and touch base with Detective Garrison to see if he's clear to join us," Clint said.

Ramona swiped at tears with her sleeve and shrugged. "I'll never feel prepared for that, but now is as good a time as any."

Ramona still had her coat on, and Clint hadn't worn one, so they were ready to roll. Sandy and I hung back. "I'm ashamed of myself for wanting to get the truth, not even thinking about the senator and how devastated she must feel," she said.

Her words gave me pause. Sandy wasn't just an ambulance chaser. She was a truth seeker too. Maybe the core reason she acted like a dog after a bone when she chased down her stories. She wanted to get to the bottom of things and share honest facts with her readers.

I removed my coat and purse from the hanger. "Sandy, I remembered my cell phone is at home, so I need to go grab it. Why don't you finish your coffee and scone in Brew Ha-Ha."

"Okay. I guess there's not much to do but wait until we get a report from the sheriff," she muttered.

Sandy settled in at the counter as I told Pinky about my errand. When I reached in my purse for the keys, I felt the baggie-enclosed note. First my phone, then the note. Heaped on stress had made me forgetful at times, but it seemed the ordeal with Ramona, at the heart of things, had multiplied my angst to the nth degree.

When I turned into my driveway, it felt ominous to park where Peter Zimmer's vehicle had sat, so I pulled in where Pinky's had been instead. Illogical or not, I couldn't help it. I climbed from my car and looked around for anything the authorities might've missed that I hadn't spotted either. Nothing.

Neighbor Eunice appeared from next door in a puffy jacket and wool cap. "Camryn!"

Oh my. "Morning, Eunice."

"I needed to see if you're okay."

"Thanks. Things feel a little raw right now, but I'll be fine before long," I said with that hope.

"I'm sure you will. So, did they figure out who the deceased man is?"

"They did, and I understand the sheriff's office will release his name this afternoon."

Eunice clicked her tongue against the top of her mouth. "We've never had anything close to this happen in our neighborhood before. My friend Sandy Gibbons wanted to know every single detail too."

Aha, the source. I'd suspected as much. "It was a big shock, that's for sure. Sandy and I already talked this morning."

"Well, that's good then. I have no idea where that woman gets her energy. She's almost as old as I am," Eunice said.

I'd wondered the same thing, many times. Sandy never seemed to run out of batteries. "Sandy is one of a kind, all right. I just came home to pick something up, so I better do that and get back to the shop."

"All righty then."

As she started to turn away, I said, "Why don't you come to our shops, anytime. I'll buy you a drink and one of

Pinky's baked treats."

Eunice's array of facial lines deepened when she smiled. "Why, thank you, Camryn. I'd love to do that."

"In fact, Sandy's down there now if you want to join her," I said.

"*Oh*. Maybe I will at that. Thank you."

We'd only had a few brief conversations over the past year, and I didn't know much about her. "Good. Hope to see you at the shop. Later, Eunice," I called out as I unlocked my back door.

I unplugged my fully charged phone and noted a few missed calls and messages. Aside from Ramona's, the others didn't hold the same urgency. Thankfully, none from my parents. I should have phoned them first thing but put it off in my feeble attempt to shield them from more bad news as long as possible. *You need to tell them.*

Back at Brew Ha-Ha, Pinky was washing mugs behind the counter, and turned when the bell dinged when I opened the door. Things had quieted. Four customers sat at a back table, and Sandy had moved from the counter to a table. Pinky followed me into my shop. "Cami, this has been the longest day ever, and it's not even ten o'clock yet."

"The old hurry up and wait thing puts us even more on edge. Besides, I'm a little worried there's going to be a media blitz about Ramona and Peter Zimmer. Who knows what the press might dig up."

Pinky let out a quiet snort. "You mean like how it relates to you, and why the ex-senator fired you, and why they left her husband's body in your driveway a year later?"

"Pinky, you do have a way with words at times," I said.

"Sorry, Cami. This whole thing is just so nerve-racking."

"Yes, it is. Majorly." I laid my purse on my service

counter and found my phone in a pocket. "Pinky, I have something to show you."

She snapped her ever-present dish towel. "What is it?"

I reached into my purse for the baggie with the green memo note inside, and held it up. "This look familiar to you?"

She took it from me and studied it like it was a puzzle. "JTK and maybe a code, hmm. Could be part of a phone number. Like if the person knew the area code and just needed the last seven numbers."

One explanation I'd surmised. "It's not your paper?"

She shook her head. "No, why?"

"I found it on the ground near where your car was parked."

Her eyes opened wide. "*No.* I know a lot of people with the first initial J, like the three Js that started stopping by last month. You know, the ones we served this morning who met in the swim class at the fitness center."

"Yes. The three Js?"

"That's what I call them but not to their faces. Their names are a little different and I can't remember what they are," she said.

I nodded. "It's always busy when they're here. They seem to know who I am, but I haven't had a chance to chat with them, or even ask their names."

"I totally understand. Not much chit chatting during the morning rush."

Before we said more, her doorbell dinged. Pinky handed me the baggie and hustled off to help her customer. I laid it on the counter, took a photo of it, and slid it on to the top shelf under the counter.

I heard Eunice's voice in Pinky's shop and headed next door. "Hello Eunice. Pinky, this is my neighbor, and I want to treat her today. Eunice, my friend Alice Nelson."

"But everyone calls me Pinky. Good to meet you," she said.

She smiled and nodded. "Good to meet you too."

"Eunice, hi!" Sandy called from her table. Eunice turned and waved.

"What would you like, my dear?" Pinky asked her.

Eunice studied the menu board. "So many choices. May I have a Columbian black coffee? That should hit the spot."

"Of course, and how about a scone or a muffin?"

She thought for a moment. "A cherry almond muffin sounds like a tasty choice."

"Coming right up," Pinky said.

"Eunice, it looks like Sandy wants you to join her," I said.

Pinky pointed in Sandy's direction. "You go ahead, Eunice. I'll deliver your order in a jif."

"Thank you." Eunice walked to Sandy's table, and they both smiled when she sat down. I filled a mug with coffee. Pinky put a muffin and packet of butter on a plate then handed it to me. "I'll grab silverware and napkins," she said.

As I set the order in front of Eunice, Sandy said, "We were just discussing the weather, since a certain other subject is off the table for now."

"The ever-changing weather is a good Minnesota topic," I quipped. "Enjoy."

7

Business had slowed a bit by the time Ramona burst into Brew Ha-Ha and scurried toward me. Pinky's expression changed from pleasant to pained in a nanosecond.

I'd almost reached security behind Pinky's counter before Ramona closed the space between us. She threw her arms around me. "Chief Lonsbury didn't come to the medical examiner's office with me after all. He got an emergency phone call just as we got there. Camryn, I *have* to talk to you." *What about Detective Garrison, what happened to him?*

It was easier to concede than to resist. I drew in a slow breath to steady my heart rate. "Okay. Let's go talk in my shop. I have a little time yet before we open."

The lights flicked on, then off again, as we crossed through the archway. Ramona took a sidestep. "What made that happen?"

I waved my hand. "Some kind of glitch with the electricity. We've had it looked at, and the electrician said it's nothing to be concerned about." Although it made me wonder if Molly was troubled by Ramona's presence and felt the need to alert me. On the way to my office for the second time that morning—first with Sandy, then with Ramona—I worried a little myself. I pulled my chair to the side of the desk, closer to Ramona, and hoped it would ease her stress a bit.

She sank down on the chair like she'd gained a hundred pounds. "I'm too scared to go home. Camryn, what if they're after me?"

"Why would you think that?" I asked.

She teared up. "I don't know. Maybe they're mad at me and killed my husband for revenge. They wanted me to suffer first, and then they'd get me next." Ramona found a tissue in her pocket and dabbed her eyes.

It seemed like a wild idea, but I considered it for a moment. "Has anyone threatened you, ever?"

She gave her head a little shake. "Well, not in so many words. I got a lot of nasty emails and phone calls from people who were upset about the way I voted on this, or that. You know about those, Camryn."

"I do. But if you've had an actual threat, you need to tell Detective Garrison."

She glanced down at her lap. "I'll think back through the last years, see if I can think of particular people, maybe come up with names."

"That's a good plan." A light turned on in my brain. "Ramona, this is a question regarding your health, if it's okay to ask. How are you managing your diabetes?"

She pulled a clean tissue from her pocket. "Not so good. I had to start insulin injections a few months ago."

She had syringes? *Hmm.* "I'm sorry to hear that."

"Peter had to help me for a while because I just couldn't inject myself. But with him gone so much, I decided I had to make myself learn to do it."

"Oh. Where did Peter go?" I asked.

"He was looking for a job for a while, and finally got one at a car dealership. It's between Orten and Brooks Landing.

He drives vehicles to other dealers, sometimes halfway across the state." Ramona referred to Peter as if he were still alive.

"Did you tell Garrison that, about Peter's job, I mean?"

She shook her head. "He wants me to come to his office at eleven. After what the medical examiner told me—and I can't talk about that yet—I needed time before I faced the detective again. I mean, how can I answer any more questions when I can't even believe that Peter's really dead?"

I had to fight the temptation to show Ramona the mysterious memo note. If it turned out to be a piece of evidence, it would no doubt interfere with the investigation, and I'd be in big-time trouble. Worse yet, if Ramona recognized whose initials JTK belonged to, or whose partial phone number it was, it would alert her that the authorities had it in their possession. If that person was her accomplice, she could warn him or her to run for the hills. It'd be self-protection on her part. If the person got caught, she would without a doubt be next, a conundrum for sure.

It was time to open Curio Finds, so Ramona made her way into Brew Ha-Ha to get a drink and a bite to eat before her meeting with Detective Garrison. I flipped on the light switch, and as I reached the front door, the lights turned off. "Molly, I've already had enough drama today," I whispered. The lights came on again. "Thank you." As I turned the key in the lock, my parents approached the door, so I opened it for them.

"Morning, Mom and Dad." I sought a casual tone as I felt tears form in my eyelids.

"Are you testing out the lights?" Dad asked.

They'd witnessed the off/on light action, but I dodged the question. "Come in out of the cold."

They stepped into the shop, and Dad shut the door behind them. Their casual, everyday personas clued me they hadn't heard about the body left in my back yard. Each gave me a hug, then Mom rested her hands on my biceps, and searched my face in her unique way. "Cami, you look troubled. What's wrong?"

I could rarely hide my emotions from her, even when I tried. When a couple of tears escaped and rolled down my cheeks, they gave me away. "Let's head to the back area by the store room so we can keep an eye out for customers, and I'll tell you what happened."

We formed a close huddle, and in a quiet voice I took them through the last night's events with as many details as I felt comfortable to give and was able to share.

Dad gave me the bear hug he was famous for, and Mom squeezed my hands in hers. "We're so sorry, dear. Why in the world would that adulterer's body be left in *your* driveway?"

It was out of character for Mom to label anyone, and I suppressed a smile. "We have no idea at this point. It's in the hands of the sheriff's office." I lowered my voice a few more decibels and added, "A lot has gone on this morning too. Ramona Zimmer is in Pinky's shop now."

Mom shook her head. "What do they say about how a bad penny keeps turning up?"

"No kidding. The thing is, Ramona does seem genuinely distraught, but I still can't bring myself to completely trust her," I said.

"You have good reasons for that too, Cami," Dad said.

"I have to say the silver lining in the D.C scandal is that it brought you back home," Mom added.

Dad agreed. "Now if we could just keep you out of trouble, even when it's not your doing, or your fault."

"No, just a string of terrible happenstances is what

they've been," Mom said.

A customer entered the shop. "Hello!" I called to her, then told my parents, "Why don't you go ask Pinky to make you a hot beverage to warm your insides."

"And face the dragon," Mom whispered.

Her second unexpected comment tickled me once again.

Customers meandered through the shop over the next forty minutes. They perused the snow globes on the shelves; most picked up at least one, gave it a shake, and watched the snow settle over the scene.

A woman selected one with two cardinals on a tree branch. "My sister collects things with cardinals. She has a clock. a music box, and lots of figurines. This will be the *perfect* gift for her." She set it on the counter.

"I think she will love it. I'll get the box it came in. Would you like me to gift wrap it for you?" I asked her.

"Sure. That's so nice of you, thank you."

On my way to the store room for the box, I snuck a peek at the back tables in Brew Ha-Ha and noticed both Sandy and Eunice were gone. Ramona sat alone at a table, her eyes glued to her phone. My parents sipped drinks from mugs at another.

At 10:49, I was alone in the shop when Ramona poked her head through the archway. "Bye for now, Camryn. Say a prayer, okay?"

An unusual request from her. I nodded in response. "Take care, Ramona."

My parents must have thought they needed to stick around until after she left because they were but a few steps behind her. "Did you talk to Ramona?" I asked.

"No. She didn't seem to recognize us when we walked past her, and we just let it go," Mom said.

"She was checking things on her phone almost the whole time," Dad said.

"It's just as well, don't you think? You only met her that one time for a few minutes in D.C., before she dashed off to a meeting," I said.

Dad nodded. "And that's why we didn't feel the need to introduce ourselves."

"You didn't notice if she made any phone calls?" I asked.

Mom shook her head. "No." She touched my cheek. "Can we do anything for you, dear?"

Besides make the Peter Zimmer nightmare disappear into thin air? "Thank you. One thing, will you tell my brothers and sisters what happened? I know they'll want to call me, or stop by, but I can't really say anything at this point. We can touch base later, or if they want to text me, that'd be fine too."

"We'll pass on what we know, and they'll understand about no phone calls or visits. We're due for a family dinner anyhow, so when things settle down, we'll plan one soon," Mom said.

"That'd be good. Also, if something comes up, like if I need to leave the shop for a good reason, can I call you to take over? Emmy went south for the month." Emmy was our occasional employee who had helped Pinky and me over the Christmas rush.

"Of course. You know you can count on us, and you be sure to do that, Cami," Dad said.

After parting hugs, out the door they went.

Pinky came in next and plunked her hands on her hips. "I'm relieved Ramona finally left. I didn't think this morning would ever end, and we still have nearly an hour to go before it does."

The morning had dragged on, even with the extra activity. "Time does *not* fly when you're *not* having fun."

"You got that right. Your parents spent quite a bit of time sipping their coffees, which was nice. Sandy and your neighbor stayed for a long time too," Pinky said.

"I don't think Eunice gets out much, so I'm glad she came and socialized a bit. Pinky, did any of them—and you know the three I mean—say anything they shouldn't have, like about Peter?"

"I didn't hear his name mentioned, if that's what you mean. I can promise you I tuned in as much as I could. Plus, I made a bunch of trips to my back room, whether I needed to or not," she said.

I tapped my temple. "Now that I think more about it, Ramona and Sandy probably should not have been in the same room, after all."

"They weren't at the same table, and both were warned not to discuss the case, right?" Pinky said.

"Right."

"Cami, have you told your city council folks yet?"

"No, and I best do that before word starts to circulate," I said.

Pinky nodded and left to help a new customer. I stared at my phone a moment and tried to decide how to phrase my message in a group text to the councilors, Gail Spindler, Rosalie "Stormin'" Gorman, Wendell Lyon, and Harley Creighton. We'd lost Mayor Frost in December and our former Police Chief Aaron Newel in January.

It'd be best to assure them it wasn't another city employee. I decided on *Hello, This isn't public information, but a man was found dead in my driveway last night, and the sheriff's office is investigating. Not to worry, it's no one you'd know. We'll talk later, and thanks for keeping this quiet for now.*

They all responded in under a minute. Gail sent a folded hands emoji, Rosalie wrote, *Oh no!* Both Wendell and Harley sent a thumbs up, and the two matter-of-fact emojis brought a smile to my face. Like it was an everyday event.

A few minutes later, Stormin' Gorman rushed in like she was pursued by an assailant. My whole body tensed, as it often did, when she arrived on the scene. Any scene.

She dashed over and grabbed me into a bear hug. "Mayor, I know you can't say anything, but I just had to know you were okay. I'm so relieved you're well enough to be at work."

"Thanks, um, Rosalie."

"Well, I have to get back to the office. You call if you need anything. You'll do that, right?"

"I will, promise."

"We need to take good care of our mayor. Bye." And off she went. The encounter had left me a bit shaken.

Clint was next to arrive. His eyes captured mine, and he managed a half smile. "Hanging in there?"

My shoulders lifted. "By my fingertips, seems like."

"A good way to put it. Camryn, what an ordeal this has grown into." He came around the counter and gave me a quick one-armed hug.

"Yeah. Ramona went to meet with Detective Garrison at eleven. If there's anything important—like a confession—to wheedle out of her, he'd be the one to do it."

He raised his eyebrows. "I agree. Garrison's seasoned and sharp as a tack."

"Clint, I found a paper in my yard this morning that we'll need to give him." I withdrew the note from the under-counter shelf.

"What have you got? He studied it a moment. "You

found this in your yard?"

I nodded. "Yes, near where Peter Zimmer's vehicle was. It could've blown in after everyone left, for all we know."

"True." Clint flipped it over and read the back. "JTK. A person's initials, or the name of a business maybe. And what looks like part of a phone number. But it could be a seven-digit code, like for a keypad door lock. It may not be connected to Peter Zimmer at all. Or it might be an important piece to the puzzle. The investigation is in early stages yet, and sounds like the county hasn't got much to go on so far."

"Like you said, it's early yet."

"When I talked to Garrison a while ago, he said they'd collected hairs from Peter Zimmer's car, but unless they have the roots, they can't obtain any DNA. And if they do get a good DNA sample, the person will have to be in the system to find out his or her identity," Clint said.

I didn't know they needed hair roots. "Hmm. I wonder, with all his dealings, whether or not Peter Zimmer has a criminal record. Sure seems like he would."

"I thought the same thing. I ran a criminal history on him, and it surprised me a little to find out he doesn't have one. Some people are smart enough and able to skirt the law. From what you've told me about Zimmer, he may have been one of those guys."

"Yeah. Deceptive is more like it. I've known a few people in my career who can tell convincing lies with the most 'not me' innocent looks," I said.

"I have a list of people who fit that description myself. I figure some career criminals must study 'how to tell if a person is lying manuals' and teach themselves what facial expressions and mannerisms to avoid. With others, sad to say, it's part of their psychopathy. They come across as charismatic, confident, and like you said, provide details that make their lies convincing and believable."

"Eew. It's scary when you put it that way, but I totally get it."

Clint held up the baggie. "I'll run this over to the sheriff's office and see if Garrison has finished his interview with your former boss while I'm at it."

"You'd think they'd be done with that by now. Is it a good thing, or a bad thing, if an interview runs long?" I asked.

"Could be either, depending on the interviewer. I'm thinking Garrison will take his time, use his practiced people skills, so Ramona feels as comfortable as possible."

"Yeah, that would help loosen her up."

"It should at that. I'll see you later." He lifted his hand on his way out the door.

I sat down on the stool behind the counter. My mind returned to the earlier conversation with Ramona. She'd said two things that raised my suspicions, made me consider her potential involvement in her husband's murder. First off, she couldn't make herself repeat what the medical examiner had told her. Why not? Plus the way she said she couldn't believe Peter was dead made me wonder if she'd taken part in his death after all.

I conjured up PG images of Ramona and Peter together. Maybe he'd given her an insulin shot, then they'd had a confrontation. As they tussled, air could have gotten sucked into the syringe. Ramona got hold of it and stuck Peter in his chest to hurt him, not to kill him.

The main quandary I had with that scenario was Ramona would've needed an accomplice. On the other hand, if she'd planned to kill Peter, she would have enlisted a person before the fact. If not, it would've been a scramble to get someone to help her after he was dead. According to Ramona, her brother was the only person she was close to, and he was halfway around the world. However, she had a long list of connections. People did unscrupulous things for the right price.

Clint called a little after noon and relayed that the sheriff had decided to hold a press conference at one o'clock, instead of a press release first, and a conference later. As the hour neared, Pinky poked her head through the archway and held up her phone. "It's almost one o'clock, time to tune in to the press conference, hear what he has to say about the Peter Zimmer case."

I'd debated whether I wanted to hear it firsthand, or wait for the recap instead, but gave in. "All right."

Pinky moved in beside me and stood next to my stool. "It'll be live on Channel Three. And others too, I'm sure, but I have Three's app on my phone," she said.

I bumped her elbow with mine. "Doesn't it seem like the conference is more of a formality because of Ramona's former position?"

"Probably, but it might help me believe it really happened, because it still does not seem real at all," she said.

"No, it can take a while till reality sets in. Even then, it's hard to believe. The good thing about a press conference is the sheriff will be in charge of the narrative, and it might help cut down on the number of media people who would otherwise hound Ramona."

Pinky shrugged. "That's true. I guess we should hope so, for her sake."

"Yes, we should. Speaking of Ramona, I half expected her to stop by again, after she'd finished with Garrison," I said.

"Hrumpf. Maybe Garrison threw her in the clink."

"*Pinky.* If he did, we would have heard about that for sure."

"I guess." Pinky clicked the Channel 3 app on her phone. A few seconds later, we saw Detective Garrison behind a podium in what looked like a sheriff's office conference room. A Minnesota flag, and an American flag, stood behind him on either side, with a deputy in front of each one.

The camera was zeroed in on Detective Garrison and the deputies. The sheriff must have been unavailable. The backs of a few heads in the front row were also visible. My eyes fell on Sandy Gibbons's, the one I recognized. I imagined how her fingers twitched as she waited for Garrison to begin.

He cleared his throat. "I'm Detective Garrison with the Buffalo County Sheriff's Office. Thank you, members of the press, and concerned citizens, for joining us. As you may know, we're investigating the unexpected death of Peter Zimmer whose body was discovered in the passenger seat of his vehicle. They did an autopsy, and the medical examiner has consequently ruled his death a homicide."

I heard a gasp. It could've been Sandy.

"So far, we have no leads and we're asking anyone with information that may pertain to this case to contact the sheriff's office without delay. You can remain anonymous. I can also assure you we have no reason to believe a threat to the public exists, as it relates to this case."

I saw a few hands go up, and Garrison lifted his in response. "I'm sorry but I can't take any questions at this time. When we learn more, we'll be sure to pass it along. Thank you."

The two deputies stepped forward to flank Garrison and escorted him from the room. The Channel 3 News camera turned to the female reporter in back. She said, "Detective Garrison was brief with his comments. That's all for now, but stay tuned for updates as we follow this case."

Pinky clicked off the app. "She should've said 'curious and unusual case.'"

"It is that, and smart of Garrison not to mention the victim's wife's name. But it shouldn't take long before the media folks put two and two together," I said.

"I agree, especially since Sandy already knows."

We were lost in our thoughts a moment, then I said, "I hope they'll be able to figure out who the initials and numbers on that memo note belong to, and if it means anything."

"So you gave it to them?"

"Yes, to Clint to give to Garrison. I think you were in your back room grinding coffee beans when he stopped by earlier," I said.

"What'd he say about the note?"

"It could be nothing, it could be something."

She chuckled. "That's about it. Huh, you'd think the experts could do a magic test and find out whose DNA is on it."

"Clint said they'd have to be in the system first. And get this, Pinky. You can't share this or people would figure out who told me."

Her eyes widened. "Okay . . ."

"Peter Zimmer did *not* have a criminal record."

"Seriously? It's hard to believe no one had him arrested for sexual assault over the years." She paused. "Maybe he changed his identity, got a new name."

"He'd still have the same fingerprints," I said.

"Yeah. I watched one of those true crime shows where a guy burned his fingertips with acid, but they grew back again. I had no idea it worked like that."

"Pretty amazing," I said.

8

Eunice surprised us both when she came into my shop.

"Hello, new friend," Pinky said.

She smiled. "Hello, to both of you."

"Welcome back," I said.

Eunice walked up to the counter. "Camryn, I went home and took a nap and when I woke up I thought of a detail I'd forgotten, what with all the commotion last night."

About the case? "What was that?" I asked.

"Well. Not too long before the police got to your place, I was at my kitchen sink washing dishes and noticed a dark-colored vehicle, like a small bus, stop in the alley. It pulled forward, so I couldn't see when it was on the other side of your garage. Then I heard a car door close and the vehicle drive away."

Another neighbor had told Garrison she'd seen one too, maybe the same one.

"Eunice, you'll need to tell Detective Garrison. You'd gone back inside your house, so you didn't hear when another neighbor reported she'd also seen one. You said the vehicle was dark colored. Not black?"

"I don't think it was black, but maybe dark gray. To tell the truth, I didn't pay that close of attention. Vehicles that don't belong to neighbors drive through now and then.

Along with more delivery vans than ever, it seems," she said.

True. "Do you remember what time it was?" I asked.

"Around six-thirty-five, thirty-six." The other witness had said 6:30 or 6:40. In that same time frame.

"Not that long before I got there myself," Pinky said. "Cami, It gives me chills to think if I'd arrived a little earlier I might have seen the killer and the accomplice, and they might've hurt me."

"Killer?" Eunice said.

"Detective Garrison had a press conference at one. He named the victim, who happened to be Senator Zimmer's husband, Peter. And the medical examiner ruled his death a homicide."

Eunice's hands covered her cheeks. "Oh, Camryn! It was someone you knew? That gives me major chills too."

"Back to the big vehicle that stopped in the alley. It may have nothing to do with this case," I said.

Pinky ducked her head close to my face. "You don't believe that do you?"

I shook my head. "No, but it's possible. Eunice, let me check in with Detective Garrison." I pulled his business card from my pants pocket. Pinky and Eunice watched me punch his number on my phone.

"Detective Garrison," he answered on the first ring.

"Detective, it's Camryn Brooks."

"Yes, Mayor."

"My neighbor Eunice is here with me in Curio Finds— you talked to her in my yard. Anyway, she remembered seeing a big dark vehicle, like a small bus, last night."

"You say she's at your shop now?" Garrison said.

"Yes."

"Okay. Ask her to sit tight, and I'll be there in five minutes or so."

"Sure, will do."

"Thanks." He disconnected.

"Eunice, the detective is on his way to see you," I relayed.

Her frown lines deepened. "I'm not sure how much more I'll be able to tell him."

"Just what you remember, so he can put it in his report," I said.

Pinky pointed at her shop. "I best go figure out the specials for tomorrow."

Detective Garrison arrived four minutes later, greeted Eunice, and offered her his hand. As they shook, I walked to the archway between the shops and noticed Pinky was alone in Brew Ha-Ha.

"No one next door, except Pinky, if you want to go in there to talk," I told them.

"Sure, let's go claim a table," Garrison said.

Eunice lifted a hand toward me. "Can Camryn come with us?"

Garrison's eyes caught mine, and I nodded.

"Not a problem," he told her.

We took seats at a back table. Garrison removed his notepad and pen. "All right, Eunice, let's go back to last night. You told Camryn you saw a dark colored vehicle, like a small bus. What time was that?"

"I'd looked at the clock at six-thirty, a few minutes before that, so it was right around six thirty-five."

Garrison nodded. "Can you describe the vehicle?"

"It was big, like a small bus, or extra-big van."

"Could you tell the color, besides that it was a dark one? Navy, gray, black?"

"Dark gray, I'm pretty sure. And it didn't have those big windows on the side, like a lot of them do. After I thought more about it, I figured it was a delivery van because I heard it stop, then a door shut a few seconds later, and the vehicle drove away."

"Any company logo on the doors?" Garrison said.

"No. But—and here's the strange part, at least it made me wonder—I remembered seeing a decal on the corner of the front passenger side window. It's the one used by medical people, you know, with snakes around a rod, and wings at the top."

"I think I know what you mean, and I'll look it up." Garrison took out his phone, pushed a button, and tapped some letters. A moment later he lifted his phone to show her an image. "Did it look like this?" he asked.

Eunice studied it and nodded.

"I guess I've never had cause to look up its name." Garrison read for a bit. "The symbol is called Caduceus—if I'm saying it right—and I've seen it posted in pharmacies, mostly. According to this article, it has two snakes around a staff with the wings at the top, which was the symbol of a Greek messenger god.

"Along the way, it got confused with the first real medical symbol, the Rod of Asclepius. That has a single snake, branch, and no wings. Huh. I didn't know any of that." He selected the photos and laid his phone on the table for us to see.

Neither had I.

As we looked over the photos, Eunice shook her head. "No. I've seen that Caduceus symbol plenty of times over the years, and like you, Detective, I associated it with medicine. That symbol on the van made me think maybe one of the neighbors had their prescriptions delivered, like a lot of us do nowadays."

Garrison nodded. "I think both pharmacies in town have a delivery service. I'll see if one has a van like that. If so, we can find out if they made a stop in your neighborhood last night."

After Detective Garrison and neighbor Eunice left, I waited on Curio Finds customers that straggled in over the next hour, until Ramona once again darkened my door. She took one look at me and burst into tears. "Camryn, the medical examiner said he'll be ready to send Peter to a funeral home tomorrow. What should I do?"

I pulled a tissue from the box on my counter, walked around, and handed it to her. She collapsed against me. I put my arm around her and guided her into Brew Ha-Ha. Pinky's eyebrows drew together at the unexpected sight we must've presented, and I read her reaction as, "Please take her anywhere besides my shop."

It made me wish we had a cot in the store room so Ramona could lie down, and I could try to block out that she was there. I helped her on to a seat at a table. "Can I get you anything to drink?"

She shook her head. "Camryn, how am I ever going to get through this?"

I shocked myself when I said, "I'll help you as best I can."

Ramona blinked away tears. "Really? Can you help me hide?"

Ah, no. "What do you mean?"

"I can't go home because the media people are after me for a story, and I don't want to talk to any of them."

I didn't want to harbor a possible fugitive at my house. "All right. How about you check into the hotel in Brooks Landing, or find one in a nearby town?" I suggested.

She gave me a little head nod. "Oh. Maybe that will work. I'll need clothes and my hygiene items."

"Tell you what. When I get done with work, I'll drive you to your house. Your neighbors don't know my vehicle.

You can get your things together, then I'll help you register at a hotel."

"You'd do that for me?" She looked at her hands a moment. "I honestly didn't realize how mean I was to you last year, when I took Peter's word over yours. And now Peter got himself involved in something bad and ended up dead. It's like this horrible crime lifted my blinders, made me face up to it, and accept the truth."

I didn't want to get into a rehash of last year's dramatic events or what happened after that. A wise man—my dad—once told me, "You need to forgive, but you don't need to forget." I took that to mean, forgive the person but be cautious when it came to his or her future actions.

"Ramona, we had pretty good years working together. So let's remember that, move past the last year, and deal with what we need to do today."

She drew in a quick breath. "Okay, and thank you, Camryn. That means a lot to me."

"Do you have any errands to run before five o'clock?"

"No. Besides, I don't want to be seen in public right now."

"All right. Where is your car parked?" I asked her.

She waved her hand at the door. "On the street out front."

"That's two-hour parking, so you can move it to the lot behind our shops. It'll be fine until we get back into town."

"Okay." She headed straight out the door.

When I joined Pinky at her counter, she plopped her hands on her hips. "Cami Jo Brooks, what were you thinking, offering to do all that for her?"

"Pinky, remember that phrase, 'keep your friends close, and your enemies closer'? It's something like that. I don't completely trust her. On the other hand, she trusts me. If she was involved in Peter's death, she might slip up, incriminate herself.”

"But still.”

"Plus, it's basic human kindness," I said.

Pinky rolled her eyes. "Okay. I'll give you that. And if you get any inside information, all the better," she added.

With Ramona hanging out in my office, it seemed to take forever as I waited for five o'clock to roll around. A few minutes to four, I told Pinky take off. She'd already put in a nine-hour day.

She tipped her head toward my office and whispered. "Are you sure you'll be okay?"

"I'm sure. We'll touch base later. In the meantime, will you talk to Erin, give her the day's updates?"

"Will do. Later then," she said.

I sent Clint a text message about my evening plans with Ramona. He must not have been able to respond, because all he sent me back was a question mark. Yes. Life in general, and my plans at the moment, were big question marks all right.

It felt both good, and a little scary, to lock the shop door and move on to the task at hand. I led Ramona through the walkway between our building and the next, to the back parking lot. I hadn't started the Subaru's engine earlier, but the outside temperature had warmed so the car would be comfortable before we'd left city limits.

With much to mull over, my brain shifted into high gear. Not a good time for that. I needed to keep my full attention on the road, and practice defensive driving skills. Twenty minutes later—after a quiet ride with Ramona, who seemed like she was in another world—we pulled into her driveway. Her motion detection lights flashed on.

"I've got my garage door opener with me." Ramona pushed the button, and as the door lifted, she said, "Go ahead and drive in."

Okay. Given our years together, I should be able to trust her, but at that moment I wondered if that were still true. What if she drew a syringe on me? She knew I couldn't run, so to avoid an attack, I'd have to think fast and plan my escape route ahead of time.

I drove in and turned off the ignition. "Want me to wait for you out here?"

"Of course not. It shouldn't take me long, but come inside with me. Please."

The chance she'd do anything harmful to me in her own home was slim, and she had apologized for her past behavior. Still, that niggling doubt what she might attempt gnawed at me. I sought the most nonchalant delivery possible when I said, "Okay."

My fears abated a bit when Ramona stepped into the house and burst into tears. "It feels so lonely already," she said.

I silently agreed. Her house did not have the welcoming presence mine did. "Can I help you with anything?" I asked.

Ramona shook her head. "Just need to figure out what to pack."

"Where do you keep your insulin?" I asked.

"The unopened vials are in the refrigerator, and then they keep at room temperature for a month." I resisted asking about the syringes.

Ramona would not appreciate me looking over her shoulder, so I hung around her bedroom door. Her bed was worse than unmade. It looked like someone had kicked off the covers a bunch of times. Both sides of the bed had been slept in. More like, the whole bed had. A possible crime scene? I'd run it by Clint.

Ramona threw a suitcase on the bed like she hadn't noticed its chaotic state. I watched as she gathered clothing from hangers and drawers and threw them in the case without care. When she went into the connecting bathroom, I followed and took a quick peek inside. Ramona caught my image in the mirror and cupped a small item—a pill bottle maybe—in her hand, like she wanted to hide it from me.

Odd. I backed away to give her needed privacy. Was it a prescription either for herself, or for Peter, she didn't want me to know about? Or worse, an illicit drug in the bottle? Was that her reason? Did I even want to know? We'd been in the house less than ten minutes and I couldn't wait to escape and never return.

I took a look around the bedroom. The doors to the spacious walk-in closet stood open and held both Ramona's and Peter's clothes, footwear, and random items. A couple minutes later, Ramona emerged from the bathroom with a small fabric container, placed it in her suitcase, and zipped it shut. She struggled to lift it off the bed, and I stepped in to help. It wasn't heavy, so it seemed she'd lost her strength with the burden she carried—whatever that entailed.

"I'll put this in my car while you take a last look around," I said then rolled the bag to the garage.

"Almost forgot my insulin." She headed to the refrigerator. By the time I'd set the case in the back, Ramona had joined me, and we climbed into the Subaru. She pushed the garage door opener button, and as I backed out, I sent up a request that I would be home within an hour, with no more drama before then.

I dropped Ramona off at her car in my shop's back lot, and she followed me to the Brooks Landing Hotel. After she'd registered, she asked if I would join her for dinner. "I'll order takeout and we can eat it in my room, or in the lobby area," she said.

"Thanks, but I need to take care of a few things." *And*

the main thing is my mind.

"Okay. We'll connect later about tomorrow . . . and Peter."

The cat got my tongue, so all I managed was a small smile, and a wave as I left. I had ignored many missed calls and messages, given the number of phone vibrates I'd gotten after Ramona and I left my shop, almost two hours before.

Home at long last, I parked in the garage, and as the door closed, I scanned the yard for any unusual activity. What if the person who'd driven Peter's body to my yard—and the accomplice who'd picked him up—had returned to the scene of the crime for whatever reason, maybe to see if they'd left any traces of their presence, like a missing memo note, for example.

The set of tire tracks left by Peter's car had been driven over, and any shoe or boot prints had been brushed away before officials stomped around the scene in their exploration. The people involved in the crime were either seasoned criminals, or they had a last-minute brainstorm that prompted them to take care of the footprints' removal detail.

I almost shed tears of joy when I stepped inside my house. It felt that good. Had it really been a mere twenty-four hours since Pinky's fateful phone call from my back yard? I kicked off my shoes, shrugged off my coat, pulled the phone from my pants pocket, and settled on the couch to return messages and phone calls.

Mom's text was first; *Just touching base.* I sent a heart emoji back to her. Erin was next. She'd talked to Pinky who gave her a summary of the day. I sent her a message how I helped Ramona pick up personal items and get checked into a local hotel. She sent me a scared face emoji back. Pinky's followed. I realized I should have included her on the text to

Erin, to save typing the same information twice. Pinky sent a mug of beer image back. *Not a bad idea,* I thought. Clint's message was, *Call me when you can.* So I did.

He answered with, "Camryn," his voice soft and sweet.

It brought long unshed tears to my eyes. "Clint," I spit out.

He recognized the emotion in my voice. "Sounds like you could use a shoulder to cry on. Is it okay if I come over?"

"More than okay." I sniffed. "Give me fifteen minutes to shower off whatever grime I might've picked up today."

"You bet. See you in twenty."

"Thanks."

I stood under a hot shower and cleansed myself from head to toe, twice. When I'd dried off and put on comfortable sweats, it amazed me how my muscles had loosened a bit. Knowing Clint was on his way played a big part in that. I heard his vehicle come to a stop in my driveway and opened the back door for him.

He stepped inside and drew me into a bear hug that I wished could last for an hour. "You smell so . . . clean. I mean, in a good way."

His comment made me chuckle. "So do you. I mean, you smell clean in a *very* good way."

Clint squeezed me tighter with one hand, lifted my chin with the other, and gave me a deep kiss that warmed every inch of my body, inside and out. A moment later, he moved his head back a few inches and studied my face. "Ready to talk?"

I nodded. "Actually, Pinky suggested I have a beer. Maybe we can grab a couple of bottles first?"

"Sure. I'm officially off-duty until morning. My assistant will cover any major issues, should they arise," Clint said.

"Assistant Chief Mark Weston is a good guy."

"No doubt about that."

I opened the refrigerator. "What would you like? I have few choices."

He rested his neck on my shoulder as he peered inside. "Hmm. I'll go with a pale ale."

I selected two bottles while Clint found an opener in the drawer, cracked them open, handed me one, and lifted his. "Here's to a better day tomorrow."

"Here, here," I said and tapped my bottle against his.

Clint took my hand and led me into the living room. We got positioned on the couch with our backs against opposite arms, heels on the cushions, and knees bent so our toes touched.

"Tell me all about it," he said.

I shared details of the day and conversations with Eunice, Ramona, Garrison, Ramona, Pinky, Ramona. "I felt like I'd lost twenty pounds by the time I left her at the hotel."

His brows lifted and his eyes twinkled when he said, "I'd say it was more like a hundred and seventy pounds."

I poked his chest. "Guess you're right." I took a sip from the bottle. "Clint, when I was at Ramona's, the state of their bed covers is what I'd considered abnormally messy. It made my suspicious mind ask the question, was that where Peter Zimmer died?"

"Oh?"

"Besides that, Ramona was acting protective of something in what I thought was a pill bottle, although I didn't get a good look at it."

His brows drew together. "Is that right? Can you elaborate?"

After I filled in more details, he said, "The tricky part is Orten is in Hennepin County, a different jurisdiction. I'll talk to Detective Garrison. He can run it by his Hennepin

County detective buddies, see what they think. If they believe there's probable cause to do a search, they'll get a judge to sign a warrant, so they can go in and look for possible evidence."

"But I don't want Ramona to know I ratted on her."

"No one has to tell her. When a detective talks to Ramona, he can ask for permission to search her house. He can tell her it's part of the investigation to help clear her of any involvement. If he needs to get a warrant, she can't prevent their legal right to a search," he said.

"My thoughts have been like a yo-yo, up and down, up and down. First I think she loved Peter and could not be capable of harming him, much less kill him. Then I imagine a scenario where they're either engaged in an activity that went from bad to worse, or maybe Ramona just got fed up with his behavior, flipped out, and killed him. I've made myself dizzy going back and forth between those thoughts." I took a gulp of beer.

"That's why we have investigators to follow leads, look for evidence, and in the best-case scenario, coax a confession out of the guilty party."

"Yeah."

"I tell you what. Why don't you sit on a pillow in front of the couch and I'll give you a neck and shoulder massage," he said.

"That would be like heaven. Thank you," I said.

"Hope so. I don't have a therapist's certificate, but I'll do my best."

I settled on the pillow and leaned my back against the couch. Clint was a natural. He worked on the knots, and loosened the tension in my tight neck and scalp. I don't know when I fell asleep, but when I woke up later, I was stretched out on the floor with a pillow under my head, covered with the comforter. I heard gentle snores lifting from the couch, and warm fuzzies ran through me.

Clint not only got an A+ for the finest massage ever, he'd also made sure I was comfortable and warm. And when I awoke, I'd have the assurance he'd looked out for me all night long. I resisted the urge to give him a kiss and hug. Instead, I laid back down under the comforter, said my prayers, and fell back asleep to the tick tock sounds of the clock.

❄

9

No idea how Clint had gotten off the couch without waking or stepping on me the next morning. But when I awoke and smelled the aroma of coffee wafting from the other room, I realized he had. I entered the kitchen and saw him at the table, his lips on a mug. He smiled and stood. "Morning."

I met him halfway and wrapped my arms around his waist. "Good morning, and it is truly that. Thanks to your expert massage I got a solid and restful night's sleep. The only bad thing was, I dozed off and must've missed part of it."

He let out a chuckle. "You didn't miss much. When you started to do little breath puffs, I stopped."

"Breath puffs?"

He demonstrated what sounded more like "poofs."

"Seriously?" I said.

"It was actually kinda cute."

I leaned my head back for a look at his face to see if he was serious. His grin didn't give me a hint one way or the other. I decided to take the high road and gave him a thank you kiss instead.

He returned it in earnest and said, "I'd rather stay longer, but I gotta head home and get ready for work. I'll let Garrison know about your questioned possible evidence in the Zimmer home. He'll want to talk to you, and then he can decide if a search is in order."

Clint gave me a quick peck and left out the back door.

As I watched water drip through the single serve side of my coffee maker, my phone buzzed.

When I saw it was Ramona Zimmer, it took everything inside myself to push the accept button. "Hello?"

"Camryn, I'm glad you answered. You know about the big decisions I have to make today, like what funeral home Peter should go to, and what kind of service I should have for him. Will you go with me?"

Lord, help me.

"Ramona, I help Pinky with the morning crowd and often do needed paperwork until my shop opens at ten."

"Oh. I wasn't sure how that worked, I mean about you actually working in Brew Ha-Ha."

"Pinky helps me too, as needed. I'll tell you what. There's a funeral home in Brooks Landing, if you want to talk to them first, unless you have another home in mind," I said.

"No, I really don't. Not another one, I mean."

"All right. You can tell the medical examiner to send Peter there. It's called Walters Funeral Services, or Walters Chapel."

"Camryn, I can't think straight about much of anything right now," she said.

"That's completely understandable. I'll look up Walters number and send it to your phone. Okay?"

"Okay. Then what?"

"We'll figure out what to do next," I said.

"All right. I'll touch base a little later then. And thank you, Camryn."

"You're welcome."

I found the phone number, texted it to Ramona, and

chided myself for feeling irritated. I'd said goodbye and good riddance to her almost fourteen months back. Instead, she'd reappeared in my life a few months prior. I'd been grateful our paths hadn't crossed again. That is, until the quagmire began two nights before. I'd spent hours and hours with her ever since, either in person, or on the phone.

When the dust had cleared from the whole awful mess, if Ramona was innocent of any wrongdoing, I'd suggest that she join her brother at his mission in Africa. As her only relative, and probably only real friend, he'd be a positive influence. He might even enlist her help for his mission work. It would give Ramona something to focus on besides Peter and his untimely demise.

Detective Garrison phoned a few minutes after nine o'clock. I was in Brew Ha-Ha helping Pinky clean up after a flurry of customers. I excused myself to take his call and answered on the way to my office. "Good morning, Detective."

"Morning, Mayor. So you know, Chief Lonsbury filled me in on your trip to the Zimmer home, and a little about your observations. If you'll tell me, in your own words, I'll note it in my report."

"Sure." I closed my office door for more privacy and began with Ramona's visits to my shop, going with to her house, her insulin dependence, the odd way she acted over what I guessed was a medicine bottle, the state of the bed covers, and added, "She didn't seem to notice the bed wasn't made when she put her suitcase on it. I know she was upset, and had her mind on other things."

"I'm sure that's true. We didn't have cause to look in her other rooms on Monday night, and no apparent reason to suspect the murder had occurred there. Since Orten is in Hennepin County, I'll talk to their detective. They can ask

Ms. Zimmer for permission to do a limited search, as a way to clear her. If she doesn't agree, they can write up a search warrant for a judge to sign," Garrison said.

I told him Ramona was staying at the Brooks Landing Hotel for an unknown period of time. "She doesn't want to be alone at her home, maybe ever again," I said.

"Hmm," he said.

"Another thing. Ramona wants me to help her make arrangements for her husband. She may have talked to the funeral home guys by now, but hasn't gotten back to me yet."

"Helpful information. Thanks again, and we'll be in touch." After we disconnected, that twinge of sympathy I felt for Ramona bubbled to the surface. Old habits die hard.

More customers had arrived in Brew Ha-Ha, so I worked with Pinky until Ramona called me again. "I'll be next door," I told Pinky as I pushed my phone's accept button and said, "Hello."

"Camryn, I got a call from a Hennepin County detective, and he wants to ask me some questions. Why, I wonder? I'm meeting with Ike at the Walters Funeral Home at nine-thirty. Do you think you can get away from your shop then?" she said.

Curio Finds wasn't as busy winter mornings as in the other seasons. Business picked up in the afternoons instead. "I'll see if my parents are available, otherwise I'll have to be back to open a little before ten."

"I understand. You know what, Ike Walters sounded very nice, so maybe it'll be okay if I go alone. I haven't had to do anything like this since my parents died. Back then, my brother was there to help, and he did most of it."

"I'm sure you'll be just fine. Ike Walters is one of the kindest men I know," I said.

"It helps to hear that. Bye."

She hung up, and I wondered how Hennepin County would approach the whole house search subject, how she'd handle the meeting with funeral director Ike Walters, and whether or not she'd have a service for Peter.

Two, instead of the usual three, women swimmers came in for their beverages, later than their normal time. "Where's your other friend?" Pinky asked them.

"Jay, I mean Jaylin, called in sick this morning," green eyes said. *Jaylin. One J name.*

"She was *not* herself yesterday. We asked what was wrong, but she wouldn't say, and that was strange," brown eyes added.

"It was so weird. She told us she shouldn't have even met us for coffee yesterday." Green eyes again.

"Josie asked her if she was ill, and Jay said, not really, but she didn't feel well," her friend said. *Josie. Two names.*

"Right, like is there a real difference?" number one said.

"We shouldn't talk about our friend behind her back like that, Journey." *Journey? Was that her real name? And how could Pinky forget that one?*

I couldn't stop myself and noted, "Journey. Not a common name."

Journey blinked her brown eyes. "Tell me about it. My mother was in love with that band, Journey. She was a teenager when 'Don't Stop Believin' came out, and decided if she had kids, her first born would be named Journey, boy or girl. Since I was her firstborn, she thought J-O-U-R-N-E-E was a better spelling for a girl. So there you have it."

"It's a unique name, and I like it," I said.

"Thanks. We had a lot of kids that shared names in school." Journee giggled. "I never had to worry about that."

Green eyes said, "We had two other Josies in my class. But since my name is spelled J-O-S-E-Y, I was the only one who spelled it like that." *Josey*.

Journee and Josey had piqued my interest about Jaylin, and how she had acted strange the morning after Peter was killed. For some reason it struck me as an odd coincidence. "I hope your friend gets better soon," I said.

"I know. She just started a part time job at a car dealership, like maybe four weeks ago," Journee said.

Car dealership? I used a casual tone when I said, "Which one is that?"

Josey wiggled her fingers. "It's called 'Your Best Deal,' about ten miles east of town."

"We laughed when Jaylin told us the name. She thought it was kinda clever," Journee said.

"Yeah, like Brew Ha-Ha," Josey added.

Pinky grinned. "If I do say so myself. So what will you girls have this morning?"

They gave Pinky their orders, and I slipped into Curio Finds. I opened the shop's door, and it seemed like a godsend Ramona hadn't called for my help at the funeral home.

As I wrapped up a gift for a customer thirty minutes later, Ramona showed up in person. She was red-faced and teary-eyed, and despite my resolve to remain neutral, a wave of sympathy washed through me. She gave me a slight nod and detoured into Brew Ha-Ha.

I handed the young woman the package. "You picked a special snow globe, and I'm sure your mom will love it."

"I agree, and thanks for wrapping it. It's really pretty," she said.

"I smiled and nodded. "You are welcome. Enjoy."

She made her way into Pinky's shop, as our customers often did.

Ramona returned with a steamy mug. As she approached the counter, I got a whiff of chocolaty coffee.

"Camryn, my whole world has been flipped upside down."

I slid off my stool and moved to the other end of the counter. "Why don't you have a seat and we'll talk about it."

Ramona set her mug down and climbed on the stool.

"How did everything go for you this morning?" I asked.

She pushed out a breath. "The Hennepin County detective surely did surprise me. He asked if their sheriff's office could search my house to make sure Peter hadn't been killed there. So they could rule that out. Can you believe it? He either needed my permission, or he said he could get a search warrant."

I struggled to maintain a poker face. "Oh my. What did you decide, what did you tell him?"

"I had to think about it and then I said he could do his search. He's going to meet me later, so I can sign the permission form," she said.

"It seems like a smart thing to do, Ramona."

"The detective said he'd like Garrison to go with him. I told him I'd give Garrison the code to the house."

"You can trust Detective Garrison, for sure."

"Camryn, you should have the code too. In case."

In case what? "All right."

"It's my zip code. Easy for me to remember." She rattled it off, a number I was familiar with.

"Ramona, you were home all evening the night Peter died, right?"

"Well, no. Remember, I was at the mall and got back around six," she said.

Hmm. "That's right, and you said Peter was gone by then. You didn't notice anything out of place?"

Her shoulders lifted. "No. I'm not the best housekeeper in the world, and the woman who cleans for me is in Florida for the week, so things maybe aren't where they should be. I don't always notice."

"I wasn't trying to be snoopy, but when we were in your bedroom, I saw it was a little messy."

A flush rose from her neck and covered her cheeks in an instant. "I don't always make the bed, if that's what you mean. I like to let it air out."

Yes, that's what I was referring to, and gave her a vague reply. "Not everyone makes their bed." However, I was a bit of a neat freak and *always* made mine.

"Camryn, I have to confess I was so scared when I found out Peter died that I couldn't sleep alone in our bedroom. I spent the night on the couch. I don't know if I slept a single wink."

"I get that. When I'm troubled, I sleep on my couch now and again myself," I said. *Like the night Peter Zimmer's body was left in my driveway.*

Ramona blinked a few times. "I don't think I'll ever be able to live in our house again. My brother is so far away, and it's next to impossible for him to leave the mission when the kids are in school. They don't have substitute teachers, not like we do in the U.S., anyway. When the students go on break, I hope Randy can come back and help me sell the house."

I touched her hand. "Ramona, we've both experienced all kinds of pressures and stressful events. Not that you've had anything close to this happen to you before, but one thing the experts emphasize is you shouldn't make major decisions—like selling your house—when you're in the middle of a life-changing event. I think losing a spouse is at the top of the list."

Tears formed in her eyes, and she was quiet a moment. "I guess. And you're right. I had to make the most stressful decisions about Peter already today. He wasn't perfect, but I'll miss him forever and ever." Peter had not deserved a loyal and faithful wife like her.

"Ramona, when you met with Ike Walters did you decide to have a service for Peter?" I asked.

"I'm not sure what to do. Peter has two brothers and a sister in Illinois, but he's estranged from his brothers. He talked to his sister once in a while, and it'll be a big shock when she finds out what happened. I haven't been able to make that call just yet."

I touched her hand. "Never easy to share news like that."

"No. If his sister wants to come to Minnesota for Peter's service, I'll ask when it works best for her. Sad to say, but I don't think she would want to travel so far when Peter's no longer here. Especially since we barely know each other," Ramona said.

I didn't want to advise her one way or the other on Peter's arrangements. "Talking to his sister is a good place to start."

"I guess so. Peter hasn't been with the car dealership long enough to make many friends there, and we didn't have other couples we socialized with here in Minnesota," she said.

That reminded me. "What dealership did he work for?"

"'Your Best Deal' is the name. Peter told me they sell more used cars than new ones," she said.

Your Best Deal? Peter and Jaylin worked at the same place? Had I been nudged to wonder about Jaylin for a reason after all? I'd driven past the dealership on my way to the Minneapolis metro area, as well as to Orten, but hadn't paid much attention to the business. I may need to stop in and check it out.

"Okay. I hope you'll be able to rest and relax a little, now that you've started to plan next steps," I said.

She stood and picked up the mug. "I'll give this to Pinky and then head back to the hotel. Maybe I will be able to sleep a little.”

“Ramona, don’t feel like you’re alone in all this. You can call me anytime.”

She attempted a smile but it only stretched a quarter of an inch.

After she left, I looked up the address and phone number for Your Best Deal, and noted they were open until six. If I couldn’t make it after work, I’d see if I had time before I opened Curio Finds in the morning.

When Pinky was alone in her shop, I approached her with a question. “Pink, do you have the last names of the three J women?”

“Gosh, no. You know I’m not very good with names, and it’s always busy when they come in. Why do you ask?”

“The letters on that memo note,” I said.

She leaned her face close to mine. “Cami, you’re not trying to worm your way into the investigation, are you? Why would you have a single reason to think one of them would be involved with Peter Zimmer’s murder?”

“I don’t have any reason. It just made me curious when you said all their first names started with J. I saw one hand you a credit card, so you’d have their last names on the receipts.” Why didn’t I consider that before?

“Yeah, they take turns paying. I run the cards and don’t pay much attention to their names. The transaction goes through, end of story,” she said.

“You have the receipts from this morning, and from yesterday, right?”

“Sure. You know how we put a clip around them and throw them in a box at the end of the day. Like you’ve done for me the times I leave early.”

“Right, and that’s what got me thinking. Now that we know their first names, we can figure out who paid yesterday, and who paid today," I said.

"I know it wasn't Jaylin either day. Besides, she always pays in cash anyway." Jaylin was on my persons-of-interest list.

Pinky retrieved the box from under her counter. A stack of loose receipts lay on top, and stacks of ones bound together were underneath them. She picked the loose ones out and laid them on the counter, picked up the first two bound stacks, and handed one to me. "Here, if you'll look through these, see if either Journee, or what's her name is in the pile."

"Josey," I said.

"Right, her. One should be in your stack and the other in mine," Pinky said.

I found Josey's receipt. No middle initial listed, and her last name didn't start with K. I held it up. "No luck with Josey."

"All right." Pinky sorted through her stack until she came to Journee's receipt and studied it a moment. "As it turns out, her last name is Bondi."

"Okay." I put the clip on my stack and passed it to Pinky. "That helps satisfy my curiosity about two of them, so thanks for your help."

"Any time, my friend."

10

I was behind my service counter when Brooks Landing City Council members, Gail Spindler, Rosalie Gorman, Wendell Lyon, and Harley Creighton filed into Curio Finds. Stormin' led the troops, with second-in-command Harley right behind her. Gail and Wendell brought up the rear. The men were quieter than the women and entered with less gusto.

In my short stint as mayor, they'd had heated debates during meetings, and I'd had to mediate more often than I would've liked or had predicted. But when push came to shove, in non-city matters, the four got along fine. It seemed their group visit was one of those times.

Wendell was in his mid-sixties with a neatly trimmed gray beard and blue eyes. Stormin' with her flaming red hair and green eyes was next in age at sixty-one, followed by Harley at fifty-eight, with beady brown eyes and a dyed blond hair comb-over. Gail was petite, a little shorter than me, with highlighted shoulder-length brown hair, and few wrinkles at fifty-something. I had appreciated her calm-in-the-storm presence on many occasions.

"Hi, everybody," I said as they gathered around the counter.

"Mayor, we wanted to see if you needed anything." Wendell spoke in a quiet voice.

I gave them a slight head shake. "That's kind of you, but I can't really think of anything."

"I've been worried sick a crazy person might come after you too," Stormin' uttered.

I noticed when Gail gave Stormin's arm a soft nudge with her elbow.

"Now Rosalie, let's not give Camryn another thing to worry about," Harley said.

"I agree, and if she ever felt threatened, we all know our mayor has a good connection with the police department in town," Gail said.

"Yes, she does, and we're grateful for that," Wendell added.

"The other thing is, Gary couldn't get away, but he wanted us to tell you you're in his thoughts and prayers," Gail said.

Gary Lunden, the longtime city administrator, had sent me messages the past two days, as had friends and family members.

"I appreciate that, thank you," I said.

"Gary is working on the agenda for Monday night's city council meeting and hopes you'll be feeling up to it by then," Wendell said.

"I plan to, sure. Keeping busy helps a lot, and I'll stop at the city office Friday to pick up the meeting packet," I said.

"I guess we'll all be doing the same, at some point in the day." Harley said.

Stormin' lowered her voice and leaned toward me. "So how is Senator Zimmer holding up? Pretty shocked, I'm sure."

As if on cue, Ramona appeared from Brew Ha-Ha, almost like an apparition. When Stormin' recognized her, she sucked in so much air I was afraid she might get lightheaded and pass out.

The five of us went mute, and it may have looked like we were in a secret meeting that no one else should overhear. That'd be a violation of the Minnesota Open Meeting Law.

Wendell made the first move. He walked over to Ramona and introduced himself. "We haven't met before, but I want to give you my sympathy," he said.

Tears glistened in Ramona's eyes as she nodded. "Thank you."

"Ramona, these are the city council members I serve with." When I said their names, each one moved closer to her and expressed their condolences.

"We should be getting on to our other commitments," Gail said. The city council seats were part-time positions, and each one had another job besides.

We exchanged goodbyes. Ramona gave me a small nod and left shortly after the councilors departed. How many times had she graced us that day with her presence already? I chided myself for feeling irked, but in addition to a shop to run, a city council to lead, and constituents' requests to respond to, questions surrounding Peter Zimmer's murder had risen to the top of my list.

With a momentary lull, I sat on the stool behind the counter, pulled out a notebook and pen, and jotted a few things down.

~Visit Your Best Deal car lot for info. Note: Garrison may have already been there.

~Ask Clint if Garrison found out more about the van with the decal.

As I wrote that, it reminded me I wanted to learn more about the origins of medical symbols, something I hadn't paid much attention to before.

I opened my laptop and did a search. Caduceus popped up first, with multiple references and pages of information that included speculation about how it became known as a medicine symbol and dated back to the 1st Century.

One source noted that the Rod of Asclepius, with its staff and one snake wrapped around it, was known as the older, and more authentic emblem of medicine associated with an Old Testament account. According to Numbers 21:4-9, "The Lord said to Moses, "'Make a snake and put it up on a pole; anyone who is bitten can look at it and live.' So, Moses made a bronze snake and put it up on a pole. Then when anyone was bitten by a snake and looked at the bronze snake, they lived."

I read a survey that found the majority of professional associations displayed the Rod of Asclepius, and the majority of commercial groups used a caduceus. Hospitals were an exception, given the majority displayed a caduceus.

In Minnesota, the emergency medical services had a blue six-pointed star with the Rod of Asclepius in its center as their emblem. Pharmacies often used the caduceus on their signs and displays. It was also the official insignia of the U.S. Medical Corps, Navy Pharmacy Division, and the Public Health Service. On the other hand, some pharmacies used the Rod of Asclepius, with its single snake.

My neck muscles tightened and my brain hurt with the new information to digest. I closed the laptop, stood, and stretched. I realized I'd seen the symbols many times in different places, and associated both with medicine, not knowing they had different origins due to a misunderstanding from centuries before.

My question remained. Who did the person in the big dark van with a caduceus symbol decal work for? A medical company that sold products or devices? Like syringes, perhaps?

I scrubbed my temples with my forefingers and switched my focus to shop business. I'd packaged a snow globe earlier to send to a customer in Wisconsin. She received our weekly emails where we featured snow globes we found in the U.S. and other countries around the world. She was our number one buyer, and either gifted a lot of people with snow globes, or had a house big enough to display her one-of-a-kind globes. Maybe she sold them. If so, that was up to her.

Neither Pinky nor I had customers, so it was a good time for me to trek up to the post office. Pinky was hanging clean mugs on a rack when I went next door. "Whacha got there?" she asked.

"Another snow globe to send to our top customer, and it looks like a good time to slip away."

"Sure, go ahead."

The post office was two blocks north. As I stepped into the brisk outside air, I took a deep breath through my nostrils and appreciated how much it refreshed my mind and spirit. On the way, I wondered about any progress the authorities had made, like if they knew Peter Zimmer worked for Your Best Deal, or if they'd located the big van with the decal.

I crossed the threshold of the post office lobby and stopped dead in my tracks when I stood face to face with Tricia Knox, Ramona's former Minnesota event scheduler. Her mouth dropped open, and her bluish-green eyes grew wide. A red stocking cap covered her curly brown hair, maybe still cropped short.

I hadn't worked closely with her, given our different roles, but what happened with legislative issues, and voting schedules in Washington, impacted when Ramona would be available to attend events, and meet with constituents in Minnesota. So Tricia and I'd had many conversations and email exchanges over the years.

"Oh! Camryn, funny running into you here," Tricia said in a fakey voice.

"Not too strange. Brooks Landing is my hometown. I thought you knew that."

"Of course. Well, I guess we sorta lost touch."

In silent agreement, we moved to the back area by the post office boxes, out of the line of traffic.

Yeah, sorta. I was shunned by staff both in D.C. and in Minnesota. "How about you? What brings you to Brooks Landing?" I asked her.

"Oh, well I needed to mail a package, and stopped by on my way home. After I lost my position last month, I got a job in Plymouth and found a house in Carson."

Plymouth was twenty-five miles east, and Carson was six miles west of Brooks Landing. A fairly long drive, but close to 300,000 people in the seven counties around the Twin Cities commuted to work in metro communities. I nodded, narrowed my eyes, and lowered my voice. "You heard about Peter Zimmer, what happened to him?"

The color drained from her face, and it took some seconds before she answered. "It was on the news. I feel so bad for Senator Zimmer. I do." It seemed she'd added those last two words to convince me, and maybe herself.

"You haven't talked to the senator about it?" I asked.

Tricia shook her head. "No. We haven't spoken since December. We didn't part on the best of terms. She was obviously upset when she lost her seat and wouldn't even give me an answer when I asked her for a job reference."

One way to lose a friendship. If they had one, that is.

"She should've given you that much, no question about it. You had a tough job, planning events then often having to change them, depending on if votes happened on Saturdays, or other things came up."

She nodded. "It wasn't always easy."

"Between you and me, Ramona could really use more support right now. I've been doing what I can to help her."

"That's big of you, Camryn. But why would you? After all, she fired you when you . . . you know . . . about her husband," she said.

I raised my hand. "Tricia, let me set the record straight. Again. Peter Zimmer grabbed me, and I used every ounce of my strength to escape. I couldn't stand the man as a person. Plus the way he treated his wife, with all the other women he chased, was repulsive."

Her eyebrows drew together. "Other women?"

"You must've heard talk about them," I said.

Her facial color went from whiter than white to a deep crimson shade. "No. I guess I wasn't in the D.C. loop." Did that mean she was one of the gullible ones Peter had managed to charm and fool?

It took me a moment to think of how to lighten the tone of our conversation. "Sorry, I didn't mean to speak ill of the dead. Tricia, I need to get this package sent." I lifted it up. "To switch to a totally unrelated subject, if you're in the market for a snow globe, or other unique items, stop by our shop. It's just down the street—Curio Finds. My friend has an adjoining coffee shop called Brew Ha-Ha."

"Thanks. Yeah, I've driven by them, and will do that some time. I better get going too. Bye."

"Bye."

Tricia took off and left me to question, what in the world? I moved out of the little alcove, up to the counter, greeted the postal worker, handed her the box, and paid the shipping cost. On the way back to work, my thoughts centered on Tricia. Our conversation and her reactions played over in my mind. She must have been one of Peter Zimmer's victims, but how was it possible she didn't know about his other escapades?

Pinky was with a customer in Curio Finds and I greeted the young woman. When we heard people in Brew Ha-Ha, Pinky went to help them. The two hours until closing crept by. Ramona hadn't returned. Given her mental and emotional overload, hopefully she had crashed and slept all afternoon.

I still struggled with the nagging thought she'd had a role in Peter's murder. Then, of all people, Tricia Knox popped up out of nowhere and showed up at the Brooks Landing post office the same time I did. Our conversation had raised my suspicions about her. Had she been in a personal relationship with Peter Zimmmer?

After Pinky went home, as the minutes passed, I felt more and more compelled to visit Your Best Deal to check it out. At five o'clock on the dot, I locked up shop then headed east in the Subaru. When I arrived at Your Best Deal, I drove at a slower speed through the lot, as though I were in the market for a vehicle. A middle-aged man with a crew cut and black framed glasses watched me from the large glass window inside. I parked and made my way through the dealership door.

The man smiled at me. "Good afternoon, what can I help you find?"

"Oh, hi. Actually, I'm still in the information gathering stage at this point." I hadn't meant for that Freudian slip to escape my lips.

He nodded a few times. "I'm Seth."

"Hi, Seth. I have an older Subaru, and my friend told me about your business, so I thought I'd stop by, see what you have in stock. Her husband worked here, but sadly, he just passed away."

"Yeah, I can see your vehicle out on the lot. You must

be talking about Peter Zimmer."

I nodded.

"When we found out he was murdered, of all things, we couldn't believe it. I guess because it's unbelievable."

"I know, it is a huge shock all right. Gosh, I hope this doesn't seem insensitive, me stopping by like this, just a couple days after his death."

"No, you're fine. Life still goes on, right?" he said.

"It does at that."

Seth leaned in a little closer. "So how is his wife holding up?"

My shoulders lifted. "It's been really hard on her, and I've done what I can to help out."

"That's good to hear. His murder didn't seem real, and then when a detective came by to ask me questions, it kinda hit me."

I played dumb. "A detective?"

"From Buffalo County. He wanted to know things like how Peter got along with people around here, or if there was anyone he had a dispute with. I told him nobody that I knew about. It wasn't like he spent much time inside the dealership. All I can say is, it's a helluva thing to happen to the guy."

"It sure is, and hard to believe, like you said." I paused a moment. "Peter seemed happy here, right?"

"Yeah, far as I know. Seemed to like driving, delivering, and picking up vehicles."

Like he did women. "I also happen to know one of your other employees. Jaylin."

Seth shook his head. "No longer our employee. She up and quit the day we got the news about Peter."

"Really? She give you a reason? I mean, I know she hasn't worked here that long. Not that it's any of my business. I'll be seeing her soon and can ask her myself."

The truth stretched a bit.

"Between you and me and the lamp post, it seemed like Peter and Jaylin were sweet on each other."

I went for a blank expression. "Oh?"

"I noticed how they exchanged looks. Maybe it was more so on his part. Jaylin was a looker. But with them both being married, I took it as flirting, nothing more."

Given Peter's inclinations, I was not so sure but nodded anyway.

Seth went on, "They started working here about the same time. And it's kinda weird they ended up leaving almost the same day. Peter died Monday night, Jaylin quit Tuesday morning. It made me wonder if finding out about his death had anything to do with her up and quitting like that."

"That is strange."

"You asked why Jaylin quit, and I guess I didn't give you a direct answer. What she told us is, Jace, that's her husband, asked her to quit." *Jace?*

It took me a few beats after Seth told me his name. "Oh. So you think the reason might be her husband thought Jaylin and Peter had a personal thing going on?"

"No clue. And if they did, why would Jace ask her to quit, seeing they wouldn't be working together anymore, not with Peter gone forever?"

"You make a valid point, Seth. Well, he must've had another reason." I didn't know Jace or have a clue what that reason might be. I was tempted to ask Seth for Jaylin's last name, but I'd told him I knew her, and he might wonder why I didn't know it. Time to take off, so Seth didn't question my real reason for the visit. I was able to slip out in a flash with a quick, "thank you," before he could ask my name, or anything else.

On the way back to Brooks Landing, random thoughts scrambled around in my brain. Ramona. Tricia. Jaylin. Jaylin's husband Jace. Seriously, another J name? Was one of them the guilty party who conspired with another guilty party, and caused Peter's death? Like Jace and Jaylin, the married couple, perhaps?

Seth had given me one answer and insights about others. Detective Garrison had been at Your Best Deal to ask about Peter; Seth thought Peter and Jaylin were sweet on each other; and Jaylin had quit her job the day after Peter died, a curious thing no matter how you sliced it. Now to uncover if her last name started with K, and if her husband had the same surname.

Clint had an evening meeting scheduled and said he'd stop over afterward. I'd be safe at home before then. I parked in the garage and crept my way to the house, my eyes on the shadowed trees and bushes. It took effort to disregard Pinky's words about a lurking ghost. Ugg.

I was about to look in the refrigerator for food options when Ramona phoned. I didn't feel I had enough energy to take the call, but if I ignored it I'd have to turn off all the lights in the house and hide, in case she came looking for me.

I pushed the accept button. "Hi, Ramona."

"Camryn, I'm glad you answered. I needed to be sure you were all right."

Did she know something I didn't? "Not to worry. I'm fine. What made you concerned?"

"I don't know. Maybe because of Peter. You know, how he was found at your house, it got me thinking you might be in danger too."

Her words made me a tad anxious so I made sure I'd locked the back door. Did Ramona say that—along with previous comments—because she was responsible for her husband's death and wanted to shift the attention away from herself? I'd walked the fine line between believing her and suspecting her involvement.

I managed to spit out, "Because why?"

"I don't know. Maybe someone was jealous of you."

I tried to process that. It didn't make sense to me, but it was as good an explanation as any.

"Jealous, in what way?" I asked.

"You know how handsome and charming Peter was. He told me how women threw themselves at him all the time, but he had resisted until you. He said that made other women mad."

Oh, dear Lord, help me not give in to the temptation to scream at the top of my lungs and break her eardrum. "And you believed him?"

"Yes, I did, at the time. I wasn't sure if it was true later on, after another staffer—who shall remain nameless—told me Peter had caught her off guard and kissed her. Then I started to wonder if Peter had lied about you after all. But I still couldn't bring myself to believe it."

How many times had we hashed that whole ordeal out? "Ramona, I can swear on a stack of Holy Bibles I did nothing to encourage your husband, in any way. He'd tried to kiss me other times too, before you caught us that day. I should have reported it, filed a criminal complaint against him, but didn't. There were enough scandals in D.C., and I wanted to protect your office. I was wrong, because when you fired me, it led to a big public scandal instead." I hadn't meant to disclose that, but the words flew out of my mouth.

We were silent a moment then Ramona let out a loud howl. She sniffed and cried over the phone. I waited a moment until she said, "I'm sorry, Camryn. If I had believed you, I could have handled it better. I probably would have won the election, and Peter might still be alive."

It was impossible to know if the last two things she said were true. "Thank you," was all I was able to utter.

Ramona made a comment I didn't catch, then we said our goodbyes.

11

My appetite had disappeared. I sank down on a kitchen chair and looked at my phone. It humbled me as I looked through the list of my Washington, D.C. contacts. A few had sent, "so sorry," messages after the abrupt end of my career, but most, like Tricia, had not said a single word. I had been deemed guilty, proven or not.

When Ramona called, I hadn't mentioned the post office encounter with Tricia, and considered what her reaction might've been. I scrolled through my contacts and stopped at Gretchen. I'd heard she'd been hired by the senator who'd defeated Ramona. Ramona's staff files would be retained for years, hopefully stacked in the office storage room.

Gretchen was smart. She knew both personal and professional information about staff in Senator Zimmer's office, and in many other legislative offices too. People confided in her, and trusted her with their secrets, because she kept them. I respected that, but since Peter Zimmer was dead, Gretchen might share things she knew without revealing sources or naming names.

I selected her number and pressed the call button. She answered after the fourth ring, as I was about to hang up. "Hello? *Camryn?*"

"Hi, Gretchen. Yes, it's me all right."

"It's been a long time. How have you been?" Her voice sounded upbeat and kind.

I gave her a quick synopsis about my positions, as Curio Finds manager, and as Brooks Landing mayor.

"Oh my, I'm sure you're great at both. Wait, Brooks Landing? Of course. I can't believe it slipped my mind that was your hometown, even with all the uproar after Ramona left, and getting the new senator settled in. That's why Brooks Landing rang a bell when we got word yesterday that Peter Zimmer had been killed and they named the community where his body was found."

"That is the sad fact, all right. And the sadder fact is his body was in the passenger seat of a vehicle left in *my* driveway."

"*No way.* Camryn, that's the worst thing I've ever heard, and you know that's saying a lot. Why on earth? How could that have *happened*?" Her voice had risen to a near squeaky level.

"The authorities are working to get to the bottom of it." I paused a moment. "Gretchen, as a little background, I'd only seen Ramona and Peter one time after I got fired, and that was last fall. Each one came into Curio Finds the same day, at different times, for different reasons. But since Peter's death, I've seen Ramona more times than I can come up with off the top of my head."

"Oh. My. God! This sounds like one of those real-life crime shows that are about impossible to believe really happened," she said.

"I agree, one hundred percent. Except it feels way worse."

"I cannot imagine what it must be like."

"Gretchen, another thing. Given all the times I denied having a personal relationship with Peter, I think Ramona finally accepts it as the truth. I was not the instigator, Peter was, as with most—if not all—the women he so called 'dated' behind Ramona's back. I'm sure she hasn't a clue how many that was. Nor do I and don't want to know."

"Me either."

"Gretchen, you were tuned in to the happenings in Ramona's D.C. office more than anyone else. My question is about the possible person, or persons, who killed Peter Zimmer. Can you think of anyone who'd have a potential motive to want him dead? And then a reason to bring his body to *my* place?"

"I can't even believe this happened to you. As far as a suspect? No one I can think of at the moment, but let me ponder it for a while. With the scores of people—men and women—who met with the senator, and all the ones who worked for her, somebody was always upset about this or that."

"That's true. Oh, and there's something else."

She sounded hesitant when she said, "What?"

"The day after Peter's death, I found a note on the ground by my driveway, by where his SUV had been. The authorities either missed it that night, or it blew in my yard the next day. Anyway, it had the letters JTK and the numbers seven three eight, dash, four six nine seven written on it. It looked like a partial phone number, but it could be a key lock code. By any chance, do you recognize what either seems to be initials, or series of numbers?"

Gretchen was silent a moment. "Okay, I got a pen and paper. Can you repeat them again?" After I did, she said, "Neither one rings a bell, but like the possible persons of interest you asked about, I'll see what I can find out. I hate to admit I don't even have my kids' numbers memorized."

"I get that. It's too easy to locate a contact and push the call button. Your help is much appreciated. Oh, I almost forgot. Guess who I ran into in Brooks Landing today?"

"Who?"

"Tricia Knox. Another person from Ramona's office I hadn't seen, or talked to, in over a year."

"Tricia? Last I heard she lived in Minneapolis."

"She did when she worked for the senator. She bought a house a few miles west of here, in an even smaller town than Brooks Landing. She commutes to a Minneapolis suburb for her job. She didn't say, and I didn't ask, what it is."

"Since she was at the Minnesota office, I didn't have as much contact with her, not like with our D.C. scheduler. I'll see what I can find out about her, the possible initials, and numbers, and I promise to be discreet," Gretchen said.

"I know you will, and thanks again. It's fine if you tell people you trust where Peter's body was found, and the reason I asked about anyone who might've had a grudge against him, *and* against me."

"Will do. Camryn, I can't tell you how sorry I am about all of this."

"Thank you for that. I'll look forward to your call," I said.

"You know it."

After we'd disconnected, my stomach started to growl. As if by magic, my appetite had returned. I opened the refrigerator door and searched the shelves. The leftover chicken pot pie from a few days before looked good and still smelled fresh. After the plate had heated in the microwave, I set it on the table, opened a bottle of bubbly water, and took a big sip.

As I swallowed bite after bite with a sip of water in between, life seemed almost normal. I credited much of that to Gretchen. It had done my heart good to touch base with her, unload my concerns, and enlist her help for leads in the search for possible suspects.

I stood at the sink washing my supper dishes when Clint's vehicle pulled in the driveway. I felt torn over how much to share about my day's adventures. Would he view my actions as investigation interference? I unlocked and opened the door. When he reached the house, my heart skipped a beat. Clint's smile coaxed one from me, one I hoped conveyed my love for him and the relationship we shared.

He stepped inside and drew me in his arms. His face was cool from the night air and contrasted with his warm kisses. I hung his jacket on the back of a chair. "Did you have supper?"

"Yup, but probably not as tasty as whatever you ate. It smells delicious in here."

"I have to admit, the chicken pot pie did hit the spot."

He nodded then studied my face. "Looks like you've got something you want off your chest."

My eyebrows lifted. "More like there are things I should tell you."

"Hmm. How about we retreat to the living room, and you can do just that."

We settled on the couch, and I began with Tricia, told him who she was, and our odd encounter.

"And her reaction made you question whether or not she'd been personally involved with Peter Zimmer?" he asked.

"It sure got me thinking about it. As far as I know, she's still single, and it seems a little strange she moved this far out from the metro. She got a job in Plymouth, and Minneapolis is closer than Carson is, so that made me wonder."

"Housing and taxes are cheaper in Buffalo County, especially in the smaller towns like Carson."

"True. Still, I'm curious if she had another reason, like a special man in her life."

"You get an A in the curious department."

"I can't argue with that." I touched his hand. "Clint, this is the part you might not like."

He leaned in closer. "Is that right? When you put it that way, it makes me a little itchy."

I shared details of my visit to Your Best Deal, told him all I knew about Jaylin. "We know her first initial is J, of course. But what are her middle and last initials? JTK, like on the memo note?"

He listened with a slight frown the entire time. "I would've advised you to steer clear of that dealership, but since it's after the fact, I won't chastise you for poking around. Let's leave it at that. However, the woman named Jaylin who worked at the same place as Zimmer and quit right after his death does seem like a strange coincidence, if that's what it was."

"I know, too strange if you ask me. Jaylin told the dealership her husband made her quit."

"Is that so? It's possible she said that to shift the blame away from herself, like to cover her real reason, whatever that might be."

"True. And to top things off, her husband's name is Jace. Another J name. I'd like to know what their last name is."

Clint shook his head. "You need to tell Detective Garrison what you told me. He must have gotten the names of every employee at the dealership so he could interview them. Jaylin should be on the list, but you can give him your take on her behavior, put her on his radar."

"I'll do that. I had more questions but knew better than to ask too many, and make Seth at the dealership suspicious," I said.

"That was wise. Besides, the whole J name thing—given the letters on the memo note—might be a coincidence and have nothing at all to do with Peter Zimmer or his death."

"I agree." *To a certain extent, at least.*

Clint glanced at his watch. "It's getting late, so I'd wait till tomorrow to talk to Garrison. What you have to report doesn't seem overly time sensitive. If Garrison asks why you went to Your Best Deal, Ramona told you where Peter worked, and you were curious, right?"

Like I was about a lot of things. "Yes, that is the truth."

I phoned Detective Garrison the next morning and shared information related to the Peter Zimmer case. He invited me to his office for a chat. The Buffalo County Sheriff's Office was connected to the jail. I had been at the jail to visit an inmate a few times, one responsible for the death of the first body I'd found the past October. Before I'd headed too far down memory lane on that case, Garrison met me at an employee-access-only entrance and led me to his cubicle.

On his back wall, framed degrees and awards took up half the space. His desk had papers piled in a variety of heights, from a quarter inch to about five inches.

He waved at the visitor's chair. "Have a seat, Mayor."

As I did, Garrison sat down at his desk and locked eyes with mine. He studied my face and managed a slight smile. My heart beats picked up speed, and without further ado, I launched into an account of my trip to Your Best Deal.

After I'd finished, Garrison leaned on his desk, closer to me. "What led you go to the dealership in the first place?"

My shoulders lifted a touch. "I was interested in what the vibe was like there. You know, if the business was respectable, or more on the shady side."

"And?"

"I didn't detect anything off at the business. Everything

seemed on the up and up."

Garrison lowered his chin a tad. "Go on."

"I gave Seth—the salesman—the impression I was in the market for a vehicle, without saying as much, and hoped when I mentioned that I knew Peter Zimmer, he would share things he hadn't told you. Whatever they might be."

"Why is that?"

"Because people often tell regular people things they don't tell cops. Maybe they're afraid they'll say the wrong thing that makes them look suspicious."

At least Garrison didn't yell at me. His voice was even when he said, "To let you know, I talked to the manager, not Seth. He was cooperative, happy to help, and he gave me the names and contact information of all the employees."

"Including Jaylin? So you found out what her last name is."

"Yes. Mayor, I know you can't seem to help yourself, but it's my job to investigate this crime. I appreciate any leads and tips you come across, but I'm the one who will chase them down, do the follow up."

"Detective, I respect that, and I'll keep my eyes and ears open for any information. Oh, and this is a related question. Have you interviewed former staff from Senator Zimmer's offices—both in Washington, D.C., and in Minnesota?"

He pushed air from his nostrils. "Still gathering information. People have moved, changed jobs."

"To give you a tip, I ran into Ramona's Minnesota scheduler at the post office here in town. She lives in Carson now. Her name is Tricia Knox."

"Okay. You happen to have her phone number?"

I took out my phone and scrolled through the contacts. "I do. At least from about a year ago." He wrote down the numbers as I recited them.

"Thanks. And to let you know, Hennepin County

detectives did a limited search of the Zimmer home and didn't find evidence to support Peter Zimmer had been killed there."

One thing to cross off the list. "I'm glad to hear that."

I walked back to the shops and entered through Brew Ha-Ha's door. Curio Finds wouldn't open for over an hour. Pinky's eyes brightened when she saw me. I'd told her I had an appointment with Detective Garrison before work. A few people sat at back tables. "I'll hang up my coat," I said.

Pinky threw a glance at her customers. "I'll help you." She followed me into the shop and waited by the archway while I slipped in, and out of, the store room.

We met by a shelf filled with antique finds. Pinky dropped her hands on my shoulders. "Okay, what's the story? Tell me all."

"All right, a couple of big things happened yesterday, and I'll tell you the second one first."

She dropped her arms on her hips. "And?"

"After work last night, I paid a visit to Your Best Deal."

Her brows drew together. "*Cami*, without telling me?"

"You had a long day, and I knew you'd want to come with me instead of going home and taking care of your own stuff." Plus, Pinky might've blabbed something to Seth that blew my cover.

She let out a big exhale. "So what happened?"

I recounted the details for the third time, and Pinky's mouth dropped open when I got to the part about Jaylin and her husband Jace. "Cami, I can't stand it. We have to find out who they are."

"Detective Garrison said that was up to him, in so many words. Now the first big thing from yesterday. I had a strange encounter with a woman—a blast from the past—who worked for Ramona too, and it got me wondering about her."

Pinky shook her head as I shared my conversation with Tricia. I'd just finished when her doorbell dinged. She squeezed my hand and dashed into her shop. When Ramona waddled her way toward the counter, I wished I hadn't followed Pinky.

"Camryn, you're here!" Ramona yelled.

Lord, give me patience, and I need it now! "Morning, Ramona. I hope you were able to get the rest you needed."

"I did, and I feel all the better for it. I wanted you to know I'm about to brave a trip to my house. My cleaning lady is back. The Hennepin detective said I was free to return home, so I'm going to meet her there this morning. I hope she can help me decide what to do with . . . things."

If she meant Peter's clothes and personal items, it seemed a little premature, given what I'd heard from others who suffered a similar loss. It was best to let a season pass and allow her brain to heal a bit to enable better decisions. Unless it was a "good riddance to Peter" gesture.

My practical mother often cautioned me about making "rash decisions." Perhaps the main reason I'd made it to my late thirties before my first serious relationship, when I'd fallen for Clinton Lonsbury.

Ramona moved her face close to mine. "Camryn? Are you okay?"

I blinked a few times. "Oh, sorry. I'm fine. Maybe I need a little more sleep myself."

"Well, I just stopped by for coffee and a muffin, and I'll be on my way," she said.

It was apparent Pinky had overheard Ramona because she said, "What can I get you, and would you like it to go?"

Leave it to Pinky.

Ramona opted for the takeout option of a large Columbian coffee with cream and a cherry muffin that I hoped wouldn't spike her blood sugar levels. She left in a happier mood, and it helped lift my spirits.

Pinky went to her back room to grind coffee beans, and I minded the store for her. Two of the Js came in, Journee and Josey. I hadn't seen either one for a couple days. I set down my coffee and greeted them. "Good morning. All set for a beverage, and maybe a baked good after your swim class?"

They both smiled, nodded, and looked up at the white board for the daily specials.

"It seems funny to have our mayor serve us, doesn't it Journee?" Josey said.

"I wear many hats, and this is one of the more fun ones," I told them.

Journee chuckled. "I'm going to stick with the Jamaica Blue Mountain Blend. Black this morning."

"You know, that sounds good to me too. I'll go with the same," Josey said.

"Jaylin isn't with you today?" I asked in a nonchalant tone.

"No. Something's up with her, but she won't say what, and we don't want to pressure her too much," Journee said.

"I'm sorry to hear that," I said.

Josey nodded. "It's strange too. Jaylin loved swim aerobics, and getting a coffee after. Not that it would hurt her to miss a few exercise days. She's the strongest and most muscular one in our class, by far. We figured she must lift weights, and we even asked her about it. Turns out, she used to be in those body builder competitions."

"Jaylin told us she lost a lot of muscle after she quit that sport, but we're impressed with how much she still has," Journee said.

"She's what my teenage son would call 'ripped,'" Josey noted.

"Wow," I said. *Strong enough to put a deceased man's body in a vehicle?*

"I don't want to gossip, but we think she might be having marital problems," Josey added.

I'd wondered the same thing. "Sadly, it's more common than you'd think."

"For sure," Journee said.

I picked up mugs, filled them, and set them on the counter. "How about a scone or muffin with your coffee?"

Journee shook her head. "No, thanks."

"None for me, either," Josey said.

"I hope Jaylin feels better soon," I said.

Journee handed me her credit card. "I know. She's made remarks about her husband. I don't think he hurts her, but he sounds pretty controlling. Don't tell her I said anything."

"No, of course I won't. Not to pry, but do you think it's things like he's telling her how to dress, how to answer the phone? Controlling that way? I have a friend who complained it's the kind of things her husband did to her."

"I think it might be something like that," Journee said.

Josey picked up her mug. "I agree. We haven't known her long enough to ask too many personal questions. Journee and I go back a few years, but we just met Jaylin when we all started the class together last month. It seems like she needs friends but doesn't seem to want to share a whole lot about herself."

"Josey and I kidded between ourselves that it's almost like she's in the Witness Protection Program." Journee chuckled, then Josey did too.

They meant it as a joke, so I smiled. It was an unusual observation, and made me consider it, nonetheless.

"My apologies if I didn't notice, but I don't remember seeing any of you in here before last month," I said.

"Oh yeah, we have been. Just not on a regular basis, like after we started that class, and we wanted Jaylin to feel more comfortable with the town and the people. She moved to Brooks Landing just before Christmas and knew virtually no one. So you could say we took her under our wing, because it's even harder to meet people in the winter, unless you have kids in school, or belong to a church, or another group," Journee said.

"Or take a class," Josey added.

"I'm glad you guys befriended Jaylin, and it's too bad she's missed how many days since she's been ill?" I asked until I counted myself.

"Like three, four?" Journee said.

Since the day after Peter Zimmer's body was found at my place. Tuesday, Wednesday, and Thursday. Three days. It seemed like three weeks.

"I sent her a text this morning, but it didn't go through. It made me wonder if she'd shut off her phone," Josey said.

"It might be nice to stop by her house, make sure she's okay. Unless she doesn't want visitors," I suggested.

They both shrugged. "We don't know exactly where she lives," Josey said.

"Just that it's on the south side of Brooks Landing, in that Pleasant Hills addition," Journee added.

"If you have her last name, you could look it up," I said.

Journee looked at Josey. "It's Klemmet, right?"

"Right. A little different, and not easy for me to remember, that's why I had to think for a second," she said.

First initial J, last initial K? Whoa. Two of the questioned letters. Detective Garrison had the original memo note, along with Jaylin's full name, so he should be all over that piece of information. Garrison hadn't told me, but maybe he'd arrested her, taken her into custody, and that's why her phone was off.

I lifted my hand a tad. "Not to gossip, but a guy at Your Best Deal told me Jaylin quit her job."

"*Really?* She said she liked it there, especially compared to the medical supplies company she worked at before," Journee said.

Medical supplies company?

"And we figured it was because her husband owns the business, and it was just too much together time for the two of them," Josey said.

"Not that she came out and said that, but that was our guess," Journee added.

"Can I ask you not to mention what I told you, or even that I said anything about Your Best Deal? Wait for her to tell you she'd quit her job," I said.

"For sure," Josey agreed.

Pinky returned with two large jars of ground coffee and eyed the three of us with an "my inquiring mind wants to know" expression on her face. "Good morning, you two. I see you've got your drinks. Hey, your sidekick is still missing," she said.

"Yeah, guess Jay's still under the weather," Journee told her.

Pinky threw me a quick glance, then focused on Journee. "Oh. Sorry to hear that."

"Thanks, and likewise. We're just about to grab a table," Josey said.

Pinky was an open book who did not cover her thoughts or feelings well. The dubious slight frown on her face might've made the women wonder if she'd overheard our conversation. They'd shared things about Jaylin they didn't want the world to know, or to get back to their new friend.

12

I'd told Pinky that Jaylin had quit her job and hoped she wouldn't blab, tell her friends I'd gotten the information snooping around at the car dealership. How would I explain the reason I went there, or the reason I hadn't relayed that to her friends?

After Journee and Josey settled at a back table, I whispered to Pinky, "Don't say anything else about Jaylin."

Pinky leaned in close to me and mouthed, "What?"

"You know more about her than her friends do, and everything I told you is confidential," I mouthed back.

"I know that."

I raised my voice to a normal level. "Pinky, you've got things under control, so I'll get ready to open my shop."

"Thanks, Cami," she said as she grabbed a rag.

At my counter, I opened the laptop, went to a search engine, and typed in Jace Klemmet, Brooks Landing current Minnesota address. The results popped up in seconds. I went to the Buffalo County website, selected Property Search, and typed in the address. Their home had been built four years before. Jace and Jaylin were listed as the second owners and had purchased it three months prior.

Where had they lived before that? I did another search, and the results revealed they had lived in three other

Minnesota communities over the past eleven years. The most recent one was Orten. *Orten, where the Zimmers lived? Had they known Peter, or more to the point, had Jaylin known him before they'd worked a short time together at Your Best Deal?*

Jaylin was on Detective Garrison's radar, so he'd likely obtained the same information, and more. At our meeting that morning, Garrison seemed more amenable to things I'd shared, at least compared to the last case when our assistant police chief had been murdered. I'd had to stay in the background on that one and did my best not to interfere in his investigation. It was more like a parallel exploration to uncover the truth, as it was with the current case.

In the last incident, after I'd learned the killer's identity in what turned out to be a half-witted and dangerous way, I vowed to be more cautious. Clint was still upset with me about that one, as well as the two before. I had to admit he was not altogether wrong. Garrison was probably miffed too, but he hadn't mentioned the four cases to me since. I liked that about him. Case closed, let's move on, not dwell in the past.

I'd kicked myself hard enough for my mistakes and didn't need others to remind me. As much as I'd tried to wipe particular things from my memory, they bubbled to the surface now and again. In fact, I was lost in thought when Pinky popped into the shop and joined me at my counter.

"The two Js just left. So what was up with the three of you? You looked like you were plotting something, and I'd caught you with your hands in the cookie jar," she said.

"We were talking about Jaylin not feeling well. I personally didn't want you to let it slip how I'd found out she'd quit her job. That might explain my expression, if I had a weird one."

Pinky put on an exaggerated pouty face. "Oh. Well, I can keep secrets, when I know they're secrets."

"I know you can, even when it hurts. A lot." I bumped her arm and laughed.

"Very funny, Cami."

"I just didn't know if you knew my dealership visit was a secret."

"I figured anything you tell me when you return from one of your spy missions is a secret. Unless you tell me it's not. Same thing with when and why you think certain people might be guilty of crimes. I dare not share that info," she said.

I gave her a hug. "Thank you. That reminds me, I haven't finished telling you about my meeting with Detective Garrison this morning."

"No, and I'd like you to note that I've patiently waited for it."

I nodded with a grin. "First off, I cleared the air about my visit to Your Best Deal. Of course, he knew Jaylin had quit. I told him about running into Tricia and passed on her phone number. He was pretty cool about the whole thing. But he told me to steer clear, let him handle the investigation, like I told you earlier."

"And you should too. Think about your personal safety. Don't forget, we have a killer on the loose. No more close calls, *please*. My heart can't take it."

"I will do my best to avert any danger."

She shook her head. "Avert? No, don't let danger even get close to you in the first place."

"A couple of things the two Js told me I wouldn't consider private. Jaylin is a former body builder; very strong. And her last name is Klemmet. Jaylin something Klemmet."

Pinky scrunched up her face. "I don't get it."

"The letters on the memo note. JTK."

"Right! You should do a search on her full name, see if it's listed."

"Of course. I like how you think. Her husband's name is Jace, so I'll see what I can find out."

People drifted in and out of the shop over the next hours, and it was good to ring up sales. Business had been steady enough, so I'd had to put any digging on hold. Mid-afternoon, it occurred to me that the Brooks Landing City Council meeting packet should be posted on the city's website. The business, the city, and the investigation all vied for my attention and concentration. *One matter at a time, Camryn Brooks.*

A little after four, I was alone in the shop and logged in to my official city email. I read over the meeting packet that included the agenda, last meeting's minutes, and the financial and committee reports. It was a relief that nothing controversial had been added to the agenda. I'd swing by my office for the printed copy later. Each city council agenda included an open forum for citizens to voice their opinions or complaints on city-related issues. People surprised me now and then with the variety of things that concerned them.

I was reading through the packet when Erin walked in. "You're a sight for sore eyes," I said.

She came over and gave me a hug. "Cami, I wish I could have spent a little in-person time with you the last couple days, but between school and evening meetings—"

I cut her off. "Erin, no need to apologize. Your calls, and text messages, were much appreciated."

Her lips curled upward. "I'm glad. So how are things going with the investigation; any progress, like leads on the suspect?"

"Not that I know of. All I can say is they cannot find him—or her—or them—fast enough."

"Her? You still have the senator on your list?" she said.

"I don't know, and I do not like the way I'm vacillating about it. On one hand, I think Ramona loved him and seems genuinely devastated that he's dead. On the other hand, I can imagine how she planned to kill her husband and hired someone to help her. This back-and-forth stuff is driving me half crazy."

Erin tapped my hand. "Try deep meditation exercises, maybe that will help ease your angst."

"Maybe. I've also got a couple of other women on my radar, besides Ramona."

"No men?" she said.

"One possibility, if the guy in question helped his wife, or she helped him."

I gave her the highlights I hadn't shared via phone calls and text messages, like the encounter with Tricia and what I'd learned about Jaylin.

Erin shook her finger at me. "Cami, you need to leave the nosing around to the sheriff's office. Or keep a bodyguard with you when you go off on your secret missions. You know that's what drives Pinky and me half crazy."

Pinky had said as much, and that was the main reason I spared my friends certain details that might scare them. It turned out for Peter Zimmer's death, since Pinky had discovered his body, the two saw and heard more details than I might have otherwise shared.

"Sorry, Erin. I have never intentionally put myself in harm's way."

"I think you honestly believe that. Cami, you're really bright, yet at times your over-the-top curiosity blocks out your common-sense smarts."

Her observation bit me a little. "You may be right. One thing I noticed since I've been back in Brooks Landing with you and Pinky—sometimes we act like we did in our teen years. You think I behave like a reckless teenager?"

"Not exactly. It's not like you were ever much of a risk taker, even as a teen. But now, when a person dies under unnatural circumstances, you're like a dog after a bone," she said.

"Thanks."

"Just an expression."

"I know, and I can't explain how that happens. Or why. It's like I feel obligated to get to the bottom of what happened to the victims, what caused their deaths. I mean who did," I said.

"I guess that shouldn't surprise us. You always stuck up for kids that got picked on or teased, from kindergarten on up. You couldn't stand it when things were unfair."

I cracked a smile. "So how did I end up, and manage to survive, all those years in D.C.?"

"Good question."

Pinky walked into the shop and exchanged a quick glance with Erin. "So are we on to do something fun tonight?"

Erin shrugged. "We hadn't gotten to that yet."

"What do you say, Cami? It's been a tough few days. We could meet the guys, or just the three of us could hang out," Pinky said.

I'd planned to do a deeper dive into information on Jaylin and Jace and Tricia but could put that on hold for the night. An evening with my friends would help make my life feel more normal.

My phone beeped. A text message from Mom. *Cami, would you like to come over for dinner?* I held it up for the girls to read.

"Well?" Pinky said.

"You two asked first," I said then, sent my mom the message, *Thanks, but I have plans with Pinky and Erin. I'll touch base with you and Dad tomorrow.* I added a heart emoji.

Have fun tonight. We love you too, Mom wrote back.

Pinky had suggested we go to Sherman's Bar and Grill for a meal after we closed our shops at five o'clock. Mark and Jake needed to cover evening shifts for other officers, and Clint thought four would be a crowd. More like it'd be three against one. Three females out for dinner with one male created a different group dynamic, no doubt about it.

Erin offered to drive to cut down on vehicles in Sherman's parking lot. She parked outside our shops at five on the dot. No last-minute customers, so Pinky and I locked our doors and climbed into her vehicle. The sun had set, and stores' lights and street lamps helped illuminate the otherwise dark night.

When we noticed only one open space in Sherman's lot we agreed it had been a good decision to carpool. "Yay," Erin said, as she pulled into the spot.

Sherman's was housed in a spacious, repurposed building, and a popular place for people all ages, the old, young, and in between. Its casual atmosphere and seasonal décor welcomed patrons. The winter theme featured antique sleds, ice skates, toboggans, snowshoes, skis, and sports equipment on the walls and propped in corners.

The host greeted us, and as he took us past the large horseshoe bar and customers at tables, many waved and said, "Hi." He led us to the largest dining room, my personal favorite. The floor-to-ceiling stone hearth and wood burning fireplace made for a cozy space. Pinky, Erin, and I took seats around a square table. A moment later, the server delivered menus, glasses of water, and baskets of honey mustard pretzels and popcorn. "Can I start you off with a drink?"

Pinky looked from Erin to me. "How about a Blue Moon tonight?"

"Sounds good," Erin said.

"Sure," I agreed.

"Okay, back with the moons in a jif," our server said.

The wonderful food and topnotch service made Sherman's one of our favorite spots. The bonus for me that particular night was the public place filled with people didn't allow more discussion on the murder.

Pinky must have read my thoughts because she leaned in close to me and said, "So I suppose we can't talk about you-know-what."

I shook my head. "Nope, can't rehash a single word about that here." I cleared my throat. "So how do you like them Wolves?" I said half in jest to change the subject. The Minnesota Timberwolves basketball team had been on a winning streak, so it was a popular phrase among the state's masses.

Pinky snorted. "All right, I'll bite. I love them Wolves. Besides, every single one of them makes me feel short."

Erin laughed. "Since you're almost a foot taller than I am, they're like giants to me. Think how short I'd look standing next to them."

"Me too." I took a sip of water and raised my glass toward Erin. "You've had a full week, huh?"

"Yes, extra busy." Under her breath, she added, "Nothing like yours, however."

Pinky and I nodded.

Erin told some highlights and lowlights, then said, "My kids are great, so that's what keeps me going when I have disagreements with parents, or others."

Our server returned with the drinks. "Do you need a few minutes, or are you ready to order?"

We hadn't looked at the menus. "Give us a few, thanks," I said.

We each had our favorite meals but checked the available choices anyway.

"Can't beat the flatbreads here," Pinky said. "But since I had a muffin earlier, I'll go with the meatloaf special tonight."

"Yes, with mashed potatoes, gravy, steamed carrots. Num," Erin said.

"Good comfort food we all love," I said.

Half an hour later, our full bellies made us feel more relaxed. "Want to hang out, maybe watch a movie?" Erin asked.

"Thanks, but I need to beg off," I said.

"Same with me. I'll be up before dawn to bake, and the last few nights haven't been the best for getting quality rest," Pinky said.

"I have to admit I agree with both of you. I think I'll go home and stare at a wall until I work up enough energy to read," Erin said.

I chuckled, then remembered the last time I'd settled in to read a book was minutes before Pinky phoned about the strange vehicle. I shook off those thoughts.

We paid our bills, then Erin dropped Pinky and me off at our vehicles.

"Thanks for the ride, Erin," I said.

"Yeah, thanks," Pinky echoed.

"You're welcome. Until next time, girlfriends."

Pinky and I climbed from Erin's car and each headed to our own. "See you tomorrow, Pink," I called out.

"Yeppers," she said.

I parked in my garage and chided myself when I eyed my property as if half-expecting an apparition to appear. Pinky had put the notion in my head, and I had yet to shake it loose. All appeared to be quiet in the neighborhood, and I spotted not a single shadow cast on the snow-covered yard. It felt good to be home, no matter what.

Erin told us in jest she thought she'd stare at a wall for a while when she got home. Once inside my house, I opted to lie down on the couch and stared at my ceiling instead. When curiosity got the best of me, I sat up, picked my cell phone off the coffee table, and looked for the name of Jace Klemmet's business. I looked at the Minnesota Secretary of State website under business filings and typed in his name. It turned out I needed the business name instead. I typed "medical supplies companies" on a search engine and learned there were over 500 in Minnesota. Where to start? It was anyone's guess.

I tried Klemmet's name and 'business owner,' with no results. However, I found two medical supplies companies with Brooks Landing addresses and planned to pay each one a visit. Of course, given the Klemmets had lived in three other cities before buying a home in Brooks Landing, the chance that Jace's company was located in town was questionable. Maybe Journee and Josey could recall the name. Or Jaylin might return to the class and coffee with her friends in the near future, and I could figure a way to broach the subject.

Another person on my radar was Tricia Knox. I selected her name in my contacts and pressed the call button. Instead of a ring, I got the reply, "This number is not in service. Please check the number and try again." Not the results I'd hoped for. I disconnected and wished I had asked her where she worked; one way to track her down at least.

I thought Gretchen might have it. Since it was almost nine, and an hour later Eastern Standard Time, I decided to text instead of phone her. *Hello, do you happen to have Tricia's personal cell phone number? I must have her old work cell number. Thanks.*

She responded a moment later. *I'm not sure but will look when I get to work tomorrow. It might be in the staff files from Senator Zimmer.*

Appreciate it, thanks! I replied.

13

Gretchen phoned me the next morning. "Camryn, I located Tricia's file and learned something new. Tricia's her middle name. Her first name is Joelle."

Another J? JTK. No way. "Why does she go by Tricia? Joelle's a beautiful name."

"I agree. Tricia listed her mother as next of kin, and her name is Joelle. Joelle Ann Knox. That must be the reason why. I know people who go by their middle names when their first name is the same as one of their parents," Gretchen said.

"That's true. I've known a couple myself."

"Anyway, I have a number that's noted as her personal cell."

When she recited the number, my heart raced, and my whole body cramped up. It was the same number as on the memo note, minus the area code prefix. "Dear Lord," I muttered.

"What?"

I didn't know what to tell her. "Oh um, sorry, Gretchen. Got a cramp that distracted me for a second. Can you repeat the number to be sure I got it right?"

"Sure."

My heart pounded that much harder when she did. I

managed to keep my voice even when I said, "Thank you. I'll let you know if I find out anything more about Peter Zimmer's murder."

"That'd be good. Camryn, we don't have to be strangers, you know. Call me anytime."

"You too. Thanks again, Gretchen."

We disconnected, and I limped around to loosen the charley horses in my legs, shook my arms, wiggled my fingers, and tried to roll my shoulders and head to loosen those muscles. I'd never had a reaction close to that after I'd gotten an unexpected revelation. The way my whole body cramped up was like a lightning bolt had shot through me.

I paced as I absorbed the latest news. Had Tricia been involved in Peter's murder? If not, why would they have what was, no doubt in my mind, her phone number written on a note found in my yard? Perhaps it was Peter's note, on his dashboard or passenger seat, and the person who'd left him at my house took it to hide the identity of his accomplice: Tricia. Or was Tricia herself the driver? If the driver—whoever it was—may have had the note then dropped it by accident. Or it could have blown from the vehicle when the door opened, and it wasn't noticed in the dark.

When Gretchen gave me Tricia's phone number, it matched had the last seven digits on the note. The number I'd given Garrison as Tricia's was no longer in service, and he'd likely found that out. There were hundreds of area codes in the United States, and if Detective Garrison had considered the seven digits as a partial phone number, he'd start with local ones first. Perhaps he'd already determined Tricia Knox had the phone number in question. If he had interviewed her, what would she have said?

My mind traveled back to my years in Washington. The senator's Minnesota staff made annual trips to the capitol to spend a few days in strategy meetings and briefings with the D.C. staff. Had I ever noticed Tricia and Peter Zimmer off to the side, just the two of them talking? It wasn't something I'd paid particular attention to. Peter was a flirt but took care not to be overtly so in public. Not when his wife was around, at least. Peter could well have interacted with Tricia behind the scenes.

Besides that, Peter divided his time between Minnesota and D.C., with the bulk of it spent in Minnesota. Ramona flew back at least two weekends a month to meet with constituents and elected officials in her district. I knew Tricia had picked her up at her home many times for meetings and events when Ramona was in Minnesota, so Tricia would've known Peter, without a doubt.

I debated whether or not to call Tricia, to find out whether the phone number Gretchen had located was still in service. Tricia didn't know my personal cell number, so if I called and she answered, I could either figure out what to say or hang up.

How many people answered calls from unknown numbers? Not me. I took every call on my official mayor's cell phone; not always on my personal one, however. If the calls were legitimate, people left voicemails or sent text messages I could respond to.

My first course of action was to share the information with Detective Garrison. He answered in the middle of the first ring. "Good morning, Mayor."

"Morning, Detective. Is this an okay time to talk?"

"Yep. What's up?"

"I found out a tidbit that may be helpful for your investigation."

"Oh, and what is that?" he said.

"I wondered if the numbers on that memo note were part of a phone number."

"Right."

"Turns out I learned the identity of the person whose initials and last seven digits of her phone number match the ones on the green memo note."

He cleared his throat. "Go on."

"It's Tricia Knox. I told you how I'd run into her at the post office. Her behavior made me curious, so I contacted a friend from Ramona Zimmer's former office. She gave me Tricia's personal cell number and told me she goes by her middle name. Her legal name is Joelle Tricia Knox, so her initials are JTK," I said.

"I'd call that a solid lead, all right. Fine detective work, Mayor. Do you know Ms. Knox's address?" That meant that he either hadn't tracked her down, or he didn't want me to know he had.

"No, just that she'd recently moved to Carson," I said.

"All right, easy enough to find. I'll take it from here, thank you."

A big smile spread across my face. Detective Garrison had complimented me on the lead.

"And to let you know, I showed that memo note to Ms. Zimmer, asked if she recognized the letters, the numbers, or the handwriting. She said the numbers looked familiar, but not the handwriting," he said.

After we disconnected, I thought about Ramona's response. Had she not known Tricia's first name? In the senator's office, we all had a work cell phone, in addition to our personal cell phone, for legal reasons. It was possible, but not probable, that Ramona only had Tricia's old work number, no longer in service.

The Friday morning patrons seemed more relaxed, overall. Maybe because it was the end of the work week for many of them, and they were winding down. When I arrived a little after eight thirty, Pinky was chatting with folks at a back table. "Hey Cami!" she called out.

"Morning, Pink. I'll be right back and lend you a hand."

"No rush." She met me as I reached the archway. I pointed my thumb toward my shop, and she followed me inside. "What's up?" she asked.

When we were out of customers' earshot, I unloaded the new information I had about Tricia. She grabbed my shoulders. "She *must* have something to do with what happened."

I shrugged. "Detective Garrison is on it. But there's a task I'd like you to take care of."

Her eyebrows shot up. "Is it dangerous?"

"Of course not. I wouldn't ask you to do anything like that. No, I'd like you to use your cell phone and call her number, so we can see if it's still in service."

"What if she answers, what would I say?" she said.

"You could ask for a woman with a different name, then apologize for calling the wrong number. If you get her voicemail, and she says to leave a message, I'll recognize if it's her voice."

Pinky lifted her phone from her jeans back pocket. "Ooh, okay. I can do that."

I'd memorized the numbers, and she pressed them in her phone as I recited each one. "Okay, can you put it on speaker phone?" I asked.

She hit that button, and after three rings, it was Tricia who said, "Hello?" in a hesitant voice.

I nodded at Pinky.

"Hi, *Kimi*?" She asked in higher pitch, an apparent attempt to disguise her voice.

"No, you must have the wrong number," Tricia said.

"Oh, sorry. Bye." Pinky disconnected.

I touched her arm. "Nice job, thanks."

"You're welcome, even if my heart was racing the whole time."

All thirty seconds. Pinky's shop's doorbell dinged, and off she went.

I got a text message from Clint. *Are you at work?*

Yes, I replied.

I'll stop by in a few for coffee and a scone.

I sent him a thumbs up back. Good. He'd be interested in the latest information. I hung up my things and returned to Brew Ha-Ha a moment before Clint arrived. He looked like a model, his long body clad in blue jeans and a brown leather jacket, sunglasses pushed to the top of his head. My heart warmed, and the beats picked up speed.

In place of a kiss, Clint took my hands in his and squeezed. There was enough talk around town about the police chief dating the mayor, so without adding flame to the fire, when we were in public view, we limited signs of affection. He took a seat at the counter. I'd update him when we had more privacy.

"Good to see you, Chief. Your usual cup of the strongest dark coffee?" Pinky said.

"You got it, along with an orange cranberry scone." Pinky drizzled them with a tasty orange glaze.

She smiled and nodded. "Coming right up."

I stepped behind the counter and set the scone on a plate while Pinky filled his cup. The doorbell dinged, and when Tricia Knox walked in, I blinked to be sure it wasn't someone else. I set Clint's plate in front of him and willed myself to remain calm as I moved around the counter.

"Hi, Tricia," I said and heard Pinky gasp.

"Camryn, hi. What a cool coffee shop."

"It sure is. My friend Pinky owns it." I waved my hand in her direction.

Pinky half smiled, and her voice lowered an octave

when she said, "Hi." I almost laughed. Partly from nerves, and partly from the way Pinky disguised her voice a second time for Tricia that morning.

Tricia nodded at her. "Hello."

"And this is our police chief, Clinton Lonsbury."

I noticed how Tricia's body jerked a touch as she tensed up.

Clint stood, and I told him, "I used to work with Tricia in Senator Zimmer's office. Tricia recently moved to Carson."

"Good to meet you, Tricia," Clint said.

"Thanks, um, you too."

"What can I get you, Tricia?" Pinky said, her voice still deep.

"Oh. I might have a coffee later." She turned to me. "Do you have a minute to talk, Camryn?"

Call me curious. "Sure. Let's go to my shop."

Tricia followed me into Curio Finds. "Wow, you sure have all kinds of cool treasures in here."

"Yeah, thanks. My parents have been collecting for years. It started out as a hobby and they turned it into a business as they neared retirement. They get snow globes and other finds from all over the world."

"Wow," she said again. "I can't believe I've never been in here before. I guess with you in D.C., and me in Minnesota, our communications were focused on our jobs, not our personal lives."

"That's true. Plus, I didn't get back to Minnesota as often as I should have." I led her to the office, and we sat by the desk. "So tell me what you wanted to talk about."

Tricia studied her hands a moment. "I didn't know who to turn to, and I don't know how much I can say, but I think the sheriff's office is looking at me as a suspect in Peter's murder."

She called him by his first name. "Why do you think that?" I sounded calm and collected, to my own ears at least.

"You know Detective Garrison?"

"I do. He's the lead investigator on the case," I said.

"Yes. He called to see if I'd be home and then came to my house about an hour ago. Pretty early in the morning. I was surprised when he asked me about Peter and where I was on Monday evening. I told him I stopped for groceries after work and must've gotten home around six-thirty, and I didn't go out after that."

The same timeframe in question. I nodded in hopes she'd tell me more.

"Then, of all things, the detective handed me a memo book and asked me to write the numbers one through ten on it. It seemed like an odd request, if you ask me."

"Hmm." I frowned, like I was thinking about it, but had figured out his reason.

"After I handed him the memo book, he glanced at it and nodded. Then he showed me a baggie with a little note inside. It had my initials and the last seven digits of my cell number written on it." She didn't mention her first name was Joelle.

In my hope for a good reaction to what she'd revealed, I frowned again. "Did you recognize the note?"

"No. I didn't write it, as Garrison must've figured out after he saw the numbers I wrote."

"And you didn't recognize the handwriting on the note?"

She shook her head. "Garrison asked me the same thing, of course. So, what do you think about it, Camryn? You look like you might have an idea."

I'd failed to maintain a neutral expression. "Did the detective tell you where the note was found?"

Her eyebrows drew together. "No?" The word was

posed as a question.

"It's not a total secret, but it wasn't broadcasted either. Peter Zimmer's body was found in his vehicle, in my driveway, and the note was discovered on the ground the next day."

Tricia jumped up so fast, it startled me and brought me to my own feet in a flash. She threw her arms around me in a death-grip hug. I had no idea she was so strong.

She finally stepped back, an arm's length away, and locked her eyes on mine. "I don't get it. Why?"

"No clue."

Tears filled her lower lids. "You found him?"

"One of my friends did, and we called the police."

She swiped at her cheeks as tears rolled down. "I feel awful for Peter, but now I feel bad for you too."

"Thanks." I paused, then said, "Tricia, not that it's any of my business, but were you close to Peter Zimmer?"

She stepped back another step, like I'd slapped her across the face. "There was a time I would have done just about anything for him."

I caught myself before my eyebrows shot up, and nodded instead. Her response had left me speechless. If I'd prodded her for more information, she may've shut down, and I wouldn't get a second chance later on.

"Tricia, this has been a big shock. I'm sorry to cut this short, but I'd better get back and help Pinky until it's time to open my shop. Please feel free to reach out, anytime."

She used her sleeve to dab her tears away. "Thanks for listening, and we'll get through this somehow." *We will*?

When Tricia and I walked through the archway and saw Ramona sitting next to Clint, we both stopped on a dime. I might have backed into my shop if Clint and Ramona hadn't turned their swivel seats toward us. Ramona looked from me to Tricia and gasped so loud we all tensed up.

Tricia's arm shot out sideways and bumped me on the hip, Clint's shoulders lifted a bit, and my stomach tightened. Pinky made a "Ooo!" face behind Ramona's back. Tricia may have noticed it too, unless her eyes were fixed on Ramona. I didn't dare glance her way to find out.

Tricia was the first one to move. She reached Ramona, bent over, and gave her a hug. "I'm so sorry about your husband. I know how much you loved him."

Ramona started to cry. "Thanks. The whole thing has been more terrible than I could ever have imagined."

Tricia nodded. I believed she could've imagined it.

"So, what are you doing in Brooks Landing?" Ramona asked her.

"I moved to Carson and came in for a coffee. Then I saw Camryn too," Tricia said. She didn't mention our first encounter at the post office.

Thankfully, Ramona did not push for more information. "Oh. Anyway, Tricia, I'm glad you're here because I need to apologize for losing touch with you, and my other staff, after the election loss. I was in a bad place for a long time." She sniffed. "And now I'm back there again, only it's way worse."

Tricia gave Ramona another hug. "Of course. As bad as that was, the election loss can't compare to what you must be going through with your husband's death."

When Ramona didn't answer, I lifted my hand toward the back area. "Maybe you two would like to go sit at a table so you'll be more comfortable."

Tricia shook her head. "Um, sorry, but I have to run." She turned to Ramona. "You have my personal cell phone number?"

Ramona frowned and glanced at the floor. It took her a moment to say, "I believe I do." *Hmm.*

"Give me a call . . . to talk, or if you need my help with

something," Tricia said.

"Okay." Ramona's lips turned downward. I would've given a hundred dollars for her thoughts at that moment. Why had she told Detective Garrison the number on the memo note only looked familiar? The interaction between Ramona and Tricia had been strained. They'd spent a lot of the senator's time in Minnesota together, yet both appeared uneasy. Their conversation was brief and uncomfortable, without a solid commitment from either one. Had Ramona suspected how Tricia felt about her husband, that she'd have done about anything for him?

Tricia had not referred to Peter by his first name when she talked to Ramona, as she had with me. Was that because it seemed too personal, like they had been closer than they should have been? Maybe Ramona believed they had.

"I gotta go. Again, my sympathies, and you take good care, Ramona." Tricia gave her a quick hug and left. She'd told Ramona she had stopped by for coffee but had left without a cup.

I mulled over Ramona's reaction when Tricia asked if she still had her personal cell number. It wasn't a tough question. Ramona should've remembered if she'd deleted it from her contacts. Or had Ramona found the memo note in Peter's possessions, recognized the phone number as Tricia's, freaked out, confronted her husband, and things went from bad to worse?

I knew Ramona hadn't written the numbers on the memo note. Her letters and numbers had loops and swirls, with a right slant. I tried to recall ever seeing Peter's handwriting on anything, notes to his wife, or on a to-do list, but couldn't. Aside from my family and close friends, that was true with most people I knew.

"What do you think, Camryn?" Ramona's words brought me back to Brew Ha-Ha.

"What do I think?"

"About how Tricia looks. I'd say not very good. Do you know if she's been ill?"

"Ah no, I don't have any idea."

Come to think of it, Tricia had appeared less than healthy both times I'd seen her, at the post office, and that morning in Brew Ha-Ha.

$$ * $$

14

After Ramona left for parts unknown—I hadn't asked where to, and she hadn't said—the next hour slipped by, as a few customers drifted in from Brew Ha-Ha to look at our merchandise. One purchased a Disney character snow globe.

Midafternoon, I found Pinky in her back room grinding coffee beans. "Hey, Pink. When you're done with that, is it okay if I go pick up my meeting packet?"

"Sure. This is my last batch."

"All righty."

By the time I got my coat on, Pinky peeked her head though the archway. "Ready to keep watch."

"Thanks. See you in a bit."

As I drove in the Brooks Landing City Office lot, I spotted a familiar woman leave the building. The mysterious Jaylin Klemmet. I blinked to make sure it was her. Had I arrived a minute earlier, I would've met her inside. What was her business with the city, I had to wonder?

I backed up to a parking spot as Jaylin climbed into a white SUV. A moment later, when she pulled out and turned north, I did the same. I followed her to Prime Fitness Center a mile away and waited until she was inside before I climbed from my car, and headed to the center myself.

She swiped her card at front counter reader and disappeared into a room halfway down the hall from the gym. I eyed the gigantic open space, filled with machines and exercise equipment. I held back a moment, then stepped up to the counter and smiled at the young woman on the other side.

What to say? "Hello, I'm Mayor Camryn Brooks, and I like to visit businesses in town, see what you all have to offer. I haven't been here yet, so would it be okay if I took a quick look around?"

"Of course, Mayor. I'd give you a tour, but I'm the only one at the front desk right now. Others are working with clients." She waved her hand toward the gym. "You can see the treadmills, elliptical and weight machines, bicycles. We also have a running track, and more equipment on the upper level. Plus a pool, sauna, and hot tub you can access from the ladies room, just down the hall on the right." The room Jaylin had gone in, was my guess. Was she headed to the pool? In that case, she'd need time to change.

"Thank you."

The woman pointed at a rack a few feet away. "Hang up your coat, if you'd like."

"I will, thanks."

After I slipped it on a hanger, I debated next steps. I'd never been to the fitness center, but knew my gray trousers, plum tunic top, and black Mary Jane flats—I hadn't put on snow boots—did not qualify as workout attire. My best line of defense was to act like I had a good reason to be there. I straightened my back and strolled into the proverbial lion's den.

It did my heart and ego good to see not everyone on the machines had "ripped" muscles, like Josey had described Jaylin's. Several carried many extra pounds. I checked out the machines and weights, like I was taking inventory. When I saw all the red faces and bodies covered in sweat, it humbled me. They strived for better fitness, something I had neglected with my own health.

I was on the other side of the elliptical machines when Jaylin walked in and headed straight to the weightlifting area. She wore a fitted, mint green one-piece outfit with spaghetti straps and shorts to midthigh. Her tanned body, with strong and defined muscles, caught peoples' attention. She did indeed look like a body builder. I swallowed my pride, left my hiding spot, and approached Jaylin as she was about to lift a heavy dumbbell.

We had never been introduced, so I said, "Well, hi!"

I'd caught her off guard. Her eyebrows lifted as she said, "Oh, Mayor." Her face was drawn and paler than her body. She glanced down at my apparel. "I haven't seen you here before."

"I'm not here to work out, although I should be." I chuckled to lessen the tension, then fibbed. "It's more like I'm in my official capacity as mayor, doing a little tour to see what all they offer."

"Oh, well that's good, then."

"It's a pretty impressive center, and you are very fit. I should start a fitness program myself," I said.

She nodded. "They have good trainers too."

"I guess when you've been in Brew Ha-Ha, we never exchanged names."

"It's always been pretty busy, but I know yours, of course. I'm Jaylin."

"Thanks, Jaylin. Speaking of Brew Ha-Ha, I guess I've missed you, if you've stopped by the last few days."

She glanced down, then lifted her shoulders. "Taking a little break. I wasn't feeling well, and today is my first day back at the gym since, ah, since Monday."

"Sorry to hear that, and I'm glad you feel well enough to work out again."

"Thanks. Things have been, um, difficult lately," she said.

"Is there anything I can do to help?"

She shook her head. "Thanks, though. Well, I better get my workout done and get home." *Get done and get home.*

"Good to see you, and don't be a stranger, okay?"

She gave me a slight nod then turned away.

I drove back to the city offices, a sturdy, one-story brick structure, built about twenty years before. The police station was housed in the same building, and the two departments shared a common front entry, then split to separate units.

I parked in the back lot and used my badge to gain access through the rear entrance. Jaylin's demeanor and words had perplexed me, and I thought about our conversation on my way down the hallway. The other councilors' office doors were closed. I stopped at Administrator Gary Lunden's office; his door was open. He was seated behind his desk and stood when he spotted me. "Camryn, come in." He came around to meet me and drew me in a bear hug that rivaled my dad's. "How are you holding up?"

"Pretty good, considering, and it'll get better. Gary, sorry to hug and run, but I left Pinky in charge of both shops, so I best listen to phone messages from the last few days and grab my packet."

"Let me know if you're not up to leading the meeting on Monday. Vice Chair Lyon can fill in, if need be."

"Thanks, Gary."

"So you know, I've briefed staff about the victim's body and where it was found. And I made each one promise not to share it with the media, nor to ask you anything about it, unless you bring up the subject first," he said.

"It's good they know about it, and I'll give them a briefing when things settle down a bit."

"They'd appreciate that." He paused, then added, "We all would."

I smiled and slipped away. The meeting packet was in the clear holder outside my office, along with a few pieces of mail. I gathered them together, keyed in to the room, and flipped on the light. The message indicator on my phone was blinking, so I lifted it to my ear and hit the play button. The monotone female voice told me I had ten new messages and no saved messages.

I listened to each one and noted their numbers on my legal pad. Three came from mayors in neighboring towns who said, in different ways, they were sorry about the homicide in Brooks Landing. Seven came from constituents who offered their opinions about how I should vote on particular issues. Not a one needed an immediate response, but I would return the calls sooner rather than later.

I thought about Jaylin's stop at the city office and went to the front desk to inquire. Receptionist Lila, a sweet woman in her fifties, had been with the city for decades. Her eyes narrowed in concern. "Mayor Brooks. How *are* you?"

The dreaded question. "Still a little shell shocked, but I'll be fine. Thanks. On another matter, one of my constituents planned to stop by today. Jaylin?"

"Well, as a matter of fact she did. She saw our ad for the human resources position and picked up an application."

What? Why hadn't she mentioned that when we chatted at the club? "Okay. I'm glad to hear that. Now I need to get back to my other job. See you Monday."

"Yes. Have a good weekend."

"You too."

When I returned to the shops, Pinky was wiping off the tables and chairs.

"Sorry it took me so long. I ended up taking a detour," I said.

"A detour?"

"I went to the fitness center."

"You what? What in heaven's name got into you, made you do that? You don't work out," she said.

"True, but after I got there, watching other out of shape people on the machines, it made me think I should give it a try. But the real reason is, I followed Jaylin there."

"You *what*?"

I filled in the details up to the reason she was at the Brooks Landing City Office.

"That must mean she plans to stick around town."

"It must. She is like a mystery woman. She's obviously having problems, likely with her marriage, from what I've gathered. I can only hope she's okay," I said.

"If she gets a job with the city, you can keep an eye on her. As I know you will."

Pinky went home at four o'clock. As I closed the shops at five and turned off the lights, they flicked back on. "Honestly, Molly." Off they went again. "Thank you." I waved it off.

The mysterious cloud around Jace and Jaylin Klemmet, given Jace's reported behavior, and Jaylin's observed behavior, along with her cryptic explanation at the fitness center, gnawed at me. I needed to go by their house to see if anything unusual or suspicious jumped out at me. It'd be less conspicuous in the dark of night.

Since Peter Zimmer's murder, I'd been more faithful to

keep pepper spray in my pocket when I ventured out, especially after dark. I felt safer with it in hand and gripped it on the trek to the back parking lot.

A light snow had started to fall in the past hour, and as flakes landed on my nose, I turned my face upward for a moment. It took me back to my childhood days when Pinky and Erin and I stuck out our tongues to catch snowflakes and blinked away ones that clung to our eyelashes. As I slid behind the wheel of my car, the temperature felt the same inside as the air outside. I started the engine then double checked the Klemmet's address on my phone as the car warmed.

Six minutes later I turned on to Klemmet's street, and saw their upscale brick home among the others. My shoulders lurched forward in an involuntary reaction and bumped the steering wheel when I spotted a big, dark van in their driveway. Exhaust rose from its tail pipe. I strained to get a good look at the vehicle through the snowfall. As it backed out, I pulled over but wasn't able to tell if it was dark gray or black. Nor could I see a decal on the side window or the numbers on the license plate.

I took out my phone, selected Detective Garrison's number, and pushed the call button. It went to voicemail after the first ring, announced he was unavailable, and if it was an emergency to call 911. It felt like an emergency, but what would I say to the dispatcher? That I spotted a van that may have been used in a crime leaving a driveway? Garrison had always answered my calls, so it was likely his weekend off. Leave a message? Call Clint?

My heart thumped in my chest. The van was driving away, and I had to put my phone down. I'd turned it off to avoid the temptation of looking at it if I got a call. We had a hands-free law in Minnesota, and my older vehicle didn't have Bluetooth. Besides being against the law, it would be risky driving and talking as big snowflakes fell at a faster rate and required closer attention. I didn't want to lose the van and fell in behind it at a respectable distance.

The van continued toward the Highway 44 intersection. A man in a red truck eased in from a side street then cut between us as we approached a stoplight. The dark van turned left on the amber light and headed east on Highway 44. The light was red by the time the truck reached the intersection, so we both had to stop. I could have made it, except for him. It was the longest light ever, and it seemed like ten minutes passed before it turned green.

The truck took a left, and I followed suit. The van had a considerable head start, so with the truck moving along at a snail's pace, there was a slim to none chance I'd catch up with the van.

About three minutes later, the truck turned south on a county road. I pressed the gas pedal, but not to the metal, given the weather conditions. It appeared the highway department had applied a salt brine to the roadway, standard practice before a predicted snowfall, so snow melted when it hit the pavement. It created a safer passage for motorists and reduced the amount of snow that crews had to plow.

After I'd accepted the reality a pursuit was in vain, I drove in to a gas station's parking lot and considered my next steps. I needed to tell Garrison and Clint about the van at the Klemmet's house. Garrison might think I was a busybody, but it could be a clue. Jace Klemmet had owned a medical supplies company, after all.

Clint had grown a tad more patient with me and my suggestions, as long as I stayed in my own lane and within the law. Chief Clint, and his assistant chief Mark, took turns being on call overnights. They each had one week on, the next one off, and seldom got called to assist a police officer during the night.

It was Clint's Friday night off but we hadn't made plans, given the one day at a time week we'd had. When I turned on my phone, I saw a missed text message from him and a voicemail from Garrison.

Clint wrote, *I drove by your shop, but you'd already left. Running errands?*

One way to put it. I decided to text, instead of phoning him. *I'll tell you about it when I see you. Want to hang out later?* I wrote back.

Your house about seven?

Seven's good, thanks.

He sent me a thumbs up in response.

I listened to Garrison's message next. "Missed your call. I'll be home the rest of the evening, so feel free to give me a call."

I pondered whether I should intrude on his Friday night personal time, or not. "Intrude," won the debate. I selected his number and pressed the call button. Garrison answered before the second ring. "Mayor, I saw I missed a call from you earlier. What's up?"

"No worries. I had a hunch to drive by the Klemmet's house, and as I did, a big dark van backed out of their driveway."

"The reason you phoned me."

"Yes, I called before it drove away."

"Dark, not black?" he said.

"It could've been dark gray."

"Did you get the license plate number?"

"Couldn't see it through the snow."

"How about a decal on the window?"

"Same deal," I said.

"Yeah. Something tells me you followed the van after it drove off."

"That I did, as far as Highway Forty-four. A truck got between us, and I lost him after he—or she, I guess—headed east."

"To let you know, I looked up vehicles the Klemmets own, and a van is not one of them," he said.

"Oh. Could've been a company van and not a personal one."

"Could've, sure. Details are still forthcoming on that, like whether vehicles were included in the sale of the business, or whether they belonged to contracted delivery companies."

Sounded like a mess to sort through. "More work ahead, right?"

"Yep. Thanks for the tip, Camryn." He was back to a first name for me.

"Sure. Glad I was in the right place at the right time."

"Right place, right time gives us leads that help solve cases far more often than you would think," Garrison said.

15

I pulled in my garage and closed the door behind me. From the alley's light, I saw large shoe prints in the snow. They started at the alley and went toward my back door. The snow had stopped but I guessed they would've been left in the last hour, or so. There'd been no messages from my friends or family members saying they planned to stop by. No package on the steps, nor was I expecting one. Strange. It could have been any number of innocent reasons someone had been there, like a neighborhood kid offering to shovel my driveway and steps. Still, I took care not to walk on the prints.

The motion detection light next to the door above the steps came on when I was six feet away. *I should have it reset to eight, or ten feet, out.* With my house keys in hand, I went up the steps and noticed a scratch mark on the lock panel. It was superficial, faint, and new. The muscles in my legs weakened. I wobbled and pressed my body against the railing for support. Open the door, or call Clint first? Either one would take more energy than I thought I could muster at the moment.

Headlights lit up the back yard. When I turned and saw it was Clint's truck, it saved me from the decision. Thank goodness for small miracles. Clint climbed from his vehicle.

"Waiting for me?"

"I guess I am." I held up my hand. "But stop where you are."

He did. "What?"

I went back down the steps, and pointed at the shoe, or boot, prints. "I know I'm jumpier than normal, but I think someone tried to enter my house."

Clint detoured around the prints, and his long strides brought him to my side in seconds. He withdrew a small flashlight from his jacket pocket and shined it on the depressions in the snow. "It appears a person with bigger feet than yours was here. But why do you think they tried to break in?"

"Take a look at the lock on my door."

He walked around the prints on his way to the house, took two steps up, and looked at the woven mat on the landing. "There's a little snow in between the links."

"Some could've come from my shoes."

Clint leaned over for a closer look at the door. "What in tarnation? They tried to pick it, all right. And maybe succeeded."

His comment released a swarm of butterflies in my stomach.

Clint shined the flashlight on the lock, the knob, and around the door. "Probably time to replace this half century old lock with a keyless entry system."

"Probably."

"I'll phone Garrison, ask him to send a deputy over to look for latent prints and get photos of the boot prints in the yard." He made the call and provided the details. He disconnected and told me, "The crime lab deputy on call will arrive in fifteen to twenty minutes. Meantime, let's get you inside via the front door."

We trouped down the path around to the front. I found

the key, turned the lock, and pushed open the door.

Clint went in first, and when I stepped inside, he whispered, "Keep the lights off and wait here till I do a search." He found a pair of vinyl gloves in his jacket pocket and slid them on. *Always prepared.* He drew his gun from its holster and cupped his flashlight against it as he made his way toward the kitchen.

Clint checked the room, then in a quiet voice said, "If anyone entered via the back door, they must've left their boots outside." He walked from one side of the house to the other and came back to the living room. "All clear on this level. Go ahead and turn on the lights."

He shined his flashlight at a lamp. I flipped the switch, and a soft glow haloed the room. "I'll take a look in the basement." He was quiet on the way down, thanks to the solid wood stairs.

I went into the kitchen and detected an unfamiliar odor in the room; a fragrance I didn't use, either in my personal care products, like shampoo or soap, or for cleaning, like dish or laundry soap. It was unusual. My muscles tensed when I had an inkling that I'd caught a whiff of that product before. But where? In a store's fragrance section? Could be. On one of my friends? Doubtful. Working in the public sector, we avoided wearing fragrances because more and more people had negative reactions to them.

I had a fleeting thought one of Sandra's children or grandchildren may have stopped by but dismissed it seconds later. Sandra's daughter had a key, and I didn't suspect other family members would break in. After I had settled in the house, and was out of town for the weekend, her daughter asked permission to use her key to pick up the last box. She hadn't been back since.

Clint joined me a few minutes later, and it switched my thoughts. He told me, "No hiding spots downstairs. Washer, dryer, furnace, water softener, empty shelves on the walls, except for laundry detergent and fabric spray on one above the washer. Clean, without clutter."

"The way I like it. Clint, this may sound strange, but do you smell something different in here?"

"Different, in what way?" He turned his head from side to side then tipped it back, his nostrils flared as he sniffed.

"Different from how it usually smells, aside from when I'm cooking. Different from any products I use. Someone must've gotten inside, for whatever reason, and left a fragrance behind. Everything I use is either unscented, or has a mild, more subtle scent, like lavender or vanilla."

"You must have a better smeller than I do. I do catch a little whiff of it now. It isn't that strong or pungent. Maybe a cologne?"

"It's vaguely familiar, and I've been trying to place it but can't. It has a hint of chocolatey coffee and something else."

"Not one of Pinky's coffee blends?"

"No."

"If a burglar was here and left his scent behind, it must've been shortly before you got home. Take a look around, see if anything is out of place or missing."

The first thing I glanced at in the living room was the cuckoo clock. Still on the wall. I did a decent check of items in the living room, dining area, kitchen, office/guest bedroom, bathroom, and closets.

All clear until I went in my bedroom and saw a small piece of paper, about four inches square, on my bed. It had a typed message that made my blood run cold. When Clint touched my shoulder, I nearly jumped out of my skin.

He stepped around me and focused on the note, the letters typed in caps. "IT WAS ALL YOUR FAULT," Clint read out loud, then snapped a photo with his phone camera.

Tears rolled down my cheeks. "What sick person would come in my bedroom and leave a note like this on my bed, of all places? What fault are they talking about? They thought I was responsible for Ramona losing the election, and then they lost their job because of it? Who would come up with a scheme this crazy to what, try to scare me? It doesn't make sense."

Clint reached his arm around me with a gentle squeeze. "I am so sorry, Camryn. You're right, a very sick person violated your personal space. There's a chance this is related to Peter's murder, but I can't come up with how that could be. The other thing is, say he *is* blaming you for the election results, why would they kill Peter?"

"Maybe they blamed Peter too, over our imaginary affair. Will this nightmare never end?"

"The second brazen act on your property, a major concern. Not to mention the risk they took. A neighbor could easily have spotted them."

"I know, and I can't count how many times I've thought, why couldn't I have been looking out my back window when they drove Peter's SUV to my house, seen the driver get out, then leave the SUV there?"

"The old shoulda, woulda, coulda scenarios that eat at us. And if you were looking out your window, they could've seen you too."

"I suppose."

Clint got a text message and checked it. "Deputy's here. He'll explore the back yard and door, then come to the front. We'll wait until he's finished outside to show him the note."

I could only nod.

"As far as the perpetrator goes, do you detect that scent in here?" Clint asked.

I leaned over, as close to the note as I dared, and inhaled. "No. Just a faint lavender scent from my laundry soap. Not the same one I picked up in the kitchen."

"A smart burglar would not have worn cologne, but he must not have thought that far. Maybe he took off his jacket for the minutes he was in the house and set it on a chair. Or, more likely, he could've accidentally brushed against something, like the wall. when finding his way around."

"That makes sense."

"Hopefully, this letter proves to be useful evidence and a good lead for Detective Garrison."

If that were true, it'd almost be worth the anguish that pushed through my body like a flood. I nodded and sucked in a sniffle.

Clint looped his arm around mine. "Let's wait for the deputy in the kitchen." He went straight to the window. "Looks like he's heading to the front."

A rap sounded on the door a moment later.

I dabbed away tears as Clint opened it for him. "Come on in, Deputy Higgins."

"Thanks, Chief. Mayor." The young deputy stepped inside and slipped off his boots. He wore a stocking cap and gloves, but no jacket. Clint had told me Kevlar vests kept officers warm enough, unless they needed to be outside in frigid temps for an extended period of time.

Higgins held up his phone. "I snapped photos of the footprints in the back yard. Part of a brand name was visible in one print, but I couldn't make what it was. I'll enlarge the photo at the office and we should be able to figure it out."

Clint nodded. "To let you know, I searched the house for a burglar; no longer here. Then Camryn looked for items missing or out of place. She didn't find anything until she went into the bedroom and found a note on her bed. On my search, I'd taken a glance in there but hadn't noticed the note."

Higgins's eyebrows lifted as he slid off his leather

gloves and stuck them in his back pocket. He put on a pair of vinyl gloves he'd pulled from a case on his belt. "Let's have a look. Lead the way, Mayor."

So I did. The white note was a stark contrast to the burgundy comforter beneath it.

After he read it, Higgins asked, "Mayor, any idea who would've written it, or a reason for the note itself?"

"No idea who, but maybe a clue about why. I worked for Senator Ramona Zimmer in Washington. It's a long story, but she fired me. After she lost the last election, her staff lost their jobs. I heard some blamed me, thought I'd campaigned against her."

"But you didn't?"

I shook my head. "No, it never occurred to me to do anything like that."

"Do you know the names of staff who blamed you for it?" Higgins said.

"No, I never got names, but you could ask a staffer that I trust."

He nodded. "All right. I'll coordinate with Detective Garrison on that part of the investigation. First off, I'll get that note bagged up as evidence. If the burglar touched it with bare hands, the crime lab has chemicals they can use to develop latent prints." He reached in his back pocket for the bag, picked up the note, and slid it inside.

We followed Clint to the kitchen. Higgins set the bagged note on the table and lifted a notepad and pen from his pocket. "I'm ready for the staffer's contact info."

I located Gretchen's information, and he recorded it as I recited it. "Thanks." Higgins put the writing tools back in his pocket.

"Deputy Higgins, Camryn detected an unusual scent in the house, mostly in the kitchen, that we believe the burglar left," Clint said.

"Yes, it got fainter after the front door was opened, but I can still catch a slight whiff," I said.

"Can you describe what it smells like?" Higgins asked.

"A little like Pinky's coffee with chocolate, and another scent besides, almost like roasted nuts."

"That's sounds pretty specific," he said.

"That's not quite it, but it's what it reminds me of."

"Camryn has a keen sense of smell," Clint remarked.

"Must have. All I detect is a faint vanilla," Higgins said.

I drew in a breath. "That's from my dish towels. It's the laundry detergent I use."

"Okay. We'll talk with neighbors, of course, find out if anyone noticed any suspicious activity here today," Higgins said.

"If I were a burglar, I'd sneak in after dusk. And since the person's mysterious fragrance was still present when I got home, I'd say he was inside shortly before that." Chills danced through me as the words left my mouth.

After Deputy Higgins left with the evidence, Clint said, "I don't want you here alone. I can sleep on the couch, or you can camp at my place until we catch the creep."

"I'd rather you stayed with me. I don't want to leave my house vacant. And your vehicle here should keep the *creep* away."

"Okay. I'll get the locks changed tomorrow and doorbells with cameras to capture images of any would be burglars," Clint said.

"That'd be good. I always felt safe, and actually comforted, living in Sandra's house. You used the right word—violated—when you said that's what he did to my personal space. Believe it or not, it almost feels worse than when Ramona fired me."

"I can believe that. Getting fired is insulting. Having

someone break in to your home is alarming."

Tears formed in my eyelids. Clint gave me a peck on the nose, drew me into his arms, and pulled me tight against him. His caring and strength assured me he would help me through whatever lay ahead.

Over coffee Saturday morning, Clint said, "Since I'm off duty today, I'll see what the hardware store has for locks and doorbells. I talked to my electrician buddy who said he'd help get them installed today."

"Thanks, Clint. Having new locks and doorbell cameras will give me peace of mind."

He nodded. "Seems to me that whoever entered your house and left that note was a coward. Instead of talking to you about whatever the issue was, he, or it could be a she, chose to pull off a scare tactic stunt instead."

"And it worked, that is for darn sure. It kept me awake half the night trying to figure out who it could be. And sleeping in the guest room is not the same as my own."

Clint laid his hand on mine. "No. Your couch is comfortable, but your little cuckoo bird woke me up a few times."

"Sorry. At times I wonder why I keep it, then I think of Sandra, and how much she treasured the little guy."

"Good enough reason to keep it."

"Clint, back to the 'it's all your fault' note. If it refers to Ramona's election loss, hopefully Garrison will come up with the names of people who blamed me for it. Even so, why would anyone deliver a note like that?"

His eyes looked both warm and intense when he said, "Camryn, if the last two crimes at your place—leaving a body and then a note—were logical, we might have an answer. Right now, authorities are still in the dark."

"You're right, if the note and Peter's murder are

connected, it makes zero logical sense. But maybe not to a person with a few loose screws," I said.

"*That* would seem logical."

"A question that bubbles up in my mind more than it should. Did Ramona have a role in Peter's death and with the note on my bed? But if the two aren't connected, was she involved in one or the other?"

"I can assure you it is my goal to keep an open mind until all the evidence is gathered, suspects and witnesses are interviewed, and the truth is revealed, however that goes down. But our trained instincts often play an important part, too. We observe body language. Or when questioning a person, he might say something he didn't mean to, then clams up. It prompts us to take another look, see if we missed it the first, or second time around," Clint said.

"Some people have keener instincts than others."

"Of course. It seems like you fine-tuned those skills in D.C., but you still need to stay aware of your surroundings." Clint gave my hand a squeeze. "How about I give you a ride to and from work tomorrow?" he offered.

"That's not necessary."

He had a more firm tone when he said, "Until this case gets solved, we'll make sure you get to work safely in the morning, and home again at night. If I'm tied up and can't do it, we'll find someone who can. It'd make me feel better."

"Clint, you don't have to make me more paranoid than I already am. After the Monday night fiasco, I've made sure to keep a can of Mace on me whenever I leave the house, including when I'm at work."

"Glad to hear that. I'm not as concerned when you're at your shop, or even running errands around town during the day. It's more after dark, in the parking lot, or on your property, given the two crimes here."

"All right." I thought for a moment. "Clint, with all the

hoopla last night, I didn't think to tell you what happened with Jaylin, or when I drove to the Klemmet's house."

Clint listened as I highlighted the incidents and inserted a comment here and there. When I'd finished, he said, "So Garrison knows about the van there, and that you followed it?"

"He does. But not that I'd also followed her to the fitness center, and we'd had a chat."

Clint shook his head then nodded.

When it was time to leave for Brew Ha-Ha, Clint escorted me to the garage, waited while I got in the Subaru, followed me downtown, parked his truck beside mine in the back parking lot, then walked me to Pinky's shop door. He even went inside, and said he needed a cup of coffee, despite the two strong brews he'd downed at my house.

Pinky's eyes narrowed when we neared her counter. "What's up? You two have really weird looks on your faces."

With people sitting around the back tables, Clint headed toward the Curio Finds archway and waved for us to follow him.

He leaned in close to Pinky. "I want you to keep a look out for anyone who seems suspicious."

Her head tilted to the side a bit. "I thought I already did. What do you mean, exactly?"

Clint saved me from explaining when he launched into the story. Pinky's eyes traveled between Clint, and me, as he relayed the details. When he got to the note on my bed, Pinky's arms flew up toward the ceiling, descended a moment later, and landed on my shoulders. "It would terrify me if someone had been in my house, and he left his scent behind besides. But like on purpose to scare you, right?"

"You wouldn't think. I know I've smelled a similar scent before but have no idea where or when. I met with hundreds of people in Washington, and waited on scores, upon scores, of people in the shops. Not to mention that many constituents stop by during the hours I'm in my city office," I said.

Pinky rested her forehead against mine. "Maybe that note isn't related to Peter Zimmer's death at all, maybe it was a guy who's mad at you for a decision you made on the city council."

That thought had crossed my mind during the restless night. "At this point, we don't have a clue."

"I can't stand it! Cami, you need to come stay at my house."

I clasped my hands around hers and slid them off my shoulders. "It's okay, Pink. We have a safety plan worked out. Clint's going to make sure I get to and from work in one piece. Plus, he and his friend are installing new locks and doorbells with cameras."

"Hmm. Maybe it's time you get a security system like I have. I don't have to worry about anyone breaking in, because if the alarm is tripped, the alert goes to the sheriff's office, and they can respond in a heartbeat. It was worth the hassle and expense of getting it installed," she said.

"I'd have to run that by the family. I don't mind footing the bill for the locks and doorbells, but I don't own the house, and I'm not even sure how long I'll live there. At some point, they'll want to sell," I said.

"I suppose," she said.

"We'll see what Sandra's kids decide to do down the road." In truth, it was the first time I'd thought about it. After I'd arrived back in Brooks Landing with my tail between my legs, I'd been swamped with managing Curio Finds, getting appointed mayor, social events with family and friends, and a budding romance with Chief Clinton Lonsbury. Add to that, I'd happened upon victims' bodies which prompted me to try to uncover those responsible. The investigative ventures had become almost a part time job for me.

Clint lifted his hand. "We don't need to figure that out today. The issue is, one or more persons committed two crimes on Camryn's property this week. The Buffalo County Sheriff's office has likely assembled a hefty list of people they've interviewed, or still need to. We can only hope they'll close in on the suspects soon."

When Pinky's doorbell dinged, her mouth drooped. I knew she didn't want to leave us on that low note.

"We'll need to set a code for your new locks. What would you like it to be? Six numbers, and not your birthday or your address, or one-two-three-four-five-six," Clint said.

"Oh." I thought for a moment. "Okay, this is random. Three-eight-two-nine-four-one."

"How are you going to remember that combo?"

"March, August, February, September, April, January. They're my parents' and siblings' birthday months, in order."

Clint's right eyebrow lifted. "Pretty sure no one will crack that code."

He left for the hardware store a short time later, sans a cup of coffee. I phoned Sandra's daughter in Iowa to tell her about the picked lock and burglary, and to get her okay for new locks and Ring doorbells. "Unbelievable! And it's more than okay to make those improvements. They're added safety features, and we'll be happy to pay whatever it costs," she said.

"That's not necessary. The man I'm dating, and his friend will do the installation."

"Nothing's cheap anymore, so I'll send you a check or subtract it from your rent."

If she sent me a check, I wouldn't have to cash it.

I ended up telling her about Ramona Zimmer's husband and his death. She hadn't heard the news, and her voice quieted when she said, "You have had a week from hell. Brooks Landing has always been kind of quaint and quiet."

"It still is, for the most part, with a major thing thrown in from time to time." A customer came in the shop. "Sorry, but I need to go."

"All right. Take good care and stay safe," she said.

16

Detective Garrison phoned a little after nine a.m., so I stepped out of Brew Ha-Ha to take the call. "Hello, Detective."

"Morning, Mayor. What an ordeal you had last night. I'm really sorry about that, and needed to see how you're holding up."

"I appreciate that. I'm doing okay, and Clint's helped me a lot."

"Yes. To let you know, we've asked our patrol units to swing by your house throughout the day and nighttime hours to look for anything that looks amiss."

"Thanks," I said.

"I gotta say, the burglary adds an unusual layer to our investigation."

"And a strange one."

"Yeah. Deputy Higgins briefed me last night, and I just read his written report. He added that you detected a foreign scent in your house. Besides the note, that's about all the suspect left behind," Garrison said,

"Weird, I know. A chocolatey coffee odor, mixed with maybe nuts of some kind, is the best way I can describe it."

"Sounds like a tasty beverage to me."

I smiled. "It does. And I can tell you that after being in Brew Ha-Ha for hours—especially when Pinky's grinding beans—the smells cling to my clothes and skin, so I know how much stronger odors like that linger."

"Yes, they do."

"That particular one was a little different than from what I've smelled in Brew Ha-Ha's coffee blends."

"Even if we could've bottled it up, it would be like finding a needle in a haystack to identify a suspect by that alone. That said, fewer people are wearing fragrances these days," he said.

"You're right. Maybe a random stranger hired by the real culprit. The message on the note was not random. It was written by someone who knows me."

"No doubt about that."

"Detective, so you know Clint and his friend are installing better locks and Ring Video Doorbells on my doors today, for more security," I said.

"I'm glad to hear that. Take care, Mayor."

"You too, Detective."

After we'd disconnected, I phoned my mother. "Hi, Mom, are you in the middle of anything?"

"Cami, you've been on my mind all morning. In fact, we'd planned to stop by to see you, but we'll be doing a little babysitting instead."

"You are the best grandparents I know. Is Dad with you?"

"Right here. You want to talk to him?" Mom said.

"Actually, to both of you, if you'll put your phone on speaker."

"So there is a reason I've been thinking about you. Something happened, didn't it? They found Peter Zimmer's killer," she said.

"Not yet."

"Hi, Cami," Dad said.

"Hi, Dad. I don't want you two to stress about this, but someone broke in my house last night and left me a strange note."

I filled in the details, then Mom started crying. "You said not to worry, but how can we not?"

"You'd better come stay with us, Cami," Dad said.

"Clint's having more secure locks installed, and sounds like he plans to be my bodyguard until they find the intruder."

"Glad to hear that, anyway. No one better to keep our daughter safe," Dad said.

"Yes," Mom murmured.

"Will you tell my siblings, if you think they should know, that is?"

"Of course they should, and of course we will," Dad said.

"I love you," I said.

"We love you more," Mom whispered back.

Clint sent me a text message at 12:35 p.m. *Mission accomplished. See you at 5.*

I replied, *Thank you!*

When I waited on customers in the shops, it helped me think about things other than the break-in. Then I'd puzzle over the foreign scent in my house and obsess about that for a while.

The day dragged on and on. By midafternoon, the crowds in Curio Finds and Brew Ha-Ha dwindled, and neither shop had patrons by four o'clock. Pinky usually left by then anyway, and I assured her I would be fine, that she should feel free to leave.

"All right. Erin will be back from her weekend retreat tomorrow afternoon. You need to tell her about this latest deal," she said.

"Of course. I told my parents who will tell my siblings. I'm not sure if the city councilors should know, or not. I'm guessing the sheriff's office will interview Ramona about it, see if she has a clue."

"Speaking of the devil, I'm surprised she hasn't been around today. It's the first time all week."

"I know. I kept expecting her to stop by. She didn't call me even once, which is very unusual. It almost makes me worry about her," I said.

"Cami, how can you even think that? As mean as she was to you."

"She did apologize, and I can't help it if I feel sorry for her. Ramona doesn't have a good support system or any real friends."

"As they say, you reap what you sow. But I have to admit, I feel a little sorry for her myself."

I drew Pinky in for a hug. "Go home and relax. It's been a long week, so do your best to clear the latest drama from your mind tonight."

I stepped back, and a smile stretched across Pinky's face. "Thanks. Jake's coming over for dinner, so that'll help a ton. We'll enjoy good food, good wine, and good music to help us unwind."

It almost made me envious when she walked out the door. I settled on the stool behind my counter when a moment later, speaking of the devil, Ramona phoned. "Ramona, hi. We missed you today."

"Really? Oh well, I've been busy almost all day. A lot of my staff, and legislators, and even some lobbyists from Washington called to give me their sympathies. It was like the floodgates opened."

"I'm glad to hear that," I said.

"I'd heard from a lot of them after the election, and

others when I cleared out my office at the end of December, but not a word since then. So I didn't really feel comfortable contacting them, either. It surely helped raise my spirits by a lot, and I don't even feel as lonely now."

It wouldn't surprise me if Gretchen had given those people a nudge. "My guess is they wanted to give you a few days to try to process everything."

"You might be right, and you know what? It got me to thinking, maybe we should have a memorial service for Peter after all," she said.

"Whatever you decide to do, I can help with the details." Another open mouth, insert foot moment.

"That really is kind of you. I'll think more about it and let you know."

"All righty." Brew Ha-Ha's doorbell dinged. "Sorry to cut you off, but I've got a customer."

"Thanks again," she said, and the line went dead.

As I crossed the archway, it lifted *my* spirits to see Clint. "Not that I'm tired, or anything, but I'm relieved it's you for two reasons. Because it's you and because it's not a customer to wait on," I said.

He grinned. "So what if I am a customer?"

I bowed my head. "What can I get you, sir?"

"A kiss?"

"My pleasure."

He leaned over for a quick smooch. "Very nice," he said.

"Mmm. So everything went well with the installations?"

He winked. "Piece of cake for my buddy and me. Mostly for my buddy."

I glanced up at the Betty Boop Oop a Doop clock. "Seven long minutes till closing."

Clint ran his hand up and down my back. "I take it you are not in the mood for a night on the town."

"Relaxing on the couch with you seems way more appealing."

"I agree. I'll help you close up the shops, so we can get you home."

As we shut off the drink machines and checked the back rooms, I told him about my conversation with Ramona.

"That's good to hear. Maybe it'll help turn her focus outward, instead of inward, like it's been since her husband's death."

My lips lifted in a smirk. "And before that, even. At least it made her feel that people care, after all. Whether they like her or not, the majority of 'em have basic human compassion."

We finished the closing up shop details, turned off the lights, and locked the doors at five o'clock sharp.

Clint reached for my hand as we headed down the walkway between the buildings to the parking lot. "So you know, I didn't see any suspicious activity around your house, or in your neighborhood today, but it'll still make me feel better to follow you home and stay with you as long as you like."

"It makes me feel better too."

The temperature had risen ten degrees during the day and my car didn't feel as frigid when I climbed behind the wheel. Clint closed my car door and waited for me to drive away before he did too.

I pulled into my garage, and Clint parked next to the door as it closed. The sun wouldn't set for another thirty minutes, but the low clouds darkened the sky as dusk approached. The house light came on when we were ten feet from the house. "Whoa, thanks for resetting that, Clint."

"You'd mentioned it, so as long as I was at it, it was easy enough to adjust the distance and sensitivity," he said.

Clint was close behind me when I climbed the three

steps. I bent over, touched the keypad on the new lock, and the numbers lit up. "Cool. I feel like we've moved forward several decades."

"You know your code?"

"Ha, ha." I punched them in and hit the open button. I heard the mechanisms moving, depressed the door handle, and pushed open the door. "Pretty slick all right. Goodbye, house keys."

"Practice the code a few times, so you can enter it fast. In case."

I know he didn't scare me on purpose, but still. To make him feel better, I repeated the process three times.

We went inside and hung our coats on the backs of kitchen chairs. Clint unstrapped his duty belt, carried it to the office/guest room door, and draped it over the knob, as he'd done many times before.

"Clint, can I get you anything to eat,?" I asked.

"Thanks, but I grabbed a late lunch. You go ahead, though."

"I'm good too. I had one of Pinky's cranberry orange scones about an hour ago." I blew out a breath. "So, for our evening entertainment, should we look at movie options, or are you more in the mood for a competitive game of trivial pursuit for two?"

"My vote goes to a movie. I feel like a sore loser when you win," he said.

"Really? You're the one who seems to know all the professional sports teams' stats and a lot on other subjects I have no clue about. But I agree with movie. Something to help my tired brain rest for the whole evening."

He wrapped his arms around me. "That goes for me too."

I woke up to the sound of Clint's phone chirping from the office/guest room, then heard him say in an official tone, "Be there in ten."

I was on my feet and at the door in seconds. The light inside was on. "What?" My voice was a hoarse whisper.

"Oh, Camryn, sorry to wake you. An incoherent man wandered into Shorty's gas station, and the on-duty officer needs assistance transporting him to the hospital." Clint strapped his duty belt around the waist of his sweatpants.

"Oh. What time is it?"

He glanced at his watch. "A little after three. Gotta fly." He gave my cheek a light peck.

It took me a moment to process that it was early Sunday morning, and Clint had started his week covering overnight calls when needed.

"Be safe," I said, as he left via the back door. After he closed it, I heard the mechanisms inside the door lock turn. He'd memorized the code.

As I stretched out on the couch again, I noted that Clint had turned off the television at some point. My mind started to churn, and sleep evaded me. I picked up the all-but-forgotten novel I'd been reading, hoping it would distract me. It had lost its appeal, however. At least for the time being. I'd try again when Peter's murder was solved, and the person who'd broken into my house was behind bars.

As my thoughts gathered, and my heart rhythm slowed to a normal rate, I lifted my phone off the coffee table, found the sleepy sounds app, and tucked the comforter around my body. The last thing I remembered was imagining myself lying on a riverbank as I listened to the gentle waves of slow-moving water.

I opened my eyes, grateful I'd slept until morning light. "Clint?" I called out, thinking if he had returned, the sounds should have woken me. The little bird chose that moment to deliver seven cuckoos. "Thanks for the time update." I dug around the couch until I located my phone in a cushion. I checked to see if Clint had left me a message. None from him, or anyone else. My parents came to mind, and I knew where to find them at eight o'clock on a Sunday morning.

I drove up the hill to the highest point in Brooks Landing to our family's church. Its majestic steeple, that rose above the one-hundred-year-old natural stone structure, was visible for miles in three directions. Another building, a mile away, blocked the full view on the north side. I parked, and a gust of crisp wind reminded me winter was not yet over. As I stepped into the narthex, organ music and familiar faces welcomed and greeted me as I hung up my coat.

I found my parents seated in their usual spot, the fourth row from the back on the left side. They looked both pleased and surprised when I slipped onto the pew beside my dad. He reached his arm around me, and I leaned across his chest to give Mom's hand a squeeze.

I felt calmer and prayed there would be no more drama to spike my adrenaline in the days ahead. It seemed I had burned through my yearly allowance in less than a week.

When the service ended, and the three of us got up to leave, I noticed Jaylin in line to shake the priest's hand. I nodded my head toward her and asked my parents, "Do you know that woman, the tan one, with highlighted light brown hair?"

"Don't believe I've ever seen her before," Dad said.

Mom shook her head. "No. Why?"

"No real reason. She comes in for coffee, and I didn't know she went to church here."

"Ah," Mom said

My parents chatted with others, as we merged with people on the way out.

"So what are your plans for today?" Mom asked as I snatched my coat off the hanger on the rack.

"Not too much. Thought I'd do a little cleaning therapy, then chill out."

"You're funny at times, the way you call cleaning therapy," Dad said.

"It is to me, and I have valid reasons today."

Mom nodded. "You certainly do. With those two . . . incidents."

"Yep."

They wrapped their arms around me in a group hug. "You better move back home for the time being, until they catch whoever they are," Dad said.

Mom added, "You're still our baby, and we want to protect you as much as we can."

I took a step back and gave each a kiss on the cheek. "I love you for that, but I have a trained police chief who is on that detail."

"Cami, I put a pot roast in the oven. At least come over for dinner," Mom said.

I noticed Jaylin as she made her way from the restroom on the other side of the narthex, "I appreciate the invitation, but it's my catch-up day." I gave them another quick squeeze. "See you soon."

I hurried outside and saw Jaylin get in the white SUV I recognized as hers. It was none of my business where she was headed, what she was up to, but I climbed in my car, and when she drove out of the parking lot, I followed her. I stayed back a ways, and when she turned onto her street, I kept going.

I felt both concerned and conflicted about her. On one hand, if her husband was abusive, I hoped she would reach out for help. I hadn't noticed any bruises on her body at the fitness center, but people had injuries on the inside that didn't show on the outside, and the psychological damage could prove more harmful in the long run.

On the other hand, I questioned if she had been personally involved with Peter Zimmer. Maybe a conflict had arisen that went from bad to worse, and she found herself caught up in a scheme against her will, one that ended in his murder. The thought gave me goosebumps, and I swallowed the lump in my throat.

Clint was finally convinced I would remain vigilant and aware of my surroundings. He declared me free to come and go from my home in daylight hours—with a can of Mace on my person—until the intruder was caught. As I drove down the alley and turned on my short driveway, my eyes darted every which way and back again. Same thing when I climbed from the car and on the walk to my house. Not another soul in the immediate area, and no new footprints in the snow.

After I'd let myself inside, I felt my phone buzz in my pants pocket. "Hi, Erin. You home from the conference?"

She ignored my question. "Cami, I just talked to Pinky. Honestly, I can't believe someone actually broke in your house."

"Erin, not to bring up a bad memory, but a bad guy broke into your house a few years ago too." The fact that her robber was dead seemed like a moot point.

"You're right, it is a bad memory. But Jerrell Powers broke in to steal my clocks, not to leave a creepy note on my bed, of all places. Why would anyone do such a thing?"

"That is the burning question, all right. The cops are on it and might be able to get DNA from it. That is, if the guy wasn't smart enough to wear gloves when he handled the note."

"Yeah. And what is that about an odd scent you smelled in your house, one that isn't in the products you use?"

I described it as best I could then said, "Not a lot to go on when you can't capture a smell and put it in a container."

"No, and you've always been sensitive to smells, Cami. More than a lot of us."

"I guess. So the good news is, I've got new keyless entries on both my doors, thanks to Clint."

"Pinky told me. Makes me think I should do the same thing."

"Tell me about your seminar, how it went."

"It was worth the long drive and overnight stay. Four sessions on different topics, like how to engage young learners and keep them engaged."

"A few of our old teachers could've benefited from a session like that."

Erin chuckled. "True. What are your plans for the day?"

"So far, I went to church and sat with my folks."

"A good place to connect, in more ways than one."

"I agree. Now it's cleaning and cooking. Nothing too exciting is my hope. How about you?" I asked.

"Mark asked me out for lunch."

"Oh. Are you two ever going to officially get back together? And don't tell me it's complicated."

"Well it *is*. I don't know. After we graduated from high school and went our separate ways, things fell apart. I sure didn't think we'd both end up back in Brooks Landing, as you know. Maybe we've put too much emphasis on our careers. Maybe I'm afraid something bad will happen to Mark on the job. I don't know," she said.

"We can't let fear control our lives. It's funny, Erin, and a little ironic that Pinky and I just started dating cops. And you're the one who dated Mark before he was a cop."

"Life is full of ironies. Like when you happened upon *my* robber's body last fall, and assistant police chief Clint was the one who responded to the scene."

I blinked. "It was an awkward introduction, to say the least. I remembered Clint from high school, but we'd never hung out."

"Plus, he moved to Brooks Landing his senior year, our junior year."

"True. Well, enjoy your lunch date, and stop by the shops after school tomorrow, if you can."

"All righty. Later, then."

After we'd disconnected, I wandered around the house, and my mind circled back to Peter Zimmer. I'd tried to come up with a mental list, or even a single person, who might have killed him, but couldn't. I had avoided the man as much as possible, had no interest in his activities, or who he hung out with. I knew one person I could talk to about him, and it would be a tricky conversation, but I picked up my phone and called Tricia Knox anyway.

When she answered, "Hello?" I drew in a quick breath. "Hi, it's Camryn. Do you have a moment?"

"Um, yes."

"I was wondering if it'd be okay to meet for coffee, or I could come to your place, if that would be better."

"Oh. You mean like today?"

"If that works," I said.

"I have plans this afternoon, but I could meet you some place in Brooks Landing, maybe in thirty minutes."

"That'd be great. How about Astrid's Cafe? You know where it is?"

"I do. See you there," she said.

"Well, that was easier than I'd thought it would be," I said out loud, and the little bird chirped out ten cuckoos in response.

17

Astrid's Café was three blocks southeast of our shops. While Brew Ha-Ha had a 1950s décor, Astrid's was more reminiscent of the 1960s, according to my parents. The eating area wasn't huge, about 24 by 36 feet, with high-back booths around the outside walls, and wooden tables and chairs in the center seating area.

I stepped inside, relieved that only a handful of people sat at two tables. I recognized many and greeted them. Tricia was seated at a back booth and waved me over when she spotted me. I slid on the cushioned seat across from her. "Thanks for meeting with me, Tricia."

Callie, a thirty something woman with sparkly blue eyes, and her dark brown hair in a bun, stepped up to our booth with menus in hand. She laid them on the table. "Good morning. Can I get you a beverage to start off with?"

"Morning, Callie. Just coffee for me today, thanks, " I said.

Tricia nodded. "The same, thanks. I already had breakfast."

Callie smiled and picked up the menus. "Sure thing, be right back."

"What's up?" Tricia said.

No one was close to us but in a quiet voice, I said, "To

get straight to the point, it's about Peter Zimmer, and who his killer is."

When her eyebrows lifted, it deepened the three lines that spanned her forehead. "I don't know what to say, except that the authorities are investigating all that."

"I know, and I don't want to interfere with them. I just thought if we brainstormed, maybe we could give them a name—or names—of who to take a deeper look at."

Callie returned with our coffees and a pitcher of cream. "Thank you," Tricia and I said in unison.

After Callie left, I leaned in closer to Tricia. "You mentioned you'd been close to Peter Zimmer, that you would've done about anything for him. That made me more than a little curious."

Tricia's face colored. She looked down at her hands, as she squeezed them together. "I'm embarrassed I let that slip. It sounded worse than it is, was."

How, pray tell? "Go on," I said.

"You know that Ramona was not always a kind person."

"That's an understatement," I muttered, half to myself. "Sorry."

"You know that I drove her to events? Half the time she wouldn't be ready, and she'd be yelling at Peter for no real reason, blaming him because she was running late. Then she'd lay into me. From my observations, it seemed like the two of them had a love-hate relationship."

"I can see that."

"Anyway, I felt sorry for Peter. I was tempted to quit, I don't know how many times. But it paid well, and I liked scheduling the events, working with all the different entities. I didn't like the drive time with Ramona, and was relieved when she stayed in D.C. Her extended weekends and other breaks weren't always easy. I just had to put up with her bad days," Tricia said.

"Yeah, we all did that. Tricia, I have to ask this. Did you and Peter get personally involved?"

"As friends, yes. As lovers, no. We started talking, then it evolved. I became his confidant, his sounding board. Like Ramona, and maybe because of Ramona, Peter didn't have a lot of friends. I heard rumors about his affairs from our D.C. scheduler, and I questioned if they were really true, or at least exaggerated. This may sound dumb, but I never asked him about it. I didn't want to know. Peter needed someone to talk to, and he told me different things he struggled with, although he didn't get into details about their marriage. Peter was male model gorgeous, yet he had deep-seated insecurities and a low self-opinion."

That took me aback. "What?"

She nodded. "He covered it up, and I know he could act like God's gift to women. I witnessed that a few times, and how he used Ramona's position to meet people when he was in Washington. My take is, he did things like that to make her jealous."

"Seriously?"

"Like I'm guessing he did with you," she said.

I tried to process if Tricia was delusional about Peter, or what. "So, here in Minnesota, he never came on to you?"

"No, he didn't."

"Tricia, what exactly did you mean when you said you would have done just about anything for him?" I said.

"It came out wrong. I meant to get him help. Even though he's gone, I'm not comfortable telling you details he told me in confidence, about his family and the abuse he suffered. The fact is, we recognized that in each other. About our backgrounds, I'm mean."

"Sorry, Tricia. I had no idea."

"It's okay. It's not like Peter and I hung out together. Our conversations were mostly over the phone. I think it made him feel less vulnerable, that he could be more forthright than if we'd talked face to face," she said.

"I understand how it can be easier to confess things over the phone." I took a sip of coffee for a moment to process what she'd told me. "Tricia, you knew Peter much better than I did. Did he ever mention anyone he didn't get along with, or had threatened him?"

"After Detective Garrison was satisfied I hadn't written my phone number on that note, he interviewed me for quite a while, asked me those same questions. Peter had never mentioned he'd had a problem with anyone to me."

"How about Ramona, did she voice concerns about anybody in particular?"

"No, not like threats, or people she was worried about. It was more general things she heard about Peter. I remember one trip when I drove Ramona to an event and she pooh-poohed gossip about her husband. She went on and on about it, said women threw themselves at him," Tricia said.

"Like I *did not*, but she thought I had. But that's behind us now. Back to that memo note with your number. Have you gotten any strange calls or text messages?"

"No. Detective Garrison asked me the same thing."

"Of course." I leaned in closer. "Something else happened Friday evening that is one big mystery."

Her shoulders twitched. "Like what?"

I told her about the break-in, the note, and the new locks on my doors.

She rubbed her arms. "Camryn, that gives me major chills."

"I know. Detective Garrison and the sheriff's deputies are on the case, but I thought maybe the two of us could try to figure out who might've had a reason to blame me, for whatever. The fact that the note was left at my house four nights after Peter's body was found has me convinced they're related."

"Must be, but how? I know you had the reputation for being a hard worker and a consummate professional. On the job, anyway." She was silent a moment. "Did something happen with anyone in your personal life? I mean, other than the reason Ramona thought she had to fire you. You don't have to give me the details if you don't want to."

I shook my head. "If another legislator or lobbyist or staffer was upset with me for any reason, we'd discuss the issue at hand. As far as my personal life, many people would've described it as boring. I avoided any D.C. drama, and the irony of that is I got sucked into what felt like an episode from a soap opera, anyway."

Tricia watched her thumbs circle a moment, then looked at me. "I have to say I'm a little miffed Peter didn't tell me the truth about that. Given what I'd heard about you, it seemed out of character, but I figured you must've fallen for him."

"Tricia, from what you've told me, it seems that Peter Zimmer was honest with you to a point. He got into what caused his past wounds, but not the unsavory things he did to try to make himself feel better, to help him cope. He needed professional help, and you recognized that."

Tears appeared on her lower lids. "I'm more convinced now, than ever, and it's too late."

I drew in a slow breath. "Back to the note with your initials and phone number on it. After giving it more thought, any idea who might have written it?"

"No. Like I told you last time, I didn't recognize the handwriting. But what hit me is; not everyone knew my initials are JTK."

"I thought the same thing, and hadn't known myself until a few days ago. It'd be on your job application, so office staff would have access to personnel records. Plus, Ramona must've known."

"I'm sure she did, but she didn't write the note."

We both knew her handwriting. "No. How about Peter?"

"I never actually saw anything he'd written, and my legal first name never came up in our discussions. Besides, Detective Garrison would've shown the note to Ramona and asked if she recognized the handwriting."

"Of course." Unless the person had disguised it.

On the drive home, I felt better knowing Tricia's relationship with Peter Zimmer had not included "benefits." If Peter wasn't the one who'd jotted her number on the memo note, then who had? I also considered what Tricia said about Peter's flirting to make Ramona jealous, and I could accept it on a certain level.

I needed to touch base with Gretchen in D.C. again, and get her take on the note left on my bed. That's when it struck me. I hadn't thought to send her the photo of the memo note. She'd be in her office at eight a.m. ET tomorrow, and I'd be her first caller of the day.

The conversation with Tricia had left me restless. I dove into home projects with renewed energy. I even braved stripping my bed to wash the sheets, blanket, and comforter, and clung to the hope I'd be able to sleep in my own bed again.

Clint phoned a little after noon. "Morning."

I warmed at the sound of his voice. "Hi. Actually, it's afternoon."

"It is, at that. Turned out to be a long night before that incoherent man settled down. He was restless, spaced out, likely under the influence. No ID, no phone, didn't seem able to talk so he couldn't tell us his name, or where he was from. I didn't recognize him, neither did anyone at the hospital. They were able to do a blood draw to check for chemicals in his system. He's in a secure room, and the medical folks will keep a close watch on him. When things were under control a few hours ago, I came home and crashed."

"That would be scary, for the poor man, and for all you professionals," I said.

"It can get tense at times, no doubt about that. We train for all kinds of scenarios, but things go sideways from time to time. How about you, Camryn? Everything okay on your end?"

"Pretty much. Nothing compared to yours, but I had an interesting conversation with Tricia Knox this morning. I'll tell you about it later."

"Interesting, hmm. I'd stop by, but as luck would have it, we're an officer short today, so I'll be helping with calls."

Poor Clint, I thought as we disconnected.

I woke up early Monday morning with two main goals—besides work and the city council meeting that night. Number one: talk to Gretchen about the break-in and send her the memo note photo. Number two: see if I could track down Jaylin Klemmet for a heart-to-heart chat. I hadn't found her cell number online, but the city would have it on her application, if she'd turned it in. If they couldn't give it to me for legal reasons, I'd bet either Journee or Josey would.

At 6:58 a.m., I selected the note photo in my phone's gallery and sent it to Gretchen, with the message, *Sorry I didn't think of this earlier. Do you recognize the handwriting?*

Her response came a few stretched out minutes later. *No, but I can ask Ramona's staffers. I still have their personal numbers.*

Thank you very much! Please give me a call when you can.

Gretchen phoned seconds later. "What's up?"

I repeated the note left on my bed story.

"Camryn, what is going on?" Her voice was louder than usual.

"That someone is blaming me for something yet to be discovered."

"It's awful."

"I had coffee with Tricia yesterday. She's as much in the dark as the rest of us."

"She's seen the note?"

"Yes, but she didn't recognize the handwriting. Neither did Ramona, unless she did, and she's lying to protect someone besides her husband. All the authorities would have to do is compare it to Peter Zimmer's signature on his driver's license."

The Brooks Landing City Hall Offices opened at 8:00, and it seemed like making a personal appearance to get Jaylin's—a potential future employee—phone number was a better option than asking over the phone. I'd also stop by Clint's office to make sure he was okay. In the meantime, Pinky appreciated a hand in Brew Ha-Ha.

When I was about to leave, to bypass the motion detector, I flipped the outside light switch from on to off, and on again. My yard lit up and expanded my view. The sun had risen a little after seven, but wouldn't be bright for another half hour, or so. With a can of Mace in one hand and the garage door opener in the other, I pressed the button. As the door lifted, I turned and backed up the last dozen or so steps, on the lookout for any possible creepers I hadn't spotted on the way.

It was a relief to climb in my vehicle, drive to the shops, and park in the back lot without a red flag incident. When I entered Brew Ha-Ha, three customers sat at the counter. I waved and called out, "Morning. Be right back," on my way to hang up my things.

When I joined Pinky behind her counter, she told me, "Thanks," as she filled to-go cups with coffee. She nodded at an older man first in line, and asked me, "Can you grab a dozen mixed muffins for this gentleman?"

"Any particular favorites, sir?" I said.

"No, two each of the six in the display case will be just fine."

"Coming right up." I filled the box with a baker's dozen, chose an apple-cranberry as the thirteenth, set it on the counter, and ran the credit card he handed me. The man pocketed his card and picked up the box. "Thank you."

"Thank *you.*" *For your business and for an idea.* I'd take a box to city staff and one to the police department to show them my appreciation.

Business was steady for the next half hour. With a lull in the action, I piled muffins and scones into two boxes. "Pink, I need to run to the city office, and I'll write these down when I get back," I told her.

"You know you don't owe me for them. Consider it a small tip for all the hours you help me out around here."

I set the boxes in a brown grocery bag. "We're a team. You cover for me, so it evens out. See you in a bit."

The outside air was brisk, but the sun had gained strength as February moved forward. On my walk to the offices, I noticed melting snow drip down the sides of buildings. Brooks Landing city offices and parking lots filled an entire block.

I entered the city office, and when I stepped up to the counter, Lila's face broke into a smile. "Mayor. Getting ready for the meeting tonight?"

"Actually, I have a request." I set the bag on the counter. "Jaylin Klemmet applied for a position here. We'd met about a matter, then I thought of something else later and realized I hadn't gotten her phone number. Are you allowed to give that to me?"

Lila's shoulders lifted. "I don't see why not. She didn't list it as private."

I wasn't about to question if it was accepted protocol or her own discretion. She looked it up, jotted the number on a post it note, and handed it to me. "Thanks." I lifted the top box from the bag and set it on the counter.

She leaned over and took a whiff. "Smells yummy. What are they for?"

"For you and Gary and other staff. I haven't brought in treats for a while."

"Thank you! They'll be perfect for our coffee breaks."

"You're welcome. I got another delivery for next door, then it's back to work. Bye."

"See you later," Lila called out behind me.

The city and police offices shared a front entry. I pushed out the city's door and pulled open the police office door. Margaret was at her front desk station. "Morning, Margaret." I smiled, and her face brightened.

Ever since I'd run into the office with blood on my hand two months before, she had been on guard. Nothing close to that happened since, but she appeared to have a deep-seated wariness whenever I stopped by. "Mayor. Good morning. How can I help you?"

I reached in the bag and withdrew the box of baked goods. "These are for you and the other employees. Pinky's creations."

"That's a nice surprise, and very kind of you. Thank you."

"Glad to do it. Is the chief in his office?"

"He is. I'll buzz you in."

Margaret pushed a button, and the lock clicked. I opened the door, greeted staff at their desks in the common area, and headed down the hallway to Clint's office at the end. His door was partially open, so I peeked inside. "Hey."

Clint looked worse for the wear, like he hadn't slept for a week. He managed a small smile. "You're a sight for sore eyes. Come in and close the door." As I shut it behind me, he came around his desk and drew me in for a warm hug.

We stepped apart and locked eyes a moment. I ran my fingers across his forehead and down one cheek. "Just a quick stop to see how you're doing. I also brought treats for your staff. And you. No offense, but you look like you could use a long winter's nap."

"It's been a *long* thirty, or so, hours." He sat down on the chair behind his desk, and I sank on to one opposite him.

"What's been happening?" I asked.

He scrubbed his cheeks with his palms. "The guy in the hospital? We still don't know who he is, due to the fact he doesn't appear to have a clue himself."

"Wow." I shook my head and waited for him to continue.

"I contacted our sheriff's office first thing and have been checking missing persons reports in neighboring counties, without success. I stopped by the hospital again this morning, and the doctors said it appeared he suffered a psychotic breakdown, whether it was caused by an underlying condition, or drugs. No detected head injuries. I took a photo that I'll send to agencies around the state."

"And you can't post it on social media sites."

"No, that would be a violation of his privacy. Of course, the opposite is true if he's listed as missing."

"I don't know how you do what you do," I said.

Clint sucked in a breath. "Sometimes I wonder that myself."

❄

18

Back at the shops, Pinky had things under control, so I slipped into Curio Finds to go through my city council meeting packet again. It took effort to give it my full concentration, but it was important to push other matters to the back burner and not miss anything. After I'd finished and walked toward Brew Ha-Ha, I heard a familiar voice. Jaylin Klemmet.

"Oh hi, you just missed your two friends, the other ones with J names," Pinky told her.

I stepped in behind her. "Hi, Jaylin."

She turned around. "Mayor, wondering if you have a minute?" Jaylin glanced toward Curio Finds.

"Sure, let's go to my office."

Given the curious look on Pinky's face, I knew she longed to follow us.

Jaylin looked almost as worn out as Clint had. I led her to my office, and she glimpsed at the tight space. "Would it be okay to talk out in the shop area instead?"

"Of course." We stepped back in the shop. "You had something to ask me?"

She nodded. "I wasn't sure who to turn to, and you seem like a good person to get advice from."

She'd determined that after our one brief conversation? "Thank you. I'll try my best, and you can trust me."

Jaylin's eyes traveled to a shelf filled with snow globes. "My husband and I are having problems. He's always been overprotective, and jealous of anyone who ever looked at me twice." With her beauty, that would be about everyone, male or female.

"Has he ever been mean?" I looked for a different word than abusive.

"He's never hit me. He just wants to know where I am and what I'm doing at all times."

"How long have you been married?" I said.

"Eleven years."

"Are you thinking of leaving him?"

She nodded. "I've thought about it. I need to get on my feet, get a good job first."

"You had a job, right?"

"Right." She gave me a summary of her short time at Your Best Deal. "I liked it mostly, because I made a friend there who seemed to understand me. My husband stopped by, caught us talking, and threw a fit when I got home. Then my friend was killed—you heard about it—Peter Zimmer, and I couldn't make myself go back to the dealership after that."

Did I have the energy to launch into the abbreviated story, as I knew it? "Jaylin, brace yourself."

Her eyes opened wide, like saucers throughout my short account of who I worked for, why I got fired, how Peter's body was left in my driveway, and that the authorities had not yet discovered who was responsible. I didn't share further details about the investigation or the break-in at my house.

She threw her arms around me. "I am so sorry. I didn't

know you knew him. I guess why would he tell me about that? There wasn't any news about where he'd been found, just that it was in Brooks Landing."

"That was to keep gawkers away, but word got out via the neighbors nonetheless."

"I suppose it would."

"Jaylin, you left your job, and quit your swim class too," I said.

"I've been mourning Peter, and I wasn't ready to tell Josey and Journee the whole story."

I understood that. "How close were you to Peter?"

"Just friends. I saw him flirt with women, but he didn't with me. We had more serious discussions. Without telling you his secrets, let me just say, he had a troubled marriage too."

"Yes. That I knew."

"Jace, my husband, has been going through business troubles he doesn't want to talk about, besides. He just sold his latest business venture. We had a medical supplies company that involved more travel than he'd anticipated.

"I think he liked to be around, so he could keep an eye on me, even though he should know by now there was no reason for that. I guess he just couldn't let it go," Jaylin said.

"Medical supplies." Had jealous Jace been involved in Peter's murder? I was about to both fish and fib when I said, "I've seen a van in town with a medical decal on the side window. That your company?"

"Could be. We also contracted with a service to do part of the deliveries. I can't think of the name right now."

I gave my hand a slight wave. "No worries, just curious." Another tidbit to pass on to Detective Garrison.

"Anyway, Jace has been debating about the next opportunity. It's a little strange, because he was meeting a buddy on Saturday for what he called 'an overnight retreat to hash things out.' He sent me a text saying they were going to sleep on it, hash things over, and he'd be home later today."

That seemed strange to me, also. A jealous husband leaving his wife for two nights. "Did he have to travel far?"

"No, just to St. Paul. He could've driven home and back again. I think he needed time for better focus," she said.

"Well, I hope he's able to land a good deal."

"Me too. Thanks for listening. We left on kind of an odd note at the fitness center. I didn't want you to worry about me," she said.

"I'm glad you came by for a chat. Turns out, I was planning to contact you."

She gave me another hug. "I feel much better, so thanks again."

"Me too."

And I hope you get that job with the city, I thought as she walked out the door.

"Your new best friend?" Pinky asked when I joined her in Brew Ha-Ha.

"After Clint and you and Erin and Mark and—"

She put her hand over my mouth and laughed. "All right already."

"Can you even grasp everything that's happened, since a week ago tonight when you stopped at my house to drop off a dish, and made that frightful discovery?"

Pinky snapped her dish towel. "I wish I could erase that image from my brain forever. I just want life to go back to normal again."

"Wouldn't that be grand?"

Clint phoned midafternoon. "How goes it?"

"Pretty good. Clint, so you know, I talked to Jaylin this afternoon and figured out a way to ask if her husband's medical supplies company had a delivery van with a medical decal on the window."

He cleared his throat. "Do tell."

"She told me their company did, and they also contracted a company to help with deliveries. Jaylin couldn't think of the company's name. Maybe the one I saw in their driveway that night? Anyway, I phoned Garrison to relay the information, and that Jace Klemmet was away on business, and could give him the name of the contracted company when he returned. All he said was, 'good to know.'"

"And it is. One reason I called is to tell you I can pick you up for the council meeting tonight."

"Thanks, but I'm going straight to my office from work. If you want to see me home afterwards, that'd make us both feel better."

"Let's plan on it," he said.

"What will you be reporting on tonight? Anything of import happen since the last council meeting?"

He sniggered at that. "According to the local buzz, there was. Since Peter Zimmer was publicly identified, I will mention his body was found in a vehicle in Brooks Landing and Buffalo County is conducting the investigation. So far they have not uncovered the location where the homicide took place, and they continue to ask anyone with any knowledge of the incident to come forward."

"Sounds like you've rehearsed that."

Another snigger. "About half a dozen times."

I smirked. "I can identify."

"You don't say."

"How about the incoherent man from yesterday morning; any updates on him?"

"Last I checked, he was still out of it. I don't know if they've gotten the toxicology report from the blood they drew yet, so we'll see. The call will be included in the medical numbers, but I won't mention specifics about any of them in my report, as per usual."

I arrived at Brooks Landing City Hall a little after five o'clock and noticed all the councilors' office doors were open. We liked adequate prep time to put other cares on the back burner and get into the right mindset before the meeting. I called out, "Greetings, everyone," as I unlocked my office door. I was about to step inside when all four of them squeezed in with me.

Wendell Lyon helped me out of my coat and hung it on the tree in the corner. Gail Spindler took my hands in hers, Rosalie "Stormin" Gorman stepped behind me, and wrapped her arms around my shoulders, and Harley Creighton shook his head.

"Are you up to this tonight?" Wendell asked.

"I am. It's good to concentrate on city business and not on other . . . things." I moved so we formed a semi-circle. "Did Gary go home for supper?"

"He left a few minutes ago and will be back by six-thirty," Gail said.

"Okay, I'll tell him later."

"What?" Rosalie leaned her face so close to mine we almost bumped noses. I lifted my hand, and she stepped back.

"It's probably not the best time to fill you in about the latest incident but thought you should hear it from me."

"Incident?" Wendell said.

I shared the burglary details and the note on my bed. Rosalie gasped, then fanned her face with her hand when I finished. Harley shook his head the entire time. Gail held my hands again and squeezed. Wendell pinched the bridge of his nose between his thumb and forefinger.

"So you've got new locks and extra protection from Chief Lonsbury. But you have no idea who broke in your house, and your only clue is the scent he left behind," Attorney Wendell said.

My shoulders lifted. "That's about it. The sheriff's office is investigating it."

"And they still haven't nailed down who killed Peter Zimmer," Harley said with a frown.

"They have a *lot* of people to interview, both in Minnesota and in Washington, D.C," I said.

"It boggles my mind," Gail said.

"Camryn, how can you even sleep at night?" Rosalie said.

"Like Wendell said: new locks, and police protection."

"If I were you, I'd have flown the coop by now," Rosalie added.

I nodded and drew in a deep breath. "Enough of my personal drama. We all need to switch gears, focus on the city business at hand."

"At least nothing controversial is on the agenda. Shouldn't be, anyway," Wendell said.

Gary Lunden came into my office half an hour before the meeting. "Evening, Mayor. Is it okay to ask how you're holding up?"

"Of course, and the answer is fair to middling. How about you?"

"Good, good. Rosalie said you gave them 'a scary update' and I should ask you about it."

I launched into yet another recap of the break-in, and when I got to the part about the note on my bed, Gary blinked a few times like he was either trying to picture it, or to erase what he'd imagined. "What an awful violation of privacy, not to mention, being a veiled threat besides. And what about that unusual smell?"

"I know. If I were going to break into a house, I'd be as scent free as possible."

When I stepped into the council chambers, I was surprised how many people were there. Gary, Clint, the fire chief, and other department heads were seated in the front row, like usual. I smiled at citizens as I climbed the two steps up to the dark oak dais with my packet, then took my seat in the middle between the councilors, two on each side.

At seven o'clock, I tapped the gavel on its wood block and called the meeting to order. "Please rise for the Pledge of Allegiance." When we'd finished, and the councilors were seated, I said, "Our citizens forum is next on the agenda. Is there anyone present who would like to address the council about matters pertaining to the city?" I looked around the sea of faces in the crowd, but no one responded.

"All right. We'll move on to the reports from our department heads."

Jaylin Klemmet walked in at that moment. She sent a glance my way, and I questioned the reason for her presence and her worried frown. She found a seat in the fourth row of chairs. I must have paused too long, because Rosalie shifted on her seat, and Harley coughed. It helped bring my mind back to the meeting.

The parks director was the first employee on the agenda list. He'd stepped up to the podium and waited until I signaled for him to go ahead. One by one, they delivered their reports, and I tried to follow along, but my thoughts divided between them and Jaylin.

Clint was last to give his report. "Peter Zimmer's body was found in a vehicle within city limits. However, the Buffalo County Sheriff, not the Brooks Landing Police Department, is the investigating agency."

"Thank you, Chief Lonsbury. Councilors, do any of you have questions for him?"

I saw head shakes and heard a "no." They knew more than the general public, and it was a relief they didn't ask him to elaborate on his report.

A younger man in the third row raised his hand. "Madam Mayor?"

I nodded at him. "Sir?"

"I have one for Chief Lonsbury," he said.

Clint turned toward him. "Go ahead."

"A lot of people are worried about that murder in our quiet town, and we can't help but wonder if we need to fear for our safety."

Clint nodded. "That is a natural concern. As far as the victim's death, he was from out of town, and we don't know where the homicide occurred."

"If it didn't happen in Brooks Landing, why would they bring his body here?"

"When they uncover who the guilty party is, we hope they will provide the sheriff's office with that answer."

The man shrugged. "Thanks."

The atmosphere in the room had grown tenser, and I hoped we wouldn't have to field other tough questions. As we moved from one agenda action item to the next, it was a relief the only comments came from councilors, and none were controversial.

The knot in my stomach eased as I tapped the gavel to close. "This meeting is adjourned at seven fifty-three."

All four councilors and I stepped down to the chambers floor, to mingle for a bit. One of my goals was to find out why Jaylin was there. As a potential employee, maybe she was interested in official city business. A few people chatted with me. Then, as if by silent agreement, Jaylin and I made our way toward each other.

When we met, she frowned, and her eyes glistened with unshed tears. "Mayor, may I have a word with you . . . and Chief Lonsbury? It's important."

"Sure. I'll check with him." Clint was talking to a citizen when I caught his attention. "Sorry to interrupt, but can you come to my office when you've finished?"

He nodded. "Of course."

"Follow me," I told Jaylin. We headed halfway down the corridor and she waited while I unlocked my door. My office wasn't large, about eight by ten feet, but was huge compared to the cracker box at Curio Finds.

She glanced around at the pictures on the walls, and the filled bookshelves in the floor to ceiling case behind the desk, and commented, "This has a nice homey feel to it."

I could take little credit for the positive vibes in either my home or my office. "I agree, thanks to the former mayor, Lewis Frost. His son didn't want any of the art or books or trinkets, and I haven't taken the time to think what to do with them, or if I want to change anything." I didn't add that poor Frosty had died in the same room, and I'd been the one who'd discovered his body.

"Oh, well it looks nice."

Her worried frown returned, as Clint gave a single knock on the open door, stepped inside, and closed it behind him. "Finally broke away."

"Chief, do you know Jaylin Klemmet?" I asked.

His eyebrows lifted a tad, as he extended his hand. "I don't believe we've ever met."

She shook his hand. "No. Good to meet you."

"Likewise. Something I can help you with?"

Jaylin sucked in a breath. "I hope so."

"Would you like to sit down?" he asked.

"I'd rather stand, if that's okay."

That reminded me of nervous Ramona when Garrison

was about to deliver the news about her husband. She'd preferred to stand, too. Clint and I both locked eyes on Jaylin and waited for her to "have a word."

"I'm worried about my husband Jace. He might be missing."

"Why do you think that?" Clint said.

"To give you a little background, he recently sold his medical supplies business and was meeting a man—I don't know his name—about a new venture—he didn't say what—in Saint Paul on Saturday. He was supposed to come home Sunday, and I got a text from him yesterday afternoon saying he'd be another day.

"But he still isn't home, and when I first tried to call him, it went straight to voicemail. Then when I tried again late this afternoon, I got the message the number's not in service. I haven't got a clue what's going on, and it makes me afraid for his safety. What if the person he met with was up to no good? Jace wouldn't just leave me without a word."

"Has he ever left for a few days before, been out of contact?" Clint asked.

Jaylin shook her head. "Never. We've had disagreements for quite a while, and he has been more distant the last week, like he had a lot on his mind."

"Did you ask him about it?"

"I finally did, a few days ago. He said selling the business and looking at the next venture was weighing him down. I'd been dealing with something that was weighing me down too—the murder of my co-worker, and friend, Peter Zimmer. I told Camryn about it earlier today," she said.

Clint nodded. "Sorry for your loss."

Tears filled Jaylin's eyes. "Thanks. Back to Jace. He is a control freak, and that includes me. He tells me how I should dress, how to wear my hair, what activities I should get involved with. At first I thought it was because he really cared. I don't know, either it's gotten worse, or it's started to bug me more. I've been tempted to leave him, more so in the last month than ever before."

"Did you discuss that with him?"

"No, at least not in words, but . . ."

Clint let the details slide. "You said Jace sold his business recently. Tell me about it and if you were involved in the operations."

"It's Prime Health, a medical supplies company. When Jace started it four years ago, I asked to *not* be listed as a joint owner, to simplify things in case we ever divorced. Not that I told him the real reason."

"So you've thought about that for a long time."

"Yes. I just felt like I didn't have a *real* reason to leave. He's a good provider." Jaylin paused a moment. "I was still part of the business. I worked in the office, took orders, paid invoices, things like that. Jace worked really long hours building the business. It finally burned him out, and he decided to sell, and did that a couple of weeks ago."

"How about you?" Clint asked.

Jaylin gripped the back of a chair. "I got a job at a car dealership, Your Best Deal. Camryn knows about that too."

"Your last communication with your husband was Sunday. Might he have had too much to drink, and is sleeping it off?"

Jaylin shook her head. "He doesn't drink. I think it's part of his control thing. He doesn't want chemicals to alter what he thinks, or what he does."

"You have photos of him?" Clint said.

"Of course." Jaylin lifted her phone from her pocket, entered her passcode, selected her photos, scrolled a few seconds, selected one, held it up for me to see, then handed it to Clint. "It's from last Christmas," she said.

The photo featured Jace standing by a decorated tree. He was taller than average and looked toned in his long-sleeved green Henley shirt and black chino pants. His gray-streaked dark brown hair, brown eyes, and chiseled features, sans a smile, gave the impression he was an unmovable force. Or maybe that was my impression from what I'd heard about him.

"Jaylin, will you text it to me?" Clint provided his work cell phone number, and he had the message in a flash.

"Thanks. Camryn, I'll email it to you so we can print the image," Clint said.

"Okay." I sat down at my desk and turned on my computer. By the time I'd signed in to my email account, the email had arrived. I sent the attached photo to my documents, then opened it.

Clint stepped in behind me.

"I actually have photo paper, along with other varieties, thanks to Frosty." I opened the middle drawer, withdrew a sheet, slid it in the printer drawer, and hit the print button.

Clint picked up the photo image when it was ready and turned to me. "Do you recognize him?"

"I don't think I've ever seen him before. No," I said.

Clint glanced from me to Jaylin. "I do, and I know where he is."

19

Jaylin's eyes looked like full moons, and her mouth dropped open. "Where?"

"He's at the Buffalo County Hospital with no ID," Clint said.

"How do you know that?"

"He wandered into Shorty's gas station in the wee hours Sunday morning and was incoherent. I was the officer who responded and took him to the hospital. We didn't know who he was because he couldn't tell us, and he didn't have his wallet and ID, or phone, on his person."

Jaylin's face scrunched up like she was in pain or confused. "Incoherent? He lost his phone and wallet, and he's in the hospital? I don't get it."

"It's unknown if he had a psychotic episode, or if he took a hallucinogenic drug."

Jaylin shook her head. "Psychotic episode? What does that even mean? He never did drugs. Ever. I don't get it. Is he hurt?"

"He had no obvious injuries, and has been in their seclusion room, one with a camera, so they can keep watch on him. They drew blood to check for chemicals, but I haven't heard any results yet." Clint paused a moment. "When did you say you got that last text message from your husband?”

She still had her phone in her hand and found the message. “Yesterday afternoon, at one thirty. I didn't ask why, I just sent a thumbs' up back.”

“That means another person sent you that message, because Jace couldn't have.”

Jaylin reached both hands behind her neck and squeezed. “I need to get to the hospital.”

“How about I drive you?” Clint said.

After I shut off the lights, and locked my office door, we all traipsed to Clint's car in the back lot. The crisp winter breeze seemed colder in the dark of night. Gary's, and the other councilors', parking spots were empty. I'd heard doors close when we'd been in my office but hadn't paid much attention to how many.

Jaylin looked at Clint's car like it was a foreign object. “I've never been in a police car before.”

A new and unexpected experience.

“Climb in the front passenger seat, Jaylin. Camryn will sit in the back,” Clint said, as I opened the door and climbed inside.

When we were buckled up, Clint turned the ignition key, and the dashboard came to life with lights and sounds. Over the radio, a dispatcher requested assistance at a medical. A moment later, a Buffalo County deputy asked a dispatcher to run a license plate.

“Oh, my. You have a lot to keep up with, seems like,” Jaylin said.

“We have our moments,” Clint said.

He drove to the hospital north of town, and parked in the emergency entrance lot, the only door open after regular business hours. I noticed, via the overhead lights, that Jaylin's shoulders shrugged forward and tensed up. “You going to be okay, Jaylin?" Clint asked her.

"Yes," she said, and climbed out.

Clint got out too, opened my door, and extended his hand to me. On the short walk, Jaylin moved like she'd aged a few decades, so I looped my arm through hers. It seemed to give her the oomph she needed to walk the distance. The sliding doors opened, and warm air dropped on us from above, as we stepped inside. Clint and Jaylin went to the reception desk, and I hung back.

Eyes were drawn to the man in uniform. A handful of people sat in the waiting area, and included a baby whose cry revealed how congested he was. A middle-aged man was bent over in his chair, as his fingers rubbed his temples. A pale, younger woman, with dyed black spiked hair, and a dozen or more piercings on her face and ears, stood against a wall. She rocked back and forth, from one side to the next.

Her movements were like Ramona's had been when Detective Garrison delivered the news about Peter, and reminded me I hadn't heard from her for a couple days. If it wasn't too late when I got home, I'd phone to see how she was doing.

After a good ten minutes, Jaylin waved me over. "They said you can go in with the chief and me. You will, won't you?"

"Of course." I was way too curious not to.

A male nurse in scrubs with a clipboard in hand opened the hallway door that led to a row of patient rooms on either side. When the door closed behind us, he turned to Jaylin. "It's a big relief to find out who your husband is."

Jaylin nodded. "They told me at the front desk that he doesn't appear to have an injury."

"That's correct. He's been X-rayed and scanned. We ran tests on his blood, focusing on chemicals that cause amnesia and hallucinations. We've also collected urine samples. Chemicals show up for a much longer time in urine than in blood." Another new piece of information to put in my memory bank.

Tears pushed out from Jaylin's ducts, and she dabbed them with her sleeve. "My husband is a health nut and doesn't even drink alcohol," she said, mostly to herself.

As we followed the nurse to the last room on the right, across from the nurses' station, patients in rooms along the way verbalized a variety of utterances, from moans and sobs, to "help," to "get me out of here." Every person who worked in emergency medicine was a saint in my book.

When we reached Jace Klemmet's room, the small white board by his door read, "John Doe." The nurse pulled a cloth from his pocket and erased it. He glanced in the small window, then pressed numbers on the keypad that unlocked the door. When it opened, Jace stared ahead from his chair, feet on the floor, and hands on his lap.

Besides the bed, the room was otherwise bare. Jace was in hospital scrubs. His complexion had color, his shoulders and arms were muscular. He appeared physically healthy, except for the blank expression on his face.

Jaylin went to him, squatted, so they were eye to eye, and laid her hands on his. "Jace? It's me, Jaylin. Do you know who I am?"

It seemed a flicker of recognition danced across his face, as he focused on her. But he didn't answer her question. Instead, he said, "Jace? Jaylin? I think something bad happened, and I don't know where I am."

The nurse put his hand on Jaylin's shoulder. "First time he's spoken or been engaged," he said in a near whisper.

Jaylin nodded without taking her eyes off her husband. "Your name is Jace Klemmet, and you're in the Buffalo County Hospital."

"Because something bad happened?" His second

reference to that.

"It seems like that's true. Do you remember who you were with? You were going to meet a man about a business." Jaylin gave his shoulder a gentle shake.

Jace lifted his hands and rubbed his cheeks. "My head hurts, like I have a fever. Can I go to sleep now?"

Jaylin touched the inside of her wrist to his forehead. "You don't feel warm, but they can take your temperature."

The nurse extended his hand to Jace. "Let's get you into bed, then I'll check your vitals."

When Jace was settled in, Jaylin kissed his forehead and told him, "Rest well. I'll be back."

The nurse entered a code that opened the door. When Clint, Jaylin, and I stepped into the hallway, Jaylin sucked in a series of sniffles. "This is the scariest thing I can think of, in my entire life."

The nurse joined us.

"I need to talk to a doctor, or other specialist who knows what's going on with his brain, his memory," Jaylin told him.

"I'll give Doctor Bruce an update, and I know he'll want to talk to you." The nurse took off down the hallway.

"Jaylin, the doctor will brief you. But, as a head's up, I can tell that from my experience, if Jace doesn't have a head injury, it would indicate he most likely ingested an illicit substance. When I responded to the incoherent man call at Shorty's, Jace was wild eyed, not focused, his breathing was rapid and ragged. He was unable to verbalize anything. I'm not going to name any drugs, but four possibilities came to mind," Clint said.

"This makes no sense. Like I told you, Jace doesn't even drink alcohol, much less experiment with drugs. Why didn't I insist that he tell me who he was meeting with? I know they call that twenty-twenty hindsight. The reality is, he didn't tell me names of other business people he met with, either. When he traveled, it wasn't unusual for him to take 'no name' clients out for meals. His professional life was one thing, his personal was another," she said.

"Did that bother you?" I asked.

"Not really. A little history here: we met through body building competitions and fell in love. As it turned out, it was about the only interest we shared. Still, the first year of our marriage was good. After that, Jace got more serious about business and wanted me to feel the same way. That's when he got more and more possessive, and jealous. He basically made me quit competitions for that reason."

I tried to think of a reply, and Clint saved me when he said, "You said you didn't know who he planned to meet in St. Paul. He sold his business and was looking at a new venture. Anything else?"

Jaylin's brows drew together. "It seemed like this meeting was different. Jace acted more nervous than usual, more secretive. All last week, in fact. I wondered if the reason was because it was a well-known company. One of Jace's idiosyncrasies is, if he said too much about a new venture, it might jinx it."

"Superstitious?" Clint said.

"I guess, but it made me consider something else. Maybe Jace was upset because I was so sad about Peter's death. He seemed jealous, which didn't make sense, since Peter was gone. Not to mention the fact we were just friends, besides. I thought maybe the main reason Jace didn't tell me what business he was looking at, was his way of getting back at me for having a male friend."

That didn't seem logical to me, but nothing about their situation made sense. I gave her a supportive smile.

Clint rested his hand on Jaylin's shoulder a moment. "We've got another mystery on our hands, all right. And we'll get to the bottom of it."

The third major mystery in less than a week, and I prayed Clint was right.

The emergency room doctor, a lanky guy in his fifties, with slicked back light brown hair, and tortoiseshell rimmed glasses, came around the corner to meet Jaylin. He extended his hand. "Missus Klemmet, I'm Doctor Bruce. It's a big relief we've learned your husband's identity, but I'm sorry we had to meet under these circumstances."

She shook his hand. "Yes, and I'm sorry I didn't suspect Jace was missing until today." She gave the doctor a quick summary of Jace's business meeting in St. Paul, about the text he'd sent on Sunday, and when she tried to call him later that day his phone was dead.

"You're here now, that's the important thing." Dr. Bruce nodded at Clint. "Chief," then his eyes landed on me.

"I'm Camryn Brooks, Jaylin's friend."

Another nod. "Of course." His attention shifted back to Jaylin. "Is it okay to talk about your husband's condition in front of the others here?"

She nodded. "Please do."

"The fact that your husband just spoke his first words in over forty hours, and he seems more settled, are positive signs. When he was brought in, he was agitated, disoriented. His eyes darted around, and he couldn't focus. His heart was racing. What one might call a 'bad trip,' a negative reaction to a psychoactive substance, like a psychedelic.

"Given his behavior, we had toxicology run blood tests on specific chemicals. They ran screens on four, and the two Jace tested positive for are lysergic acid diethylamide, or LSD, a hallucinogen and central nervous system stimulant, and Rohypnol, a central nervous system depressant.

"Both are powerful, and both are illegal in the United States. Rohypnol is known for causing amnesia. So combined with the sensory distortions of LSD, he may have no memory of whatever experience, or possibly dangerous situation he was in. Your husband is strong, fit, in top physical condition. If he wasn't, he might not have survived," Dr. Bruce said.

Jaylin's tears rolled down her cheeks in full force. "Survived? You mean someone drugged him . . . and tried to *kill* him?" she managed to utter.

I dug in my pocket for a packet of tissues, handed it to Jaylin, and put my arm around her shoulders, as she dabbed at her cheeks and nose.

Dr. Bruce's shoulders lifted. "In any event, we can thank the Man Upstairs Jace is safe and sound in the hospital."

"I can't imagine who Jace could've gotten involved with," Jaylin said.

Clint gave her a moment. "Jaylin, you and Jace are on the same cell phone plan, right?"

"Yes. Why do you ask?"

"Because you could request a printout of your incoming and outgoing calls, his as well as yours. We'd need a court order to track down who the numbers belong to, but our office could call the numbers, and see if they ping on a local tower," Clint said.

"Oh, okay," she said.

Dr. Bruce adjusted his glasses. "In the meantime, we'll do all we can to help your husband heal and hope to move him from the security room soon."

"I feel the need to stay close to Jace. He's been acting on the strange side for the last week. He needs to get better and tell us what's been going on, and maybe I can help," Jaylin said.

"So you're planning to stay at the hospital?" Clint asked.

She nodded. "I'd never be able to sleep at home tonight."

"Camryn and I can drive your car here, so you'll have it when you need it."

"You don't have to do that but thank you." She looked down a moment. "Wait. I wonder what happened to Jace's car? He left home in it, bound for Saint Paul, and you found him early Sunday morning in Brooks Landing, Chief. How did he get back to town, if he was in no condition to drive?"

Clint shook his head. "Another burning question. I can tell you that no abandoned vehicles have been reported in the area. Now that we have his identity, we can check his vehicle registration, and plate number, and send a statewide request to locate it."

Jaylin nodded and dug in her small purse for her car key, minus an actual key. She handed it over. "It's the white Kia in the main lot. Do you have a push button start in your vehicle?"

"No, it's an older model."

"You just put your foot on the brake and press the ignition button."

Simple enough, right?

Clint drove me back to the city office and parked next to Jaylin's vehicle. "Let me start it for you, so it warms up a bit."

"No need, but thanks." I got out of his car and into Jaylin's. The push button ignition was slick. I backed out of the spot, and Clint followed me to the hospital. After I'd parked, he waited nearby as I went inside and delivered Jaylin's key fob to the emergency room receptionist. "Please get this to Jaylin Klemmet. She's inside with her husband."

"I surely will."

"Thanks."

As I walked toward Clint's car, parked in the closest row, I got an uneasy feeling and glanced around. The parking lot had tall light poles, but dark areas loomed around the edges. Two parked vehicles, one on the far right, and the other in the middle, left the lot seconds later. Had one of them followed us? It seemed Peter Zimmer's body in my driveway, along with the break-in, and strange note on my bed had made me paranoid.

"You look troubled," Clint said when I was back in his car.

"Just imagining things."

"Like what?"

"It sounds dumb, because you're driving your cruiser, but it crossed my mind that we could've been followed."

"Maybe not so dumb, after all. While you were inside, I talked to Detective Garrison, filled him in on the situation. He'll be sending a deputy to provide personal security for both Jace and Jaylin Klemmet."

"Clint, do you think they're in danger?"

"You heard Jace say—in his not fully coherent state— that he thought something bad had happened. Whatever it was, it seems the plan went sideways, and Jace somehow got away from the bad guys, who in all likelihood did try to kill him. When that person finds out he's still alive, he'll likely try again."

"This is too scary. And what about Jaylin?"

"Could be they've kept watch on their house, maybe figured Jace would make his way back there. If they'd watched, and knew he hadn't, they could've followed Jaylin, thinking she'd lead them to Jace."

Chills traveled down my arms. "Dear Lord. How did you land on all this?"

"It started bubbling in my brain when Jace made that comment, and the doctor said the drug combo should've killed him."

"Maybe we shouldn't have brought Jaylin's car here."

"I'll talk to Garrison about moving it to a secure location and tell her to stay put for the time being. Let's collect your vehicle and get you home."

On the short distance to my house, I looked in the rear and side view mirrors about two hundred times. Clint drove in behind me and parked in front of my garage. I pressed the close button and stepped outside. We walked arm in arm, and it was a comfort the light came on, ten feet from the house. Both of us glanced around as we climbed the two steps to the landing.

"Doesn't appear anyone tried to break in. Have you gotten any Ring Doorbell alerts?" he asked.

"Not that I know of, but my phone has been on silent most of the day and I didn't think about it. Let's check the feed."

We stepped inside, and I flipped on the light, slipped off my coat, and hung it in the living room closet. When I returned to the kitchen, Clint was on a chair at the table.

I moved in behind him, wrapped my arms around his shoulders, and nestled my chin against the side of his neck. "Long day, huh?"

He covered my hands with his. "You know it, for you and me, and Jaylin, especially. After seven long days before this."

"Clint, do you think Jace will come out of this, get his memory back?"

"We can hope and pray he does. A big concern is why he kept his business dealings under wraps. Who knows what else he's been hiding from his wife. There's gotta be more to the story, than he fell in with the wrong people," he said.

"For sure. The Klemmets may have a dysfunctional marriage, but watching Jaylin at the hospital, it was obvious how much she cares about Jace."

Clint nodded. "I agree. And speaking of dysfunctional, you haven't given me any Ramona reports the last day or two."

"That's because we haven't talked since Saturday, the longest stretch since Peter's death. And no, I didn't tell her about the break-in. I meant to touch base after the council meeting tonight, but my plans changed."

"As they say, 'no news is good news,' so I'd take that as a good sign."

I nodded. "Ramona has heard from staff and other people she knew in Washington, and that's helped lift her spirits, by a lot."

I held up my phone, tapped the app, and handed it to Clint. "Shall we look for visitors?"

"*What in tarnation?*"

His loud volume startled me. "What?"

Clint moved in beside me and played it again. At 7:22 p.m., a very tall and bulky man, dressed in black, with a ski mask drawn over his head and face, approached the door. It seemed when he spotted the new doorbell camera, it shocked him because he lifted his arm to cover his face, then turned, fled to the alley, and headed south.

When my body started to tremble, Clint pulled me against his muscular chest.

"It must be someone who knew I'd be at the city council meeting during that time," I said.

"Yeah, helps that the video is time stamped. Good thing we got the doorbell installed when we did."

"Thank you for that."

"I don't know if we can get a good enough view of his eyes, or mouth, or shape of his nose under the mask to identify him, but we can see the way he moves, the way he walks, the way he favors his left leg, with a slight limp. I'll get a copy of this, send it to my officers and to Garrison. Someone in our office, or the sheriff's, might recognize him. Let's just say, stranger things have happened."

Clint sent the video to his phone, and to Garrison's with the message, *Things are ramping up.*

"Clint, don't you think it was the same guy who left the note on my bed, seeing how the new doorbell surprised him? What more could he be up to?"

"We've gotta locate him to get that answer." He squeezed my hand. "We will find him. Meantime, I don't want you outside alone in the dark. The guy is a coward, sneaking around when he thinks you're not home so you can't confront him. Still, we're not taking any chances."

I felt too worried and weary to disagree.

After we ate a snack, Clint and I cuddled on the couch, and made a pact to talk about anything except the current circumstances, like Peter Zimmer's unsolved murder, the burglary, the attempted break-in, and the mystery surrounding Jace Klemmet's health crisis.

At ten thirty, Clint kissed me, and said, "Go get ready for bed. I'll snuggle beside you until you fall asleep."

20

I woke up with a start. It was still dark out. I patted the empty spot where Clint had lain then turned to look at the alarm clock. 6:41. I watched it change to 6:42. As the short video of my would-be burglar, captured by the doorbell camera, played through my mind, a lump formed in my stomach. I didn't recognize anything specific about him, but his body type fit a long list of men I'd known over the years.

The fragrant smell of coffee helped push the video from my mind and prompted me to roll out of bed. Clint? I picked the robe off a hook, slipped it on, and headed to the kitchen. The man himself was backed up against the counter, phone to his ear, and a coffee mug in the other hand. He gave me a smile and slight nod. "All right. Thanks for the info. Later, then."

He stuck the phone in his pocket, set the mug on the table, and gathered me in for a warm hug. "You sleep okay?"

"I did, knowing my personal protecter was near. How about you?"

"Your couch is more comfortable than my own bed," he said.

I smirked and took a step back. "That Garrison on the phone?"

"Yeah. He's got a deputy stationed with the Klemmets.

They moved Jaylin's vehicle to one of their garages during the night."

"Poor Jaylin, caught up in this mess." I filled a pod with coffee grounds, set it in the single brew side of the coffee maker, and hit the start button. I watched coffee start to drip in a cup, then turned to Clint. "Have you heard any updates on Jace, like if he's regained his memory, at least enough to tell authorities what had happened to him?"

"No. Garrison will be heading to the hospital to check on him this morning."

"Good. You know what? Life is ironic at times. Before last Tuesday, I hadn't spoken to Jaylin, except to take her coffee order. And then these unexpected circumstances drew us closer. She's the one I'm most concerned about at the moment, even more than Ramona. Then we have Peter's killer and my intruder still at large."

Clint looked at me over the top of his coffee mug. "Why is that?"

"I guess because she is facing so many unknowns."

My little cuckoo friend popped out seven times with his alert.

"That bird can startle a guy in the middle of the night, in a quiet house," Clint said.

"I know, but he's also helped, if it seems *too* quiet." I picked up my phone from the counter. "Instead of waiting for Garrison's report, I'm going to send Jaylin a text."

"That works."

I found her contact and wrote, *Wondering how you're doing.*

She responded seconds later. *Still with Jace. There's a deputy outside his door. I'm trying to be brave, but I'm scared.*

I read our conversation to Clint as we went along. *I would be too, but they'll keep you safe. Any change in his condition?*

He was restless so they gave him a sedative to help him sleep. Fingers crossed when he wakes up he'll remember what happened.

I sent a folded hands emoji back, lifted my filled cup, and took a sip. "Clint, switching to Ramona, she'd mentioned maybe having a memorial service for Peter, and I wonder if she'd made a decision, yes or no. I want to check on her anyway. I'll give her a call later."

Clint followed me to the shops, made sure I got inside safely, then headed off to work. I was earlier than usual and was happy to see Erin sitting at Pinky's counter with a cup of brew. "A little pick me up before school?" I asked her.

"Cami, hi! Yes, my usual high-tech coffee. Pinky's in the back room getting goodies. The seven o'clock rush about depleted her supply here."

I spotted customers at back tables. "I'll hang up my things, then give you guys the latest."

Erin's eyebrows lifted. "Oh boy."

My long skirt had pockets, so I slid my phone in one, and headed into Brew Ha-Ha. Pinky smiled. "Erin said you were here and had more news."

I waved them into Curio Finds. "I'll make this as fast as possible." I couldn't tell Jaylin and Jace's story without permission, so I found the ring video on my phone, and held it up for them. "It happened last night when I was at the city council meeting."

Pinky gasped and twisted her dish towel with both hands.

Erin grabbed my arm. "Cami, come sleep at my house until they catch this guy."

"Thank you, but Clint will stay with me until they do.

He also insists someone is there every time I leave and return to my house."

"That's a relief. My body can handle only so much stress. You had more practice with that, working for you-know-who, you-know-where," Pinky said.

I smiled on the inside and nodded.

At the sound of Brew Ha-Ha's doorbell, the three of us headed through the archway. When I saw the two Js, Journee and Josey, a ripple of apprehension rolled through me. How would I act, what would I say if they mentioned Jaylin?

Pinky was in the dark about the Jaylin and Jace situation, as much as her friends were, and she asked them, "So your friend's still not going to class with you two?"

"We don't know what's going on, but we don't want to ask her about it either," Journee said.

"And let's be honest. If she caught the bug that's going around, we want her to stay home until she's well," Josey added.

"She came in yesterday and looked okay, so that's why I asked," Pinky said.

Journee and Josey glanced at each other and shrugged. I didn't want Pinky to tell them Jaylin had talked to me in private, so I jumped in with, "What would you ladies like this morning?"

After a quick glance at the menu board, they gave us their orders. Pinky and I prepared them, and they took seats at a back table. I went into Curio Finds to work on bookkeeping and customer orders.

At 9:00 a.m., I sent Jaylin a text, *How is Jace and how are you?*

She responded, *He is stirring more and mumbling words I can't quite catch but the doctors say they're good signs. I'm hanging in there.*

Let me know if you need anything.

She sent a heart emoji back.

I figured it was an okay time to call Ramona, but it went to voicemail after six rings. With all she'd been through, her sleep schedule could understandably be off. An hour later, I decided to send her a text instead. *Checking to see if you need anything.* No response. At 9:30, I phoned again. It went to voicemail on the first ring, like it was turned off, or out of battery.

Something felt off. Without a word from Ramona for days, it brought to mind what Jaylin had experienced. Jace had been in a life-threatening situation, and some evil person had texted Jaylin from his phone to mislead her. Why? Jaylin hadn't suspected Jace was in trouble until she couldn't reach him by phone. She later learned her husband had been taken to the hospital without his phone, and without the cognitive ability to have sent the message she'd received.

Was Ramona in trouble? She'd seemed in better spirits the last time we'd talked , but I knew she was struggling over her husband's death. She was not in a stable emotional state and did not like being alone . What if she'd given up hope and harmed herself? The thought made my temples pulse and my heart pound. I tried to convince myself the explanation for the dead phone might be as simple as, given all the calls from former staff and others, it had run out of battery, and Ramona had forgotten to plug it in before she went to bed.

Curio Finds was supposed to open in thirty minutes, so I didn't have time to get to her house and back by 10:00. I called my parents' home phone, and Mom answered. "Cami, hello. Your dad and I were just talking about Peter Zimmer's murder, wondering if they have any leads."

"Not that I've heard."

"Nothing about your burglar either? No, you would've told us."

"I surely would've. Mom, I'm calling to see if you'd be able to mind the shop so I can go check on Ramona."

"Is she ill?" she said.

"I'm not sure. She hasn't called for a few days, and I haven't been able to get a hold of her this morning. I just want to find out if she fell or . . . something."

"Shouldn't you phone the police to do that?"

"I'll call them if I need to, after I get to her house."

"Okay. We'll be there soon, dear."

"Thank you, Mom."

I popped into Pinky's shop. "My parents are coming in to cover for me for a while. Don't freak out, but I'm going to do a wellness check on Ramona."

She snapped her dish towel with added vigor. "You're *what*?"

I explained my reason, and Pinky shook her head. "Maybe she doesn't want to talk to you, or to anyone."

I couldn't tell her about Jace's situation, and how it had heightened my fear. "Her phone seems to be turned off, and I feel the need to visit her, that's all."

"What if she doesn't open the door?"

"I have the code to her house," I said.

"Oh."

I headed to my office, and phoned Clint. "Camryn."

"Hi. My parents are going to run the shop so I can head to Ramona's, see if she's all right. We haven't spoken since Saturday, and her phone must be dead."

"You're not thinking she is, are you?"

"Not necessarily, but she may be ill or injured," I said.

"I'm covering a shift, so I can't leave town to go with you."

"Not to worry. If anything happened to her, I will call

nine-one-one, and then you, all right?"

"All right. If anything looks suspicious, do not enter the home."

My parents unlocked the Curio Finds door and let themselves in a few minutes before ten, just in time to open the shop. I gave them a smile. "That was fast, thanks for helping me out."

"It's kind of like the other way around. You taking over for us has been a godsend," Mom said.

"It sure has," Dad agreed.

"Glad to do it. I'll take off," I said.

On the drive to Orten, I tried to block out unbidden images of Ramona in a variety of grim states. She'd seemed upbeat the last time we'd talked, but her emotional state could drop from high to low, in a flash. That's what worried me—her rock-bottom lows.

I turned on her street. The curtains and blinds were still drawn, at 10:20 in the morning. If she were home, her vehicle would be in the garage. I decided to park on the other side of her driveway, to keep it open for others. In case. The temperature was mild, so I left my coat in the car.

My heart rate sped up on the way to her door. I pushed the bell and heard it ring, but no movement inside. I counted to thirty and pushed the bell again. Still no interior sounds, so I punched in the five-digit code—her zip code—one even an amateur thief might try.

When I opened the door, a dreaded scent hit my olfactory. The same one an intruder had left in my house the past Friday. It stunned me. Random thoughts and questions crisscrossed in my mind. Why was that smell in her house? Who had been there? In all our years together, I'd never detected that scent on Ramona or Peter.

I heard the back outside door open and close. What was

she doing outside? As an unexpected guest in her home, I had no choice but to call out, "Ramona?"

"Camryn?" She came into the living room and was not alone. The man behind her looked like a giant in comparison. I'd seen him a couple times in Ramona's office. Was he a lobbyist, or a staffer from another office, maybe? He stared at me with a "if looks could kill" glare. The giant was puffing on a pipe, the source of the scent that filled the air and my nostrils. My heart raced, and my muscles tightened. *Him.*

Ramona's eyebrows lifted as she asked me, "What are you doing here?"

It wasn't a difficult question, but the reason seemed trivial in light of the current situation. Was Ramona in cahoots with the giant? To buy a little time, I answered her. "You didn't take my calls or respond to my text. When I tried again, your phone was either turned off or dead. I just wanted to be sure you were okay."

"Oh. I guess I'm not even sure where my phone is," she said.

The giant finally spoke. "You gave it to me earlier." But he didn't produce the phone to prove it as he laid his pipe on the coffee table.

Ramona's brows drew together and her eyes glanced upward. "I did?" She turned to the giant. "Claude, you know Camryn Brooks, right?"

His stare down seemed to intensify. "Yes."

I fingered the can of Mace in my skirt pocket, ready to pull and aim, if he came after me. The problem was, we'd all take a hit if I pressed the button. Could I escape, make it to my car, and call the cops? I guessed the chances of that were slim to none. The giant's strides would be twice as long as mine. And as much as I'd tried, I couldn't run, at least not fast enough to make a clean get away.

Ramona and the giant appeared to be on friendly terms, but friendly to what extent? My brave inner self awakened. I jutted out my chin, and said, "Well Claude, at least now I know your name. What I don't know is, why you broke into my house and left that creepy note on my bed."

Ramona jerked. "What do you mean, your house? *What note?*"

When he took a step toward me, Claude seemed four inches taller and a hundred pounds heavier. It was do or die. "Ramona, *run!*" I yelled. But she remained as still as a statue.

I backed up toward the bedroom wing, to put space between Claude and Ramona. He followed me. She stayed put. I fingered the trigger on the Mace, pulled it from my pocket, pointed it at his face, and gave him a full blast. A bit of mist drifted back to me. My eyes burned and blurred.

Claude howled and groped toward me. Before I made it to a bedroom, he swung at me, managed to grab a handful of my hair, and tugged. I was scared and angry, and the adrenaline spike gave me enough strength to deliver an effective, sharp elbow blow to his belly. He bent over, with the added pain. My eyes watered, and my nose ran. I swiped at both, as I dropped to the ground to escape. Claude caught my foot and dragged me back toward him.

"Ramona!" I yelled.

I sensed, more than spotted her near to us. Then I heard a crash, and a crack that sounded ominous, like a heavy object hit Claude's skull. He made an "Ugg" sound and dropped to the ground. Thank God it wasn't on top of me, or I would have suffocated in no time. I struggled to see clear images with my tear-blurred eyes and resisted the urge to rub them—a major no-no that would make my eyes burn even more so.

Ramona cried out, "Camryn, I'm worried that I killed

him."

"I doubt that. Did you get sprayed?"

"No, but that stuff's in the air and is hurting my eyes and nose."

"Sorry, but go call nine-one-one. *Now*."

"I don't have my phone."

I fished mine from my left pocket and slid it across the carpet in her direction. I heard her mutter something, and a moment later she had a dispatcher on the line. I crawled past Claude and I blinked away tears, thankful I'd only had a small snootful.

Ramona gave them her address, said we weren't in imminent danger, and closed with, "Hurry!"

"The police will be here in a couple of minutes." Ramona helped me to my feet and slipped her arm around my waist as we looked at the giant, asleep on her floor. "His head's bleeding," she said without emotion.

My vision had cleared a bit. "What'd you hit him with?"

She pointed "That chair."

A heavy dining room chair lay on its side on the floor. "I'm pretty certain you saved my life."

"I don't know what got into Claude, why he went after you like that."

Good question. "Who is he?" I asked.

"He was a lobbyist for a pharmaceutical company and often came to D.C. We were friends, of sorts, had dinner now and then. He knew Peter, too. I'm embarrassed to tell you this, but he said I was too good for Peter, that he brought me down."

I had to agree with my attacker on that observation.

A loud knock sounded on the front door. "Orten Police!" a male voice sounded, and two officers, a male and a female—both in their thirties—stepped into the entry. The male said, "I'm Officer Peterson, and this is Officer Somers."

I nodded, and Ramona whimpered.

The officers looked from Ramona and me huddled together, to Claude on the carpet, blood mixed in with his brown hair on the side of his head. "Are you two harmed?" Peterson said.

We both shook our heads, and I said, "Caught a little Mace when I sprayed him."

"He was after Camryn and tried to hurt her," Ramona added.

Claude moaned, as if in protest.

"The ambulance is on the way. We'll have the EMTs assess and dress his head wound," Somers said.

"Officers, if you find two phones in his pockets, one belongs to Ms. Zimmer," I said.

"Okay." Officer Peterson's phone buzzed. He answered, "Peterson. . . Thanks." He disconnected, and said, "A Buffalo County deputy will help provide security for the suspect at the hospital." He went over to Claude, took a closer look at his head, checked his pulse, but didn't comment.

21

Officer Somers took out a memo pad. "Let's go into the kitchen, so I can get your names, dates of birth, addresses, the victim's name, and brief summary of what happened."

We settled at the kitchen table. Ramona's voice was shaky, and her hands trembled as she gave the officer the info she needed. As the adrenaline started to drain from my body, I felt shakier myself and was glad to lean my arms on that table.

After I'd answered her questions, I said, "I have reason to believe that man—Claude—broke into my house in Brooks Landing and left a note on my bed last Friday. When I confronted him about it, he came after me."

Officer Somers looked at her notes, then studied me a moment. "Ms. Brooks, are the authorities handling that case?"

"Yes, and another felony crime Claude might've been involved in."

Ramona let out a high pitched shrill that startled Somers and me. She tensed, and I jumped. "No, no, no! You don't mean Peter's murder? Camryn, why would you say that?"

A knock on the front door saved my response for the moment. "We'll come back to this," Somers said, and headed to the living room. I peeked around the corner and watched more officials arrive: two EMTs with a gurney and two Buffalo County deputies joined Somers and Peterson.

The EMTs attended to Claude, took his vital signs, and put an oxygen mask over his face. "How long has he been out?"

Peterson glanced at his watch. "The call came in at ten thirty-two, so maybe a minute before that. Nine minutes."

Voices chattered from their radios.

"He's starting to stir," an EMT said.

They discussed next steps.

"Any way you slice it, the chances that he'll be a happy camper when he wakes up is zippo," Peterson said.

"Yeah," one muttered.

"Let's get him situated before that happens," an EMT said.

"Can't cuff him behind his back, so for everyone's safety, we'll cuff his hands to the side rails," a deputy said.

Somers stepped in to help as the other four got into position. With some effort, they managed to lift, and position, Claude on the gurney. A deputy found two phones in Claude's front pockets.

"I believe one of those belongs to Ms. Zimmer," Somers said, then called out to Ramona, "What color is your phone, Ms. Zimmer?"

"Lavender," Ramona answered. I supposed he had to confirm that, but the thought that Claude had the lavender one and Ramona had the black one tickled me.

The deputy handed it to Somers, who handed it to me, and I carried it into the kitchen.

When I returned, I saw a deputy withdraw a wallet from Claude's back pocket, and flip it open. "Got his ID. Claude Heffron."

His partner withdrew a small evidence bag from a

pouch on his belt. The deputy dropped it inside, then laid it on Claude's stomach. He was semi-conscious, as they cuffed each of his hands to the gurney's side rail.

Peterson made a phone call, and when he disconnected, told Somers, "A deputy and I will ride along in the ambulance. We'll be in touch."

"Copy," she said.

Somers helped the team by holding the door open for them. With the curtains drawn, I couldn't see the action outside. Somers watched for a few minutes, then closed the door. I heard Peterson's voice on the radio say, "County, we're en route to HCMC." Hennepin County Medical Center in Minneapolis.

One deputy came back inside, his phone in his hand. "I'll take a photo of the scene for my report."

"I'll do the same," Somers said.

"Officer Somers? I need to make two phone calls. One to my parents who are filling in for me at our shop. And one to Chief Clinton Lonsbury. He knew I was coming here to check on Ramona and he'll be wondering."

She nodded. "Sure, go ahead. Save the details until I've finished taking your statements, okay?"

"Okay. On second thought, it'd be better for me to text instead."

The deputy and Somers took photos while I sent a brief message, *Still at Ramona's for a while yet,* to both Clint and my mother.

Officer Somers and I headed back to the kitchen. Ramona had her arms crossed on the table, and her forehead on her wrists. "Ms. Zimmer?" Somers said.

She lifted her tear-streaked face. "My life has fallen apart. I lost my husband and now come to find out one of my long-time acquaintances could've been involved in his death. For sure, he tried to harm my best friend." *Me?*

I grabbed a few tissues from the box on the counter and gave them to her. "Ramona, you saved my life, and I will owe you forever. But how in the world were you able to lift that heavy chair, and swing what must've been higher than your shoulders and with enough force to knock Claude out?"

"He was bent over, so his head was more like shoulder level. I can't explain where my strength came from."

"Adrenaline gave you that boost, sent extra oxygen to your muscles. Happens in 'fight or flight' situations," Somers said.

"I've never experienced anything quite like that before, or been more terrified," Ramona said.

I'd been in many "fight or flight" situations I would rather have purged from my memory forever.

Somers held up her pad and pen. "I'm going to take your statements separately, if you'll wait in the living room, Ms. Brooks. It won't be long."

I looked at the blood stained carpet, then dropped down on a chair, and thought about Claude. I had a vague recollection of meeting him, and remembered how he smelled, more than how he looked. I'd met with lobbyists on a regular basis in D.C., and didn't recall ever seeing him at a meeting in Ramona's office, or at legislative conferences, policy forums, or networking events.

Yet, Ramona said Claude was in Washington often. Maybe other staff met with him. When the two came in from her back yard—what were they doing out there anyway, and where was his vehicle—my initial observation was he wanted to be more than just friends with her. How ironic. The man who sought a close relationship with her was likely a psycho.

I wanted Officer Somers to finish with Ramona so I could tell Clint and Detective Garrison about Claude. They needed to dive into who he was, where he lived, his past and present positions.

It had only been minutes, but seemed like an hour when Ramona returned to the living room. Her face was blotchy, her eyes red and almost swollen shut. "Your turn."

I nodded and touched her shoulder on the way by. "Ms. Brooks," Somers said when I took a seat across from her. "You're the mayor of Brooks Landing. Is it a coincidence that you, and your town, have the same name?" I figured the question was meant to put me at ease.

"No. My great-grandfather founded the town decades ago."

"Ah. I understand you worked for Ramona Zimmer when she served in congress. And she shared why she fired you, and that in light of recent events, she learned she was wrong."

I nodded. "It was rough, but as it turned out, I'm where I should be in life."

"You said you believe Claude Heffron broke in your house and that he was likely involved in a felony crime, possibly a murder, given what Ms. Zimmer said. Tell me about the break-in first."

I took her through the details, and noted the unusual scent, both in my house and in Ramona's when I'd arrived earlier.

Her eyebrows lifted a titch. "And the murder?"

"I'm still trying to process that." I told her why I thought the murder and the note were connected. "I think he must blame me that Ramona lost the election. But why would he kill Peter? Was he jealous? I don't know.

"I have a vague memory of meeting him in the senator's office. It sounds strange, but I remember how he smelled from that unusual pipe tobacco. Claude didn't smoke in the office, of course, but the smell clung to his person, the way a strong perfume might."

"I get that. Go on," Somers said.

"I'm certain Claude broke into my home, but at this point, I can only suspect he was involved in Peter Zimmer's murder. That's why I need to talk to the Buffalo County detective, so they can start an investigation on him."

Officer Somers stood, offered me her hand, and we shook. "I have all I need for now. I'll let you go so you can contact the detective." She lowered her voice. "Are you going to be okay, after what happened?"

I blinked a few times, when I felt tears sting my eyes. "Yes, thanks for asking."

She tipped her head in the living room's direction. "Your friend is pretty distraught, so it'd be good if someone stayed close to her for a while."

"I agree."

"I gave Missus Zimmer contact information of a cleanup crew to remove the victim's blood. She said she'll ask her cleaning lady about that first."

All I could do was nod.

After Somers left, I asked Ramona to pack an overnight bag. "I want you to stay with me a few days until everything gets sorted out."

"Okay." I followed her to her room, and we made a wide berth around the blood on the carpet. I noticed blood spatter on the wall too. Her room was still a mess, but in light of the morning's events, it didn't bother me in the least.

"Camryn, you should change your sweater, in case any Mace landed on it. I have one I got as a gift that I've never worn, and it should fit you just fine." She opened a drawer and removed a camel-colored merino wool pullover with a mock neck collar.

"Thank you. It's so soft." I stepped into the bathroom, slipped my sweater over my head, and put on Ramona's.

When I returned to the bedroom, I saw Ramona had changed her top as well.

On the ride to Brooks Landing, I asked Ramona about Claude. "Why was he at your house?"

"He called and asked to stop by. I thought it'd be nice to have company."

"There wasn't a car in the driveway, so I was surprised to see you weren't alone."

"I told him to park his work van in the garage since it's supposed to snow later," she explained.

"His work van?"

"For his medical supplies company. He just bought the business, and it was included in the sale."

My vision started to blur, and I had to pull over.

"What's wrong?" she asked.

"Maybe nothing, but a big dark vehicle with a medical logo on the passenger side window was seen in my alley the night Peter was found in my driveway. What color is Claude's?"

"Dark gray. I didn't see any logo when he drove in, but I couldn't see that side. You don't think Claude was involved in what happened to Peter, do you? Whatever reason would he have?" The skepticism in her voice rang out as clear as a bell.

"No idea at this point." I willed my body and mind to calm down because I knew in my heart of hearts Claude Heffron had been involved, all right. The up side: he was in police custody, chained to a hospital bed.

Then another thought struck me. Say Heffron was involved in Peter's murder, that meant he either *had* an accomplice, or *was* the accomplice. *The other person is still out on the loose.*

I closed my eyes and said a prayer. A welcomed sense

of peace washed through me and settled my nerves.

"Are you okay?" Ramona asked.

"Yes. Just needed a moment." I shifted into drive, scanned for traffic, pulled back on the highway, and was in Brooks Landing thirteen minutes later. I dropped Ramona off at the shop's front door, drove around to the lot, parked, grabbed my coat off the seat, and walked to Curio Finds.

My parents both stood behind the counter with "what's going on?" looks on their faces. No one else was in the shop.

I gave a small wave. "Hi. Where's Ramona?"

"We heard her voice next door," Mom said.

"Okay. I hope you can cover for me a while longer."

Mom and Dad looked at each other and nodded.

"Good. A major thing happened. I need to talk to Detective Garrison. And Clint."

"Oh, dear. That sounds serious," Mom said.

"It is, and you can thank Ramona for saving me from injury, or worse."

Mom gasped. Her hands flew upward and landed on her chest.

Dad's frown line deepened. "Cami, what happened?"

"Ramona can tell you and Pinky all about it." I went to the archway and saw Pinky and Ramona by a table. "Hey," I called to them, and waved them into Curio Finds.

Pinky sensed the worst, given the way she wrung the dish towel in her hands. "What is it?"

"Ramona, I need to leave for a while, so I want you to tell them the story. Okay?"

She looked at me with a sad puppy face. "Okay."

"Cami!" Pinky protested.

I lifted my hand. "See you later." I slipped on my coat, and out the door I went.

It took but a few minutes to reach the Buffalo County

Sheriff's Office, and I stepped up to the reception window. "Hello. It's Camryn Brooks. Is Detective Garrison in?"

"Let me check." She had Garrison on the phone in seconds, told him I was out front, said, "Okay," and hung up.

"He'll be right out."

"Thanks." I called Clint, relieved when he answered. "Hi, can you come to the sheriff's office? I'm meeting with Garrison."

"What in tarnation? Never mind, I'll be right there."

Garrison appeared at the counter. "Mayor. Official business?"

"A new development. Clint's on his way too."

Garrison opened the door for me, then turned to the receptionist. "When Chief Lonsbury gets here, send him back."

"Will do."

Clint arrived after we'd sat down at Garrison's desk. The intense look on Clint's face made it impossible for me to stay seated. I stood and lifted my hands. "All right. There was an incident at Ramona's." I took them through the whole story, from the time I'd arrived, to the time I left Ramona in the care of Pinky and my parents.

Clint made an occasional soft, grunt-like sound but he didn't interrupt. When I finished, he took me in his arms. "Thank God you're safe. Now if we could just keep you out of dangerous situations altogether."

Garrison blew out a breath. "The positive side is it's filled in pieces of the puzzle. That said, it gets a little complicated with the different jurisdictions involved. The Orten Police will be charging Heffron with the assault against you, Camryn."

"It's a cluster," Clint said.

"Yep. Orten will no doubt tap into Hennepin County's

resources. They'll need search warrants for Claude Heffron's residence, his van, currently in Ramona Zimmer's garage, and his business location. Meantime, I'll write up a criminal complaint naming Heffron as the suspect of your burglary here in Brooks Landing. Then I'll head down to HCMC and check on his status," Garrison said.

Clint gave me a ride back to my shop, despite the fact it would've taken me the same time to walk back. He parked in front of the shops, and said, "I need to go in and thank Ramona."

"Clint, at Officer Somers' suggestion, I invited her to stay with me for a few days. She's not in a good place, mentally or emotionally. First her husband's murder and then having to knock out a guy she thought wanted to help and befriend her."

We went in the Curio Finds door, and I was relieved no customers were inside. My parents and Ramona were seated in a circle of folding chairs we kept in the back room. "Mission accomplished," I said.

As they greeted Clint, Pinky came in, beelined toward me, and threw her arms around me. "Cami Brooks." She paused a second, and her voice cracked when she added, "That's all I can say, or I'll cry."

I noticed my parents—yes, my dad too—and Ramona all had tears in their eyes.

"You're a brave girl, and it's a good thing you used that Mace," Dad said.

I laid my hand on Ramona's shoulder. "Ramona is the true heroine in that battle. I gave Heffron a shot of Mace, but she knocked him out and saved both of us from . . . whatever," I said

Ramona sniffed. "I thought Claude wanted to help me, but he was no friend, at all."

"Ramona, thank you," Mom said.

Clint's phone rang, and he stepped away to take the call. When he came back, he pulled me aside, and in a quiet voice said, "Jace Klemmet is coherent and wants to talk to a police officer." My heart rate doubled its speed.

Clint had just walked out the door when I got a text from Jaylin. *Jace is awake and saying scary things.*

Things he needed to tell the police. *Do you want me to come there, wait with you while he talks to them?*

If you can, she wrote.

Yes. Be there soon.

"Mom and Dad, I need to go help a friend for a while, if that's okay. I promise I will not be in any kind of danger."

"Of course, dear. It's fun to mind the shop and look at how you have things arranged," Mom said.

"We'll be just fine," Dad agreed.

"Ramona, what about you? Want to hang out here, or go to my house?"

"I'll stay here."

Pinky left to help customers. I grabbed my coat and took off.

Clint's car was in the hospital lot. I found a spot, went inside, and checked in at the hospital's front desk.

I'm here, I texted Jaylin.

In the waiting alcove across from the patient rooms.

The arrow on the wall pointed me in the right direction. Jaylin's pale face contrasted with her red-rimmed eyes. She stood and threw her arms around me. It was an emotional day for a lot of us. "Chief Lonsbury's with Jace."

Detective Garrison arrived, glanced at us, gave a quick nod, and headed into Room 203. It seemed he'd been detoured before he left for HCMC, as he'd planned.

Jaylin spoke in a quiet voice. "I didn't know any of this

until a half hour ago, so I'm still trying to process it all. Jace told me Monday night, a week ago, he had an appointment to deliver his work van to the guy who bought his business. When Jace arrived, Claude said his friend had passed out in his sauna—"

I cut her off. "*Claude*? His last name?"

Her shoulder lifted. "He didn't say."

"Sorry, I interrupted you. Go on." My head and heart pounded.

"Okay. Well, Claude didn't want his friend to drive, and he'd already helped him into his car—in fact, the car was running—and he needed to drive him to his home in Brooks Landing."

"Where does Claude live?"

"Just east of Orten," she said.

Seriously? Ramona didn't mention that. "Then what?"

"He needed someone to follow him, so he could get a ride back home, and asked Jace to do that. He said he would."

"Did Jace drive the van there?"

Jaylin thought a moment then shrugged. "He must have. The original plan was, when Jace delivered the van, Claude would give him a ride home. And he did, after they got back to Claude's. Anyway, the next day we heard Peter Zimmer had been killed, and that his body was found in Brooks Landing. I'd lost my co-worker, my friend, and couldn't face going back to work. I told you how upset Jace acted, and how I thought it was because of how I felt."

"Yes."

"Turns out, he had started to worry that Peter was the one in the sauna, and that Claude had killed him—although he had no idea why—and he'd helped, by picking Claude up at what turned out to be your house."

"Why didn't Jace go to the police?" I asked.

"He thought his imagination had run wild. But it ate away at him. He wanted to clear his conscience, make sure he hadn't helped a killer, so he asked Claude about it a couple days later. Claude laughed, said the guy was fine, that his wife made sure he got into the house okay."

"Sounds like Claude's a practiced liar. But I'm a little confused. What happened with the meeting in St. Paul, and how did Jace end up back in Brooks Landing, given his altered mental state of mind?" I said.

"Jace said Claude was the one who'd talked to him about a potential business venture. They planned to meet at Claude's and ride together to St. Paul, where Claude would introduce him to the owners. Instead, Claude drugged Jace at his house. The last thing Jace remembers is Claude saying they should have a drink before they hit the road," Jaylin said.

"After what the doctor told us about the drugs in his system, it's a miracle Jace survived. And he has no idea how he got from Orten to Brooks Landing?"

New tears formed in her lower lids. "No. All Jace is sure of is that Claude figured out a scheme to get him to his house and planned to kill him before he went to the police."

I drew in a deep breath. "Jaylin, you need to brace yourself. As soon as you said Claude's name, I suspected he was the same Claude I had an encounter with this morning. Claude Heffron, and he is a monster."

Her eyes widened. "*What?*"

Without getting into details about Ramona herself, I told her how I'd met Claude at Ramona's that morning, and why I suspected he'd broken into my house; how I'd confronted him, how it had escalated into a dangerous showdown—Claude against Ramona and me.

Jaylin reached over, took my hand in hers, and squeezed. "As awful as that is, I call it two wins. You and

Ramona are safe, and that evil man is in the hospital under guard.”

"And there's no doubt in my mind, he's the one who killed Peter Zimmer.”

“And then tried to kill Jace,” she said.

$$\text{❄}$$

22

Jaylin and I each nursed our thoughts, and watched staff go in, and out of rooms, until Clint and Detective Garrison emerged from 203. Both had furrowed brows and slumped shoulders. They wore expressions that were difficult to read, maybe a combination of relief and sadness.

Jaylin and I rose from our seats. Clint glanced at me, while Garrison focused on Jaylin. "Your husband went through a lot in his quest for the truth," he said.

The way Garrison summed up Jace's condition was almost poetic.

Jaylin wiped her nose with a tissue. "If our relationship had been better, if we'd been closer, Jace would've told me his suspicions about Claude. Maybe I could've convinced him to go to the police."

"It's easier to see things after the fact," Clint said. He looked from me to Jaylin. "You two have compared notes about Claude Heffron, right?"

"Yes," we said, as one.

"Everything that monster did is hard to grasp. And why?" Jaylin asked.

"We're determined to get to the bottom of it," Garrison said.

"And we have our suspicions," Clint added.

"Did Jace remember how he got from Claude's house to Brooks Landing yet?" Jaylin asked.

"No. All he knows is that he somehow escaped, maybe hitched a ride back here. We're hoping that particular memory will return soon, for his sake even more than ours. In any event, we have witness testimony, and that's all we need to charge Claude Heffron with interference of a body, a gross misdemeanor. And Hennepin will charge him with murder," Garrison said.

Three jurisdictions had charges to file against him.

"Jaylin, were you able to get your phone records, so we can check them out?" Clint asked.

Her mouth dropped open. "Sorry, I totally forgot. I'll take care of that today."

It seemed my parents had cozied up to Ramona. My dad was in Curio Finds when I returned. "Your mother is next door, having lunch with your friend." It took me a second to realize he meant Ramona. "I picked up soup and sandwiches at the deli. They're still eating. When I finished, I came back to mind the shop."

"Thanks, Dad." I slipped off my coat, and hung it in the back room.

Mom and Ramona sat at a table. Pinky hovered nearby. "Cami, you're back. Everything okay?" Mom asked.

"Better, anyway. My friend's husband is in the hospital but he's coming around."

Literally.

"I'm glad to hear that. Ramona's staying with you for a few days, so why don't you two come over for dinner after work." She turned toward Pinky. "You know you're always welcome too."

Pinky's body twitched. "Thanks, but I got a little behind on my baking and need to catch up."

I tried to keep my expression neutral while I thought it through. "Gosh, Mom. That's sweet of you, but after this morning, and what my friend is going through with her husband, I may need to go back to the hospital."

All I longed to do was go home, climb into bed, pull the covers over me, and wake up in a week or so. Then I thought about Jace, and changed my mind.

"Ramona, how about you?" Mom asked.

Say yes.

"Me? Oh, well I'd love to. I haven't had a homemade meal for . . . I can't remember when."

"That's settled then. You can come home with Eddie and me. Cami can pick you up when she's done."

"Okay," Ramona said.

My parents left around two o'clock and took Ramona with them. Pinky poked her head through the archway. "The suspense is killing me."

I waved her in and gave an overview of what Jace had said, so far.

"And you helped get the guy who got him," she said.

"Yeah." Believe it or not.

The hours seemed to creep by as I waited for news on Claude Heffron's status, and whether Jace had remembered any more details. Detective Garrison and Clint came into Curio Finds a little before five o'clock. Pinky had left at four.

"I asked Chief to meet me here so I could tell you both at the same time," Garrison said.

"Wanna go sit at a table next door? I'll lock up and shut off the lights," I offered as we headed that way.

How did I know Molly would turn them back on and then off again? I sank down on a chair next to Clint, across from Garrison.

"They got Heffron's head stitched up, and he's shackled to a hospital bed. He lawyered up, so it delayed Hennepin. I hung around for a while, but no question that he is going down for Peter Zimmer's murder, for making Jace Klemmet his hapless accomplice, then attempting to kill him."

"Ramona didn't know where Peter had been that night, but now we know he was at Claude Heffron's house, probably in his sauna, so Heffron could take good aim at his vein," I said.

"There was evidence his hands had been bound, so he couldn't defend himself, not with his hands anyway," Clint added.

We chatted for a few minutes, then Garrison stood. "Well, folks, it's been a long nine, or so, days. I know it's gotta seem a lot longer to you, Camryn. And to you, Chief."

I nodded, and Clint said, "Sure does."

"Catch you around the bend," Garrison said. Brew Ha-Ha's doorbell dinged when he left.

Clint leaned in closer. "So what are your plans for the evening?"

"I'm going to check in with Jaylin, see if she needs anything. Then I'll collect Ramona from my parents' house where they'll be feeding her supper. Hopefully, she'll want to get as much sleep as I do."

Clint stood, reached for my hand, and pulled me to my feet. He drew me into his arms for a comforting embrace. "I'll stay clear of your house and your *guest* tonight, if it's okay with you."

"It is. I'm hoping, with Peter's killer in custody, Ramona will start to feel better tomorrow, or the next day, and be ready to return home soon."

"It'll help if she gets involved with something—anything—maybe finds a good job."

"She'll need to. Outside of her position, Peter was her whole life. If she has a service for him, it'll bring some closure."

Clint's phone buzzed. "It's Jaylin Klemmet." He pushed the accept button. "Hello? Okay, I'll be right there."

"What?"

"Jace remembered the rest of what happened to him."

"I'll meet you there," I said.

Clint was in Room 203 with Jaylin when I knocked on the door. "Come in," Jaylin said. Jace was sitting up in his bed and smiled when I walked in. I hadn't seen him since he'd regained full awareness, and the change was like night and day.

"You're Camryn. Jaylin's been telling me what a help you've been to her," he said.

I smiled. "Thanks. We're all very relieved you're better."

"Same here. I guess they pumped a lot of nutrients into me. Jay also told me you helped put the guy who assaulted me in the hospital."

"I had a small part. Ramona Zimmer had the major role."

"A team effort," he said.

"Jace got more of his memory back."

He nodded. "Yes. You tell her, Jay."

"Jace was lying by a tree, and felt like he was stuck in a dream, and couldn't wake up. He was able to stand though, and made his way to the nearest building with lights. Jace went inside, but everything was distorted, and the lights were too bright. He could hear a little, but he didn't understand what anyone said. He couldn't talk. And the next thing he remembered he was here, but didn't know it was a hospital for a while."

I choked up as I laid my hand on his. "Welcome back."

The next two weeks were packed with happenings. Claude Heffron was in the Hennepin County Jail, awaiting trial. The detectives had interviewed him with his attorney present. Heffron would not admit to any crimes. Hennepin County conducted a search of his property. In the sauna, they spotted a few blood drops that, when tested, matched Peter Zimmer's. The soles on one a pair of his shoes were identical to those found in my yard. Neither Jace Klemmet's phone nor his wallet had been recovered. Neither had Peter Zimmer's phone.

With the evidence and witness statements listed in the criminal complaints, along with reports and records, the judge set his bail at $10 million. Clint told me he could pay a bail bondsman ten percent of that—$1 million, the bondman's fee for paying the full bail amount—and get released from jail with conditions until his trial.

Detective Garrison gave me his opinion. "Since Claude Heffron won't talk, we can only surmise that he was obsessed with Ramona Zimmer. He knew Peter, and must've invited him over to relax in the sauna, then killed him. And planned it on the night Jace Klemmet was set to drop off the van."

A chill ran down my spine. "So calculated."

"Premeditated, no doubt about that. When they interrogate Heffron's phone they'll be able to see who he called, and the times he placed those calls."

"Claude blamed Peter for his escapades and thought I was involved with him. Then he decided both of us were to blame when Ramona lost the election because of all the backlash over the scandal?"

Garrison's shoulders lifted. "As I said, we can only surmise."

Ramona decided against a public memorial service for her husband. Instead, a few of us gathered by her parents' graves, where Peter's ashes would be buried beside them. None of his family members made the trip to Minnesota to say goodbye.

Ramona was ready to sell her house, but her newfound therapist talked her into waiting at least six months. In the meantime, she planned a trip to Africa to join her brother and hired a neighbor to keep an eye on her house, inside and out.

Jace had been released from the hospital, and Jaylin said his close-to-death experience had given them a new perspective on their lives and their marriage. When she'd sat with him in the hospital, she remembered how much she had loved him, and still did. The spark that had attracted them had reignited.

Jaylin and Jace agreed to work on their damaged relationship and had started seeing a counselor. In an unexpected turn of events, the paperwork for the medical supplies company hadn't been filed, so Jace was still the owner. Jaylin told him they would make it a joint venture, that she'd be his partner.

On Saturday night, almost four weeks after Peter Zimmer's body was left in my driveway, Pinky, Josh, Erin, Mark, Jace, Jaylin, Clint, and I gathered at Brew Ha-Ha to decompress and celebrate Jace's return to health. We'd invited Ramona who wasn't up to it, and Detective Garrison who had another commitment.

Tasty appetizers and treats filled two tables. Bottles of sparkly wines, with and without alcohol, were on another. We all needed the traumatic events put to rest.

When it came time to toast, Jaylin poured herself and Jace each a glass of bubbly water, held hers up, and cleared her throat. "We have an announcement. Jace and I got the biggest, and best, surprise of our lives. When he was in the hospital, I suspected something, but couldn't grasp it at first. Turns out, we're going to have a baby! Doctors told us years back it would be a miracle if I ever got pregnant."

Jace patted Jaylin's tummy and raised his glass. "Here's to our little—or should I say our big—miracle."

The women got teary eyed, and the men were close to it. We all cheered, clapped, toasted, and hugged the expectant parents. They say, "all's well that ends well."

In light of the Klemmet's renewed relationship, that was most certainly true.

Other Snow Globe Shop Mysteries

Snow Way Out. Since childhood Camryn has loved the sparkling beauty of snow globes, and now sells them. They're so popular, Cami and her friend-coffee shop owner Alice "Pinky" Nelson decide to host a snow globe making class. After everyone has left with their own handmade snow globes, Cami spots a new globe left behind on a shelf that features an odd tableau-a man asleep on a park bench. On her way home, she drifts through the town park and is shaken to come upon the scene from the globe-a man sitting on a bench. But he isn't sleeping. He's dead. And Cami is a possible suspect. After her friends come under suspicion, Cami plows through clues to find the cold-blooded backstabber before someone else gets iced.

The Iced Princess. It's that time of year again—the Christmas rush is about to begin and Curio Finds Manager Camryn Brooks and her friend Alice "Pinky" Nelson need to hire additional help. Their former high school classmate is not quite who they had in mind. Has the rich socialite worked a day in her life? Molly begs for the job and they hire her. On her first day Molly is in her own little world and Cami worries she may flake out. It turns out far worse: Cami discovers Molly poisoned to death in the shop. There is soon an avalanche of suspects as Cami shovels through the clues.

Frosty The Dead Man. Mayor Lewis Mayor Lewis Frost, Frosty to his friends, has controversies swirling around him. City council members wonder if Frosty is trying to snow them. After one councilman storms off in a huff, the mayor asks curio shop manager Camryn Brooks to consider a seat on the council. Later, Cami goes to his office to discuss the proposal and her blood runs cold when she finds Frosty dead, and the snow globe she sold him earlier that day is in sparkling shards on his carpet—along with a large diamond. Does the snow globe which features a peculiar tableau hold a clue to Frosty's demise? One way or another, it's up to Cami to shake things up before the killer's trail goes cold.

Cold Way To Go. The last thing Curio Finds Manager Camryn Brooks expected was to get appointed as Brooks Landing Mayor. Her first tough assignment? Call out the police chief about his extensive absences. On a dark, frigid January afternoon she heads to Chief Newel's office and finds him licking an envelope. A moment later, he drops dead. A Buffalo County detective is called to look into the suspicious circumstances, but Cami feels compelled to conduct her own investigation, and finds herself face to face with a killer.

Christine Husom loves to hear from readers and visit book clubs and attend other events. Feel free to contact her at <u>christinehusom@aol.com</u>, and visit her website, <u>www.christinehusom.com</u>

www.ingramcontent.com/pod-product-compliance
Lightning Source LLC
Chambersburg PA
CBHW061615190726

48288CB00007B/2329